KILTING AROUND

CATHRYN FOX

COPYRIGHT

Kilting Around
Copyright 2023 by Cathryn Fox
Published by Cathryn Fox

Discover other titles by Cathryn Fox at www.cathrynfox.com. Please sign up for Cathryn's Newsletter for freebies, ebooks, news and contests: https://app.mailerlite.com/webforms/landing/c1f8n1
ISBN: 978-1-989374-96-2
ISBN Print: 978-1-989374-95-5

GAVAN

"What the hell am I really doing here, Finn?" I ask my cousin as he fluffs up a bouquet of flowers and frowns as he stands back to examine the flaccid white pedals.

"What is the matter with these magnolias? They were perky before you walked in." He angles his head my way, his eyes narrowing as he runs his gaze up and down the long length of my tired body. "I dinna believe they're happy to see you, Gavan."

"Finn..." I grumble not in the mood for his sexual innuendos. After a long-ass flight across the pond, I'm not interested in discussing my sex appeal on flowers. "What the hell is going on?" I ask again.

Finn's arms drop as he fully turns to me, his jaw agape like I just asked him to figure out the square root of six hundred, or something equally bizarre. Even if he spewed the right answer, I wouldn't know. Yeah, I studied business at Boston University. We both did. But I wasn't in it for the math. No, I studied business so I could run a successful Public House (pub) someday here in Boston.

"What dinna you get?" he asks as one hand flops over to present me with his palm.

Dinna.

Born and raised in Glasgow, we're both Scottish, but sometimes he leans into his accent a little more than I do.

"I explained it all to you on the phone," he continues as he takes a small step closer, like he's examining my pupils. "You don't have another concussion, do you?" He shakes his head. "I warned you about the dangers of playing football. You're far too aggressive on the pitch."

I grumble under my breath. "I do not have a concussion and you didn't explain anything to me," I say, getting the conversation back on track. "All you did was call me and tell me to get my arse to Boston because you had some emergency. So here I am. What's the emergency?" I glance around the extravagant Beacon Hill office space, take in the floor-to-ceiling ornate columns, as well as the blue and white color scheme covering the walls and furniture. The place looks like it jumped right off the cover of some interior design magazine. Finn always did have a flair for the dramatic, but he made Finn-tastic Affairs into one of Boston's most sought after event planning businesses, so clearly his theatrics are working for him.

"Was it a nice flight?" He folds one hand over the other and innocently blinks at me. "How's the weather been in Glasgow?"

Shite, I'm going to strangle him...slowly. I glare at my *former* best friend. "Are you sick?"

"Darling, no." He waves his hands up and down his body. "Do I look sick?"

"You're looking a little peely-wally." It's a lie. He doesn't look pale, at all. In fact, he looks fit and healthy as always. "Why are you wearing a kilt? It's three hundred degrees out there."

He smooths his hands over the tartan wool. "It's all part of the image here at Finn-tastic Affairs." He gives me a little wink. "We Scottish are exotic, dinna you know? The women go crazy for it. Always wanting to know what I'm wearing beneath this kilt and if the carpet matches the drapes."

"You care about that why?"

"Don't be cheeky, cousin, and yes, I realize a gay wedding planner is cliché, and I'm okay with that because it's good for business. You would not believe how many women want to convert me. It's a fun game and good for my bottom line." I raise my brow and he laughs. "Not *that* bottom, and don't worry that pretty head of yours, you'll get used to wearing a kilt in no time at all." I'm about to rebel, but he twists his hips to flare his kilt.

"What are you doing?"

"Showing you that everything here at Finn-tastic Affairs is authentic."

"What you're showing me is your tadger." For some reason my cousin does love to show off his parts.

"Exactly. You can't wear anything underneath the kilt—too hot for that anyway—and of course, your dangly bits will be itchy at first, but—"

"Finn!" I stare at him and try to get him back on track even though I know I'm not going to like what he has to say. "Why would I need to get used to one?" I reluctantly ask and brace myself for the answer.

"When you take over for me, of course. Seriously, Gavan, are you sure you don't have a concussion?"

"Finn, you're really starting to piss me off."

He purses his lips. "Doesn't take much."

With my patience approaching zero, I push up to my full height and stand eye to eye with him. Wait, did he just say... "What did you just say about me taking over here for you?" I glance around his frilly boutique and snort. Maybe he's the one who injured his brain on the pitch. Either that or I heard him wrong.

"Just for the next month." He hugs his hands to his chest. "Oh, Gavan, I can't wait for you to meet Alistair. He's just...everything."

Yeah, and so was Danny, and Robert, and Kent...or was it Kurt...but I keep that to myself. His flavor of the month isn't really the issue here, and if he doesn't get to the details as to why he needs me to take over—which I have no intentions of doing—I'm going to beat it out of him. But this is Finn, he likes to take the winding back roads of Scotland to get to the point.

I fold my arms and offer him my best scowl as I plant my feet. "Go on."

"It's not every day I get invited to go to Fiji, you know."

"I'm sure it's not."

He smiles, his eyes half closed, like he's dreaming of a faraway place, and I'm guessing he's envisioning himself sitting in a cabana in the South Pacific. I wouldn't mind being there myself right about now.

He snaps back to attention and circles his desk, three efficient steps taking him to his seat. Well, would you look at that. He can be direct when he wants to be. He flips a page in what looks like a planner.

I plop down into the chair across from him, and put my boots on his desk. He frowns as he glares at me. "Gavan, really. Were you raised in a barn?"

"Yes." I was raised in Da's pub, serving up drinks since I was a wee boy—much like my cousins were raised in their parent's pubs since food, cooking and Scottish culture is big in our families—and we did have a pasture with sheep out back, and there was a barn. That's close enough, I guess.

He rolls his eyes and shoves my feet off his gorgeous oak desk. "We leave tomorrow, which is why I needed you here today."

"To take over your business?" The idea is simply too ludicrous for me to even entertain.

He clicks his tongue and taps his head. "See, you're getting it. Not so dense after all."

"Forget it, Finn." I jump up, and turn toward the door, ready to leave as fast as I arrived. "This conversation is over."

"Gavan, nae..." The pure panic in his voice stops me dead in my tracks. Christ.

I turn back to him and try not to soften as pleading eyes lock me in place. "Not only have you lost your mind, you have no idea what constitutes an emergency, because this..." I glance around his show room. "...is not it."

"Gavan, I need you."

His pleading look pierces something deep inside me. Shite. "What do I know about your business, and even if I did agree to this and I'm not saying I am, I'm not wearing a kilt. Don't you have staff for this sort of thing?" My gaze goes to the empty offices off to one side and the abandoned receptionist's desk.

"My staff are all busy with other events, and my receptionist is out until Friday. This is an emergency, and well...as much as it pains me to say this...you owe me, Gavan."

Ah, and here it comes...the ace he's been holding for years now. "Finn..."

"You'd be dead, you know?"

I didn't know I was allergic to bees until I was seventeen and disturbed a hive down at the lake. If Finn hadn't loaded me into his truck and whisked me off to the hospital, I wouldn't be standing here having this insane conversation.

"D-E-A-D, Gavan," he reminds me, driving the point home by painfully enunciating each letter.

"Yes, and how unfortunate it is that I'm not."

He angles his head and eyes me, and I can almost hear the wheels turning in his busy brain. "You remember that time I found you in the sheep pasture." He tips his fingers to his lips, suggesting I had too much to drink. "...with your pants to your ankles." He briefly closes his eyes, a cheeky grin curling his lips. "Oh, if those sheep could talk."

"I was taking a piss, Finn. I wasn't shagging..." Christ. I pace back and forth. "You're resorting to blackmail now?"

"I wouldn't call it blackmail, exactly."

"What would you call it?"

He looks offended for a second, but as I stop pacing and hold my ground, he drops the act and switches tactics. "I'm your cousin and best friend. You should want to help me out, Gavan."

"*Former* best friend."

"Fine." He steps closer. "Former best friend..." He taps my nose and I swat his hand away. "...you can disown me after you do me this favor."

"You've lost your fucking mind. I don't know the first thing about planning an event, or whatever it is you even do."

"Oh, it's so easy. A monkey can do it."

I growl and stand nose to nose with him, but I'm so tired, the fight is draining out of me. "First you pull the death card on me, then you try blackmail and now you're calling me a monkey?"

He must sense some shift in me, because a smile spreads across his face, like he knows he's got me right by my dangly bits, and dammit, I'm worried he does. He's my cousin and best friend, and I wouldn't be alive today if it wasn't for him. I owe him, but more importantly, he's family and I'd do just about anything for family.

Family is the reason I'm living in Glasgow and not Boston. My dreams of opening my own pub were put on hold indefinitely after Da's stroke. I had no choice but to go back home and help out at the pub he poured his heart and soul into for years. I love the man who single-handedly raised me after Ma fucked off when I was a young lad. I should be home helping him, not standing here having this debate with Finn. They both need me, but the circumstances don't even compare.

Finn, however, has a dozen cousins on his mother's side of the family. I know he and I are the closest but he could have called any one of them.

"You'll have to pretend you're me, of course."

"Oh, of course." Isn't this just getting better and better.

He eyes me. "We're the same height and build. You'll just have to dye your hair orange. Pretending to be me will be easy."

"I'm not...wait, what? Why the hell do I have to pretend I'm you?"

"The Johnsons." I glare at him, and he huffs. "The Johnsons are Boston royalty, Gavan. They own Johnson Fidelity, a multibillion-dollar investment company. Why do you not know these things?"

"Because these things are not important to me."

He throws his arms out. "Sarah's wedding will be talked about for decades."

"And this has what to do with me?"

"They want me, and me alone to plan the wedding. My staff simply won't do." He puts one hand to his chest and his chin lifts an inch as he splays his fingers. "My reputation precedes me. I'm the best in the business, and no way can I turn away an account of this magnitude. I must give the Johnsons exactly what they want."

"Then you'd better skip Fiji if this is so important to you."

"Gavan..."

I fold my arms. "Finn..."

"Lucille Johnson will be here in five minutes," he continues, completely ignoring my protests. "She's the bride's sister. I— or rather you—will be working closely with her for the next few weeks while I'm away. She's a ball buster, so we must present her with our best Scottish charm."

Scottish charm?

"Fuck that."

"Word of mouth is everything amongst the rich, Gavan." A bell over the door jingles, and he looks past my shoulders. "Shite, she's here now. Quick, you need to hide." He hurries out from behind his desk, and shoves me into a closet, leaving the door cracked. "Watch and learn."

Two sets of footsteps sound on the marble floor as he hurries across his wide expanse of space to meet her. "Ms. Johnson, darlin', how ye daein? Yer looking as gorgeous as ever. Please have a seat."

A chair scrapes and I peek through the crack in the doors to catch sight of a pretty young woman. She smooths her hand over her skirt as she lowers herself into the plush leather. I inch the door open a bit more, let my gaze move over the length of her. Dark lashes blink over bright blue eyes as she slides a loose strand of silky dark hair behind her ear. Maybe bonnie lass would be better words to describe her, and while she exudes confidence that doesn't give anyone the right to call her a ball buster.

But she is rich and we all know they live in a different realm than the rest of us, and expect people like Finn—and me—to run circles around them, and cater to their every need. I've experienced their sense of entitlement firsthand at my da's pub. Rich, vacationing Americans wanting a real Scottish experience. Of course, I plan to give them that when I open my own pub here. Although that dream is getting dimmer and dimmer.

"Please call me Luce. It's nice to meet you, Mr. Duncan."

"It's Finn, of course."

She offers him a brilliant smile that probably costs more than Da's pub brings in every month. "I've heard great things about your company."

Finn smiles back and putting on his best Scottish charm as he casts a fast glance my way as if to say, told you so. "Aye, word of mouth is everything. Can I get you a refreshment? Perhaps a cool glass of fizzy juice?"

Jesus, he's not just leaning into his accent and heritage, he's falling all over it.

"No, I'm fine, thank you." She opens her bag and pulls out a tablet. "I'd like to get straight to business."

"Aye, of course."

"I do love your accent." She leans forward, like she's sharing a secret. "Did you know I have a bit of Scottish in me?"

"Nae, dinna know that."

I try not to fidget as they make small talk before they get down to business and begin to set a timeline and discuss venues. As the minutes tick on, it gets harder and harder to breathe in the small space, and I'm two seconds from busting out of the closet and blowing his plan, when the bell over the door jingles. I listen for a second longer, and when I hear only one set of footsteps on the marble floor, I say, "Can I come out of the closet now?"

Finn chuckles as he swings the doors open, a cheeky grin on his face. "Darling, is there something we need to talk about?"

I step from the closet and glare at him. "Not funny."

"Did you watch and learn?" He reaches out and touches my hair, examining the length. "We'll have to think about a trim as well."

I swat his hands away. "I can't be you, Finn."

"Of course you can." He playfully wags a brow. "Did you hear Luce say she was part Scottish, and wouldn't yae know it, cousin, she's just your type. Unless of course you really are coming out of the closet."

If I was coming out, I probably wouldn't have been admiring Luce or thinking about how I might go about putting a little more Scottish in her.

"Bloody hell, Finn. Yer off yer heid."

"I am not crazy. I've given this a lot of thought." He efficiently claps his hands. "Now, let's get at your transformation. Make you a wee bit more braw, like me."

I grumble. "I just...why can't I just be me?"

"Are you daft? I already told you why." He gives an exaggerated huff. "You need to work on your listening skills, Gavan, or should I say, Finn." He chuckles.

I glared at him. "No, what I need to work on is saying *no* to you."

"Do I need to remind you that I—"

"Saved my life. No, I get it." I shake my head hardly able to believe I let him arm twist me in to taking over his business —pretend to be him. "If I can't pull this off and you lose the account, it's not on me and you cover all expenses while I'm here."

Finn grins at me. "You'll do it then?"

I roll my eyes, because yeah, he knew I was going to do it the second he asked. "Yes, I'll do it."

"You'll play the part *and* wear the kilt?"

"Yes, and yes." But I draw the line where Luce is concerned. I won't be putting any Scottish, or anything else, in her. Nothing good could come from that, which means she's hands off—no touching, no kissing, no shagging.

Unless, of course, she asks me to.

LUCE

"I wouldn't call him eccentric," I say to my sister and press my phone harder against my ear to block the street noises as I hurry down the sidewalk. I should have worn a hat. It's unseasonably hot for May and the humidity is playing havoc with my flat ironed hair. I'll no doubt resemble a hedgehog by the time I enter Finn's showroom. Not that I'm trying to impress him. I mean, the man is nice to look at, and well built, but I'm no longer into men—thanks to being such a bad judge of character—and he's not into women, so there's that.

"What do you think he wears under that kilt, Luce?" Sarah asks with a chuckle.

"Don't know and don't care." I dodge a guy texting as he comes straight at me, and glance up to see the big Finn-tastic Affairs sign overhead. "I'm here now. I'll let you know what venues are available as soon as I know. We're going to go over all that today." Sarah continues to ramble on about her preferred wedding venue, and I don't mean to be rude, but I end the call while she's mid-sentence. She'll probably talk for another thirty minutes before she even realizes I'm not on the other end.

I love my sister, I really do, which is why I agreed to plan this wedding for her—in four months—with the help of Boston's number one event planner. While Finn is excellent at his job, or so I heard, my sister insisted I be involved in every step along the way. Yay me for having such great organizational skills, which lend beautifully to my job as a financial advisor at our family-run investment company.

While my finance career has nothing to do with event planning, I agreed because I love Sarah and would do anything to help her pull off her dream wedding, even on such short notice. Glen Baxter, nephew of the man who owns the New England Patriots—a well-known lawyer—proposed to my sister in April. Mom suggested a September wedding and Sarah readily agreed. What my younger sister wants, my younger sister gets. I'm as guilty as the rest for spoiling her. At least the wedding is taking the focus off my previous bad choices and my future as a spinster.

I pull open the door and the little bell overhead jingles. I head toward the back of the showroom, and slow my steps at the sound of Finn's voice. Wait, is that his voice? It sounds a bit deeper than yesterday. Maybe it's spring allergies. I've been plagued with them myself.

I walk around a large pillar and Finn has his back to me as he stands behind his desk, waving his arms erratically as he glances out the tall window overlooking a backyard gazebo.

What is he saying and who is he talking to?

I come to a resounding halt, as he belts out, "I must be off ma trolley. I'm a damn eegit."

Is he calling himself an eegit? Does that mean idiot? He continues to throw his arms out, gesturing to no one in particular. I wait, and when it doesn't look like his ranting is about to stop any time soon, I clear my throat, and he spins, his eyes wide, surprised as they land on me.

"I didn't mean to interrupt." I check his ears to see if he's wearing a headset. Nope. Apparently, he was just talking to himself. Maybe Sarah was right and he is a bit eccentric. Not my business. He's good at what he does and that's all I care about.

"I dinna hear you come in."

"The bell rang." I point over my shoulder and move toward him. There's something different about him today. I let my gaze move down the long length of him, but still can't quite pinpoint what's off. Off? Maybe the word is *on*, because wow, he looks a bit wider, harder, a delicious morsel any girl would want to gobble up, and dammit, I forgot my spoon.

You're off men, girl.

Were his legs that muscular yesterday? I'm not sure. I'm also not sure why I'm suddenly wondering what he's wearing under his kilt. Damn you, Sarah. I shake my head to get it on right and meet his gaze. My God what is the matter with him? He looks like a deer in the headlights.

"Is everything okay?"

"I...yes...I mean, aye." He covers his mouth and coughs. "I might be coming down with a cold."

"Oh, sorry. Should we postpone?" A wave of panic moves through me. I can't afford to put venue shopping off for another day—not with the wedding only four months out— but if the man is sick.

"No, I'm sure it's nothing." He waves his arms about, and while I've seen him do the movement yesterday—he likes to talk with his hands—today he looks like he's trying to ward off a demon that only he can see. "I put together a list of venues like we discussed, and I made a few calls."

He gestures for me to sit and drops into his chair. He places a thick index finger on a sheet of paper and slides it across the table to me, but I'm not looking at the paper. Nope. I'm looking at the streak of orange dripping down his cheek. Is he feverish? I mean, even if he was, he wouldn't sweat orange, right?"

"You ah, have a little something..." Before I can help myself, I lean across the table, and brush my thumb over his cheek. I come away with a streak of...dye? Does Finn dye his hair orange?

Panic moves over his face a second time, and he glances over my shoulder, zeroing in on the door, like he's about to bolt.

"Finn?"

He focuses back in on me, the fear almost gone from his face when he says, "I guess I didn't rinse away all my special shampoo." He rips a tissue from the box on his desk and scrubs it over my finger. "It helps keep the orange bright and luxurious," he explains.

I'm familiar with purple shampoo for blond hair but not orange shampoo for orange. Then again, I don't know any gingers, and I only know about the purple shampoo because Sarah uses it.

He runs the tissue around his forehead and face, and looks pleased when it comes back clean. I glance at the list of venues, and when I see Cypress Country Club, I point to it.

"Are you saying this is available in September?" Hope fills me. You must book the Cypress years in advance, and I'm not sure I have this kind of luck.

"Nae, it's on the list because you mentioned it." My heart sinks into my Louis Vuittons, and I lift my head to find Finn frowning.

"I'm sorry, lassie."

Aww, he's so genuinely sweet. "It's okay, it's not your fault."

"There are plenty of other places available."

I pucker my lips and look the list over again. "I know, Sarah had her heart set on Cypress."

He goes quiet, thoughtful for a moment, and he seems as disheartened as I am. No wonder he's the best at what he does. He truly cares about his client's desires. "Why don't we head down there. You never know what I can pull off wit' me Scottish charm."

I laugh at that. "Maybe a peek at what you wear under your kilt will sway minds."

Oh. My. Freaking. God.

Why the hell would I say that? I smooth my hand over my frizzy locks. Did the sun fry my brain as well as my hair? I don't know, but what I do know is this early morning version of the man I met yesterday is throwing me off somehow. I blame my sister for bringing up what he wears under his kilt.

"I mean..."

"Aye, I know what you mean. It's a lifelong mystery for sure." He stands, and I follow him up, my chin lifting to meet his gaze. I don't think I noticed how green his eyes were yesterday.

"Do you know that only two percent of the population have green eyes and the highest concentration comes from Scotland." What am I doing? "It's actually a genetic mutation." He folds his barrel arms across a broad chest, his lips twitching. "I'm not saying you're a mutation." My laugh comes out sounding crazy and manic. "I mean, look at you. You're not a mutation at all. You're really well built, and...well, you're tall, and well, red hair is a mutation too..."

Shut up, Luce.

"You seem to know an awful lot about mutations."

Yeah, probably because I am an oddball myself. My mother and sister are gorgeous natural blondes, tall and thin and vibrant and vivacious. I have short black hair, and I'm vertically challenged. You know what they say about short people: you gotta hand it to them, because they can't reach it any other way.

I wouldn't exactly say I'm the black sheep. But I don't have their people skills, obviously—heck, my sister is the 'face' of Johnson Fidelity, while I'm kept in the back room running numbers. I do however, excel at what I do, and it impresses my folks. God knows I wouldn't want to disappoint them—again. I just wish finance was my passion, or that they'd get behind what I'd really like to do with my life. Not that they want to know, or I'd tell them. I'm not ready to be disowned.

We have staff for that sort of thing, Luce.

"Wait, are you curious?" he asks, pulling my drifting mind back to the present.

"Curious about what?"

He bends and grips the hem of his kilt. "What's under ma kilt."

"Oh no, of course not."

Dear ground, please open up and swallow me whole.

"I mean, if yer curious." He arches a brow and inches the wool up a bit.

"Not," I say and hold my hand up, unable to tell if he's being serious or not. Something tells me it's the former and that he's the kind of guy who blurts out whatever it is he has on his mind.

He wags his brows. "Curiosity killed the cat."

"Satisfaction brought it back," I announce in response. I have no doubt this guy knows all about satisfaction—in bed. Why the hell am I even thinking about such things? Oh, probably because I haven't been touched in so long. After my last boyfriend—who is currently in prison for embezzlement—I decided being single was my best option.

How's that working out for you, Luce?

Well, I'm standing here fantasizing about my sister's gay wedding planner. So yeah, working out just fine, thank you very much.

His Scottish chuckle— can a chuckle be Scottish?—curls through me and tugs at something deep between my legs. Alrighty then.

"I'll drive," I say and practically run to the front door. "My car is in the lot." I jerk my thumb to the right, toward the two-tiered parking garage where I left my vehicle, as I steal a fast glance over my shoulder to see if he's coming. I can't help but think something is wrong as he walks—or rather shuffles and twists, and rubs his thighs together—a pained look on his face. I don't know what's going on under that kilt, but I'm thinking some kind of ointment might be in order.

"Did you want to change for the ride?" I ask.

Relief moves over his face, and his mouth opens. I'm sure he's about to say yes, but then, like he's remembering something distasteful, a scowl pushes back his smile, and he grumbles something about a stupid promise he made. At least I think that's what he said. Hard to tell through the grumbling.

"I'm fine," he murmurs and dangles a set of keys around his finger.

"I don't mind waiting. It's really hot out there, and that thing looks itchy."

"You dinna know the half of it, lassie."

I stare at him for one more second, and shrug. "Suit yourself."

He steps outside and shoves a key into the lock. He grouches some more as it only goes halfway in. He tugs it out and tries another key.

"New lock?" I ask.

"New to me," he answers, and I note the way the women on the street admire him as they walk past. As he struggles to lock up, I give him another once over, and take far too much pleasure in the way his tight black T-shirt showcases muscular arms and a broad back. I get the sense that those muscles are homegrown and not born in a gym. As a boy in Scotland did he work a farm? As I consider that, I picture a wee little Finn herding sheep. As my mind drifts, I note the way he's staring at me. I stand up a little straighter. Damn, what did he just ask?

"Sorry, what?"

"Top or bottom."

Oh my God. Is he asking me my bedroom preferences? Why would he be asking that? Yeah, sure I was staring, possibly drooling a little, but what I do—or haven't done in ages—in the bedroom is none of his business.

"Well, which is it?"

"Finn..." I begin, a wave of heat moving into my face, and it has nothing to do with this current heat wave.

He gestures with a nod to the parking garage. "Where did you park, top or bottom?"

"Oh," I blurt out. "Bottom...bottom."

"What did you think I meant?" He angles his head. "Wait—"

"That," I say quickly. "That's what I thought you meant." I hurry down the sidewalk, aware of his presence behind me. He keeps pace and stays close, and I start jogging like a damn lunatic. Not my smartest move, considering I'm in my Louis Vuitton's. My stupid heel catches in a crack in the sidewalk, and I let out an ungodly squeal as I go down. I'm seconds from faceplanting when a strong set of arms wrap around me and swoop me up.

"Got you, lassie."

"Thanks," I say, breathless, but not from jogging.

His arms tighten around me as I slip lower, and his warm scent, a mixture of the Scottish Highlands and what every girl's fantasies are made of, curl around me.

"What's your hurry?" He winces. "Oh, shite..." He shakes one leg out and I jiggle in his arms. "Twisted up my dangly bits."

Dangly bits?

Oh my God is he referring to his...

"Ah, that's better." Gorgeous green eyes narrow in on me. "Why were you running?"

"I...uh...in a hurry. I have to get back to the office by two. A... meeting." I slide my hands around his neck to hold on, as a group of young men and women start snapping pictures of us. "Oh, no. This is so embarrassing," I groan and bury my face in his neck. "I can't even imagine how they're going to caption this fiasco."

"What? You've not seen a lad in a kilt before?" he shouts, making this about him and not me, and I have no idea why, but I start chuckling. "You better piss off before I really give you something to caption, and yer not gonna' like it."

One hand lets go of my bottom as he gestures with his middle finger, and I slide a bit lower...and just like that, while I might not know what he's wearing under his kilt, I know what he's *not* wearing....and he's wrong. They are going to like it.

I briefly close my eyes and silently lecture myself not to spend one single minute thinking about his naked...dangly bits beneath the itchy wool. Nope, not going to spend one single minute thinking about it.

Two minutes though, yeah, I might spend two...

"No, I did not do a spectacular job," I yell into the phone. "Acting is not my thing and yesterday was a complete disaster." I don't bother telling Finn about the stiffy—one I'm pretty sure Luce was aware of—judging by the look of horror, at least I think it was horror, that crossed her face. Christ, every time she wiggled against my tadger, it thickened a little bit more. What can I say, I'm a man and she's a bonnie lass.

"Oh, come on, Gavan. I'm sure you were marvelous." I shake my head and pace around Finn's showroom. "You secured the venue they wanted, didn't you?"

"Yes, but only because Sarah Johnson wanted it and apparently, what the Johnsons want, they get. All we had to do was show up and ask. One look at Luce, and it was a game changer."

"I told you they were Boston royalty."

Truthfully, I don't care who they are. Someone else's wedding shouldn't get bumped because they decided at the last minute that they wanted the country club instead. Fucking rich people. So obnoxious, walking around like they're better than everyone else and putting on airs. Bloody fake. Speaking of fake, who am I to talk? I'm pretending to be someone else so Finn can get what he wants. I'm nothing but a lie, and for a guy who prides himself on truth and honesty, this doesn't sit well with me. I rake my hand through my hair, and grumble when a few orange strands tangle in my fingers. I shake them off and grunt as they fall to the floor.

"I think there was something wrong with the dye we used."

"There was nothing wrong with the dye," Finn says. "You just didn't leave it on long enough."

"My hair is falling out. I think we left it on too long."

Finn exhales an exaggerated huff. "Gavan, I don't remember you being such a complainer."

"Are you fucking kidding me?" After the shit I went through yesterday with Luce, and everything else I'm doing for him, he has the nerve to say I'm a complainer. I don't deserve an Oscar for my less than stellar performance, but I at least deserve thanks. I drop down into his plush chair and put my feet on his desk.

"Get your feet off my desk."

I go still and my gaze darts around the room. Does he have a nanny cam set up or something? "My feet aren't on your desk," I say as I slowly and quietly lower my boots to the floor. The itchy ass kilt scrapes my balls and I scratch them. Who in Scottish history thought it was a good idea to go bare under the damn thing? Did they think it made them tougher or something? "How do you wear this fucking kilt all day?"

"Stop being such a baby, our heritage and traditions—"

"I know all about our heritage and traditions."

"Rub a little salve on your bits. I keep some in the top left drawer."

I tug the drawer open, and find a huge tub of salve. "You couldn't have told me that before you went to Fiji?"

"Slipped my mind."

Yeah, sure. I screw the lid off, dip into it and sigh with pleasure as I soothe a big dallop over my balls. "Speaking of Fiji. How is it, and how is...Albert?"

"It's Alistair," he admonishes.

"Right."

"Fiji and Alistair are both amazing. We are having so much fun. Guess who we ran into on the elevator."

"Ah, dinna ken." Not only do I not know, I don't care.

The sound of ice clinking in a glass comes through on the phone as he excitedly says, "Come on, guess."

"Santa Claus?"

"Gavan," he begins, the joy leaving his voice. "Why do you always have to be such a bawbag?"

Scrotum.

He's fucking calling me a scrotum. Jesus.

I silently groan and scrub the back of my neck as a tension headache threatens.

"I guess that's what happens when you grow up on the tough streets of Glasgow," Finn says with a sigh.

"You grew up on those same streets, Finn, and I'm the one who fought your battles." I can't even count how many guys I kicked the shit out of for making fun of Finn and his flamboyant ways.

"Fine, but that still doesn't mean you deserve to know who I ran into now."

"Good." I push to my feet, and wipe my brow. His shop is airconditioned but with the floor to ceiling windows, it's hard to combat the sun shining in and heating the place. "I'm going back to your place for a swim."

"Before you go," he says quickly, and I can visualize him tossing his hand out as he points a finger at me. "How did things go with Luce?"

That gives me pause. "Fine, why?" Did he set this whole trip up just so he didn't have to deal with a woman he called a ball buster? She didn't come across like that at all, and she didn't even have to get assertive at Cypress. They heard her name and bent over backwards to accommodate her needs. Is there another side of her that I haven't seen yet? Will she go all hulk when she doesn't get her way? "What's going on, Finn?"

"Nothing. Oh, Alistair is waving me over, and he's got a huge banana—"

"Finn!"

He laughs. "A banana split, Gavan. You didn't let me finish. What was it I said about your listening skills?"

The phone goes dead. Listening skills, my ass. He was trying to fuck with me, trying to get a rise and we both know it. I take a step around his desk and the salve is squishy, and makes a sucking noise with each movement. Great, I sound like I'm working on a big slurpy between my legs. Fuck me. I hike the kilt up higher than any man should, anxious to get out of it. I shove my phone, as well as Finn's phone, into my pouch, gather up the salve, and head toward the door. It opens and in walks a well-dressed middle-aged woman, who is about to adjust her silk scarf over her shoulder but stops abruptly when she sees me. Oh boy, this looks like it's going to be fun.

Channeling my cousin, I ask, "How can I help ye, lassie?"

She narrows her eyes, her lips pinched, and then suddenly catching me by surprise she laughs. Hard. The sound fills the big room, and I glance down. Are my wee bits showing? Did I hike my kilt up too high?

"What's so funny?"

"You." She bends forward, and holds her stomach as she laughs harder.

I've been called a lot of things before, and I guess funny is one of the nicer things.

"Gavan, I take it," she says and my muscles tighten.

Shite. Is my cover blown? Wait, that's a good thing right, and I can end this daft charade. But then Finn would have to come home, and he really did sound like he was having fun and I don't want him to lose a business he spent years building.

"Do I know you?"

"I'm Stefanie..." her laugh dies down and she wipes her eyes as she nods toward the receptionist desk. "I can't believe Finn actually talked you into this. I guess I owe him a Benjamin."

"You took bets?"

She clears her throat and sobers quickly. "Yeah, uh. So how is the Johnson wedding coming?"

"Good, we secured Cypress Country Club."

Her eyes go wide. "Wow, you're good."

"Luce is good. I didn't have much to do with it."

Her brow raises at the mention of Luce. "What was she like?"

Okay, now I'm really starting to get worried. "She was very professional."

"Uh huh."

"What's that supposed to mean?"

"Nothing," she says as she glides across the room and takes her seat. She puts on a pair of glasses and wakes her computer.

I jerk my thumb out. "I'm heading back to Finn's for a swim. My next meeting with Luce isn't until Sunday. We'll be going through the invitation books, and hopefully placing our order. This morning I arranged for an engagement shoot for Sunday." Thank God Finn has good contacts who will drop everything for him. It's impressive, really. When I went back to help Da, Finn stayed here with barely a penny in his pocket and made something of himself. I'm actually kind of impressed by his fearlessness. "So I have the rest of the day off?" She glances up at me, because yes, those last words came out like a question.

"If there's an emergency, I can get you on Finn's phone."

"Ah, yeah, and I have mine too just in case." I touch my pouch, and give her my number. I feel like I'm leading a double life with two phones. That thought makes me laugh because yeah, I really am leading a double life. I'm no James Bond, but the late and great Sean Connery—a fellow Scot—would be proud, or not. Stefanie writes my number down, and I don't expect for there to be any emergencies, although, like my cousin, she might not know what constitutes one and I am waiting on the contract from Cypress. Luce wanted to get that signed right away, before we work on the invitations.

"Finn took a few invitation books home last week. Can you gather them and bring them back when you return?"

"Yeah, sure."

I wait a second longer, and when she ducks her head to hide behind her computer and I hear her snicker, I step outside. She's right. I am ridiculous. The salve begins to warm on my balls, as I climb into Finn's car and drive the short distance to his impressive home. His business is obviously doing well if he can afford such a place in Beacon Hill. I ease into the driveway, and the neighbor waves as I walk into the aircondi-tioned house.

I toss my keys, and set the salve on the side table. After kicking off my boots, I drop my kilt to my ankles. As it pools around my feet I exhale a happy sigh, thrilled to rid my body of the heavy wool. I wish I could wear pants. But I'll need the kilt for the photo shoot, and then later for when Luce and I will be picking out invitations to pick out. I reach into my pouch and pull out my phone. I punch in Da's number and with my arse out and my dangly bits well, dangling, I walk through the house and open the back door. Finn's yard is private, which means I won't be giving the neighbors a scare.

"Gavan," Da says as he answers, sounding happy to hear from me. Guilt swamps me. Is he hoping I'm finished up here and headed home?

"Da, how are you?"

"Fine, fine. How is Boston? What was Finn's big emergency?"

"You don't want to know," I grumble, and walk around the inground pool, considering my best way in. Ladder or cannon ball?

He chuckles. "Sounds like Finn is up to his old tricks."

"Yeah," is all I say. Finn is known for his dramatics, but if Da knew I dyed my hair and was parading around in a damn kilt, he'd no doubt tell his entire pub and I'd be the laughing stock of Glasgow when I returned home. A good Scot would never let me live it down. "How is Freya making out?" I ask, wanting to change the subject. He goes quiet for a second and my throat tightens. Freya is one of Da's best customers, and when I heard from Finn and dropped everything, she offered to stand in for me. But what does she know about bartending?

What do I know about event planning?

"She's good, son. Working out just fine." I hear a woman laughing in the background. "Don't you worry about me. You tend to your business there. No need to rush home."

"I'll be home in a couple weeks," I tell him.

"No hurry, son. Take as long as you need. You might want to start thinking about setting up shop there in Boston." My heart pinches tight. Does he think I'm just going to abandon him? I'm not Ma. I'm not going to fuck off when he needs me. He's the only parent I have. "At least take a look around."

"Yeah, sure," I say. Maybe I will. I don't know. Then again, maybe if I do find a nice place, I can finally convince Da to leave Scotland and come to America with me. That way I can look after him and he'd be a great asset to my business.

Another chuckle trickles through the phone and something that sounds like a slap reaches my ear. "Everything okay?"

Da laughs, but his voice is distant, his words not for me when he says, "What ya doing there, lassie?"

"Da?" I wait a second. Christ, what are they doing? Ugh. Maybe I don't want to know, but it is nice to hear laughter.

"Gotta go, Gavan." The call ends and I stare at my phone for a second, wondering what just happened. I shake my head, toss the phone onto one of the lounge chairs, and tear off my T-shirt and socks. I run, and hug my knees to my chest and jump into the refreshing water. I stay underwater and swim to the other end of the pool.

I push to my back, and close my eyes letting the sun shine down on me. Maybe it will dry up the rash on my parts. With my ears underwater, I float, and take deep breaths, hoping when I open my eyes I'll be back in Glasgow.

An ungodly scream pierces my calm, and my lids fly open to find Luce standing on the edge of the pool, a look of horror spreading across her face. Shite. I try to flip, and take in a mouthful of water, as she looks at my dick like it's the Loch Ness Monster's...wee baby cousin.

Fuck me. The water is cold, and I've got shrinkage. Can't a guy catch a break?

"Luce," I sputter, and stand up, hiding my dangly parts below the surface. "What are you doing here?" I push my wet hair off my forehead, and blink fat droplets from my lashes.

"I'm sorry," She holds her hands up, palms out, and begins to creep backward. "I didn't mean to interrupt. I should go..." She turns and her heels tap on the concrete pool deck as she darts for the open gate.

"Wait, no. It's okay." Her steps slow. "What are you doing here?" I ask, when I notice papers in her hand.

"I...the contract came through." With her back still to me, she lifts her hand and waves the papers. "They emailed them to me, and I thought I'd get them to you and get them signed off. Stefanie told me where I could find you. I rang the bell, and I heard a big splash back here. I didn't know you'd be... um, well...naked."

I hurry from the water, and glance around, but find only my T-shirt. I snatch it up and hold it in front of my dick.

"Let's get it signed then," I say, before she can bolt and I blow this contract for Finn. Wait, why is her body twisting like that? Is she fucking laughing?

"The water was cold," I explain.

"Yes, yes, I'm sure it was," she says, her voice uneven and shaky as she tries to pull herself together.

"You think it's funny now, do you?"

"No, no, not at all."

I shift the shirt, and glance down and see the white salve all over my parts. I guess the stuff was waterproof. "It's not what you think?"

"What do I think?"

"That I was...you know...chugging."

"Chugging?"

"Touching myself." Her body shakes harder, her sweet ass jiggling beneath a mid-thigh tight skirt, that showcases her sweet, heart-shaped ass.

Stop staring, Gavan.

"Hey Finn, listen. What you do in the privacy of your backyard is your business. This is on me, not you."

Her calling me Finn instantly reminds me I'm supposed to be acting like my cousin. "It's salve, lassie. For ma rash. It's the damn kilt. If you dinna believe me, turn around and I'll show you."

"I think I've seen enough."

I shake my head, and resist the urge to tell her she's not seen anything—thanks to the cold water. But I bite my tongue, because Luce is an important client and while my dick loves the idea of putting a bit more Scottish into her, I can't blow this for my cousin.

Shite. Why the fuck would I use Luce and blow in the same sentence? More importantly, the last thing Finn would be thinking about is giving this bonnie lass the horn, which means the stiffy I got yesterday when picking her up, and the one growing between my greased-up legs right now is going to be a little problematic and raise all kinds of questions.

How the hell do I get myself into these kinds of messes?

4

LUCE

I wave the papers. "Do you want to put some clothes on, and we'll get this signed, or I can meet you at the office later?"

Or we can go to your bedroom, and you can practice your signature on my body, with your tongue. I leave that delicious thought off, for numerous reasons.

"Let's get it done right now. Just give me a second."

I stand completely still as he hurries inside the house. Once he's gone, I slowly turn, and fan my hand in front of myself. Holy Hell, I didn't expect to see him stretched out in the pool—bared to the world. I've seen naked before but never that kind of naked. Lordy, when I came through the gate, and walked toward the pool, my gaze went straight to his face, but it quickly strayed downward. The second I saw all that salve on his...parts, I screamed, not at all sure what was going on, but I feared he was having some kind of breakout, or immune system attack, or battling the worst rash known to mankind.

Why the hell would he wear a kilt—with nothing underneath —if it gave him a rash like that? I realize he's going for a certain Scottish flair with his business, and everyone seems to love it, but still. He comes back out, dressed in khaki shorts and tugging on a clean T-shirt. I try not to stare at him as he lifts his arms and in that manly way men dress, tugs it on and adjusts it over his shoulders. Yummy.

You're off men.

I pull myself together as I quickly lecture myself. What is it about Finn that keeps reminding me I'm a girl who hasn't been touched in forever? Even if I did want to start something with him, he's not into women. He's totally the wrong kind of guy for me, which must be why I'm drawn to him. I'm so good at choosing the men who are bad for me. Nevertheless, nothing can or will happen.

What about that boner he got yesterday, Luce?

Maybe that wasn't about me, though. Maybe he was thinking of his partner, or there was a good stiff breeze up his kilt or something.

Stiff...

I resist the urge to chuckle. God, when did I become so juvenile?

"Again, I'm sorry," I say when he finishes dressing. "Should we head inside?"

He grumbles something under his breath—my God, he likes to grumble—and I follow him through the sliding doors. The air conditioning washes over me, but does little to cool the heat inside my body. We head to his kitchen and my gaze moves around his top-of-the-line equipment.

"Gorgeous," I say and admire his range. "You must cook." I turn to him, excited about that. I do love to talk food, and share recipes. He narrows his eyes, his muscles tight. I laugh. "You don't know if you cook?"

"Aye, I cook. I make a mean mac and cheese. I'm about five minutes from getting hangry."

"Hangry and a mad rash. That's probably a combination a girl does not want to see."

"You're right about that, lassie. Join me?"

"Aye," I say teasing him. "With a stainless-steel 30-inch all-gas Thermador, I thought you might be a budding chef or something?"

He shrugs. "I get by."

He starts opening cupboards and closing them again. Does he not know where he stores things? He could, of course, have a personal chef who has the day off. That must be it.

"How do you know so much about ranges anyway?" he asks.

Cooking is my passion, but I don't tell people about it, and I especially don't bring it up around my family. They think kitchen work is beneath me. Finn finally finds a pot and fills it with water. I put my hand over my mouth to stifle a laugh as he stands in front of the state-of-the-art range, and stares at it like it's an alien from outer space and he's trying to figure out how to communicate. He turns a knob, and nothing happens. He turns it back and curses under his breath.

"You need a goddam engineering degree to work this thing."

"Is it new?"

"New to me."

"Ah, I see. How about I cook for you then?"

He turns to me, his brow drawn together. "No, you're my guest. I can cook for you."

"I really don't mind, Finn." I walk up to the stove, and turn on the flame. He jumps back and I wink. "I guess you don't have the right touch."

He mumbles something about having the right touch as I put the lid on the pot. I lean against the counter and try not to fidget as he stands close, crowds me. "Are you stuck on mac and cheese?"

"No, it's just easy. To be honest, I was going to use a box."

I laugh. I find it hard to believe a guy as fit as him lives off boxed food. "Would you mind if I looked in your fridge and made something a little more gourmet?"

"Will it have cheese in it?" he asks, arching a brow and looking like an adorable little boy full of hope.

I laugh and he grins at me. "You bet."

"Be my guest, then." He waves his hand toward his fridge.

I step up to it, and admire the spotless, stainless-steel appliance. I run my hand up and down the long, sleek handle. "You're working with some great equipment, Finn."

"Thank you," he answers without a beat, and that's when I realize what I'm doing with my hand, not to mention the words coming out of my mouth. Shit. I turn to find him grinning at me. "I was talking about your appliances."

Do not think about his equipment, Luce.

Dammit, I'm thinking about his equipment.

"Of course. What else could you have been talking about?" He smirks at me, and I have to say I like this playful side of him. In fact, I'm enjoying everything about getting to know him, especially how he was willing to go to bat and put on his best Scottish charm to get the country club. I loved how happy Sarah was when I told her.

"Nothing." I bend, and pull out one of the drawers. Was that a groan? No way did Finn just groan. I look at him and he tears his gaze away fast.

"Stubbed my toe," he says quickly, and I eye him a bit longer, not sure if he's telling the truth. He must be, though. Me bent down and digging in his fridge isn't going to pull a groan from him.

I turn my attention back to the contents of the drawer, and wow, he's working with some great products here too. For a guy who doesn't cook, he sure has high-end ingredients. I pull out numerous types of cheese and set them on the counter, giddy about my find.

"You do love cheese," I state, as I begin to unwrap the gruyere first. I note the loaf of thick cut grain bread in a basket. "How about grilled cheese?"

"That's gourmet?"

"The way I make it, it is, and I can probably get it done in four minutes or less, before you reach hangry." He folds his arms, skepticism all over his face. "Let me prove it to you."

"Aye lassie, prove it to me." I admire his smile "What can I do to help?"

"I could use something cool to drink."

"I'm on it." He pulls open the fridge and grabs the jug of lemonade.

I admire his backside and turn fast before he catches me. "Sometimes you sound so American and other times you're all Scottish."

His shoulder muscles tighten as he opens a cupboard and pulls out two glasses. "I went to school here in Boston." He pours the lemonade and hands me a glass. "I picked up on the local lingo."

I take a big drink, and as I lick a bead of moisture from my lips, I don't miss the way he's watching me. Okay, probably my imagination. I'm reading things that aren't there. "I read that on your website."

He nudges me and winks. "Checking me out, were you?"

Oh, he has no idea...or maybe he does.

"I always do a thorough investigation before I hire someone."

Understanding moves over his face, and for a second there I think I might have offended him.

"Why are you handling your sister's wedding?" he asks, walking through the door I just opened.

"She's busy, and she asked me to."

He gives me a cheeky grin and says, "If she asked you to jump off the building, would you?"

"You sound like my mother." I chuckle. "But yeah, probably. What my baby sister wants, my baby sister gets." I catch the way he's looking at me. Damn, do I sound like a jealous old spinster? "I just mean, I love her. She's the baby of the family. Three years younger than me, and I don't mind helping out.

She's busy with her fiancé and she's a model, not to mention the face of the firm."

One thing I don't say is that Sarah and I were always very close growing up—her and I against the world—and there's a part of me that harbors a lot of guilt for going off to university. I studied hard, immersed myself in my classes and even though she was busy with modeling during her high school years, I could never be there for her like I used to be. I promised to always be the best bigger sister a girl could have and I think I failed at that. I guess that's why I'd do anything for her now, even plan her entire wedding.

"I've seen the commercials. Don't you work full time, too? I believe your title is financial advisor."

"Now look who's checking who out."

"I like to know who I'm working with. But that doesn't answer my question. Why isn't your sister planning her own wedding? You're the first sister I've worked with. Most brides love to work directly with me."

"Better organizational skills, I guess." I shrug. "And it's not been so bad." Do I admit that I actually like being around him, even though I barely know him? He has a reputation as being over the top and eccentric, and while I see it sometimes, every now and then I catch a glimpse of what I can only assume is the real Finn. I like that guy. I think we could be friends, and I'm a little short on those lately.

Okay, it's true, and I hate to even think about it, but it's been a while since I had a best friend. Why you ask? Well, the guy I dated before Mr. Embezzlement had an affair with my best friend behind my back. Want to know who that guy was? Ryland Baxter. Does the name ring a bell? It should. Ryland Baxter is my sister's fiancé, Glen Baxter's, older brother. I'll have to face them at the wedding. God, I hate lying, cheating people, especially guys who use me to get to someone close to me or to work their way into our family business.

"Anything else I can do to help?" Finn's words pull me back.

"Can you butter the bread?" He goes back to the fridge to get the butter and gets to work on the bread. "You have to butter both sides."

"Yeah?"

"It's my secret to the crunch."

"Ah, I had no idea I've been doing it wrong all these years." His stomach grumbles and I laugh. He butters both sides of the bread and I grill one side, and flip it over, putting the cheese on the crisp bread. I glance at him as he watches. "Breathe a word of this and…" I make a slicing motion across my neck and he laughs.

"Your secret is safe with me."

"You're good at secrets, Finn?" It's odd, but I do get the sense this guy can keep a secret and that's admirable. I trust so few people today.

He swallows and his throat makes a sound. "Yeah, the best."

"I'm pretty good with them myself." So were my last two boyfriends and my best friend. I finish up making the sandwiches and he roots out two plates. I slice the bread into fours and arrange them on the plates.

"Fancy," he teases.

"You're one to talk. Everything about your home and your shop is fancy."

"You don't like it?"

He feigns insult as he places his hand on his chest, those dark lashes of his blinking over totally offended, wide green eyes.

I stare at this man, a different version of the one I first met in his office. "Lucky for you, I like fancy."

I like him.

He grins, about to pick up the plates, but I hold a finger up to stop him. "One more thing." I go back to his fridge, grab the big jar of pickles and place one on each plate.

"Ah, now it's gourmet. Before the pickle, I thought it was just a grilled cheese. You had me worried for a bit." He winks and carries our lunch to the table. Smiling—I honestly don't know how long it's been since I smiled like this, was so at ease with someone—I bring our drinks over and smooth my skirt over my thighs as I sit. He takes a big bite into his bread, pretty much demolishing the first triangle.

He shakes his head. "Luce, I have to say, I think your skills are going to waste."

My stomach knots. I'm good at my job. It's the only thing my parents praise me for, and sometimes I still feel like a little girl in their eyes, always trying to impress them. Sarah never had to try. She could bungle a cartwheel and land on her face and they'd still fall all over her. I know this because we were both in gymnastics together and I'd witnessed it first-hand.

"I'm not kidding, Luce."

I toy with my sandwich, and pull a napkin from the holder on the table. "What do you mean?"

"If you can make a grilled cheese taste so good—best grilled cheese I've ever eaten, by the way—why are you wasting your skills in finance?"

I roll one shoulder like it's nothing, even though my insides are dancing. Honestly, the compliment means a lot, as does his faith in me.

"I'm pretty good at my job too."

"I have no doubt. Something tells me you're a natural at everything you do."

"I don't know about that." I don't think I'm a natural in the kitchen. I probably wouldn't win any cooking game shows. But I work hard at it, and every weekend, I bust my hump, secretly apprenticing at Prime, one of Boston's top steak houses. My entire life, doors were always opened to me because of who I am. I'm not naïve enough to believe otherwise. Just once I want to make it on my own merit, which is why no one at Prime knows who I really am. I'm enjoying the anonymity, and when the head chef yells at me, I kind of like it. It's fun just being one of the staff, and I don't want preferential treatment.

"I like to fool around in the kitchen," I say, shrugging off his compliment.

"Oh yeah?" His grin is playful and full of suggestion.

I roll my eyes at him. "Not like that."

He goes dead serious. "What do you mean, not like that?"

Oh, God, is he messing with me? Or am I the only one with sex on the brain? "Nothing. I just…I didn't mean anything."

"For what it's worth, I like fooling around in the kitchen too." Okay from the gleam in his eyes, he's definitely talking about sex. "Someday I'll make you mac and cheese."

Or not.

Which is good. I do not want to fool around with Finn in his kitchen.

Yeah, you do, Luce.

"How long have you lived here?" I ask, redirecting the conversation. My damn libido needs a moment to cool down, not to mention a good scolding.

He closes his eyes, like he's trying to remember. "A couple years. I think."

"You think," I laugh. I bite into my sandwich and moan. "Damn, that is good."

"Told you."

I sit back in my chair. "Was it hard leaving Scotland and your family to come here?"

"My cousin and I went to uni together. My da is back in Scotland."

"No siblings?"

"No, and I'm trying to convince my da to come here."

I wipe my greasy fingers on the napkin. "Why?"

"He had a stroke a few years ago." He sits up a little straighter in his seat, and I note the sudden tension in his body, the concern in his eyes. "He works too hard."

"What does he do?"

He perks up a bit when he says, "He runs a neighborhood pub, and raises sheep. I helped out for years."

"You enjoyed that."

He smiles. "I did. It's hard work, and with his stroke..." Fear mingled with sadness moves over his face and my heart squeezes tight. "I don't want to lose him."

Without thinking, I reach across the table and put my hand over his. I want to ask about his mom, but since he didn't bring her up, I won't either. I get the feeling she's not in their lives. "You're really worried about him."

He nods, and when his gaze goes to my hand, I suddenly feel foolish for touching him. I drag my hand away and busy myself with wiping condensation from my glass of lemonade.

"Where did you go to school?" he asks.

Okay, so he doesn't want to talk about himself. "Harvard."

"Impressive." He finishes another quarter of the sandwich in one bite. The man has a big appetite, and I was right, those muscles didn't come from a gym. They came from hard labor.

"I actually just finished my MBA." Shoot, why did I say that? He's going to think I'm fishing for compliments.

"Double impressed. Where did you find the time to learn to cook with your heavy schedule?"

"When I was younger, sometimes our chef would let me sneak into the kitchen and help out."

"Sneak?" he asks, picking up on the one word I probably shouldn't have used. I steal a glance at him. Will he think I'm a spoiled rich kid with every opportunity in the world, complaining that my parents didn't want me in the kitchen. He's a guy who clearly busted his ass.

"Oh, I just mean, Mom and Dad had us so busy with other things, there wasn't a lot of time for cooking, and they didn't really see the sense in me learning since we had an amazing chef working for us."

"But you snuck into the kitchen because it was important to you and you didn't want your parents to know because you didn't want to upset them." I wince, and he adds, "There's a lot in that to be admired, Luce."

Once again, his compliment fills me with pride. I open my mouth, about to tell him about my secret job, but quickly stop myself. I really don't know him well enough to be sharing secrets and I probably said enough already.

"Thank you."

"Do you always live up to the expectations others put on you?"

Wow, he nailed that pretty quickly.

His face holds genuine interest, not judgement, and for that I'm grateful. "Apparently. How about you?"

"Yup," he says so honestly and woefully, we both start laughing. "It's not easy, but you know that."

This time he reaches across the table and gives my arm a supportive squeeze. My entire body reacts to his touch, and I pray to God he can't see the quiver going through me. But it's more than that. I barely know him yet find him easy to talk to, nice to be with. I think Finn might just be one of the good guys, but dammit, he's playing for the other team. Not that I'm looking for a relationship.

A comfortable quiet envelops us, both lost in our own thoughts, and when he shifts in his seat, uncomfortable, I say, "Maybe you should rethink the kilt. You looked a bit...sore."

"Worried about my dangly bits, Luce?"

"Apparently, someone has to," I tease. "You could at least wear something underneath."

He takes a big drink of his lemonade, sets it back on the table and asks, "How is that authentic?"

"It'll be our little secret."

He smiles, and my heart misses a beat. "You won't tell?" he asks his voice an octave lower, a whole lot sexier.

"I won't tell, Finn. I'm good at secrets." A strange warmth moves through me as I promise to hold his secret close. "There's no shame in wearing underwear beneath your kilt. I don't walk around without panties under my skirts."

Oh, God, why did I say that? More importantly, why is there a hungry look spreading across his handsome face, a look that makes me think he's currently picturing me panty-less beneath my skirt.

5

GAVAN

My doorbell rings and it pulls me from the rich, seductive fantasy dancing around inside my weak brain, and filling my blood with hunger.

Pretend you're me, he said. It will be easy.

Easy, my ass. I'm sitting here imagining the sexy lingerie Luce must wear under her tight skirt and frilly white blouse that almost gives me a hint of her cleavage, and I'm liking it a lot and that's a problem. I have no idea how I'm going to stand without her noticing my stiffy.

"Do you want me to get that?" she asks, picking up on my distress, and I hope she doesn't know what's causing it.

"No, I'll get it." I stand, and quickly put my back to her, adjusting my shorts as I slowly walk down the long hallway. By the time I reach the door, my boner is under control and while I'm not religious, I throw up a silent prayer of thanks. I swing it open, and my gaze drops to take in the three young girls around the age of ten, all dressed in the same uniforms. Ah, girl scouts.

They offer me up dazzling smiles as I take in the badges sewed to their scarfs. As a young boy, I wanted to join the boy scout organization, but there was no time for it. I was too busy slinging drinks behind Da's bar, long before I was of legal age. Speaking of Da, I never should have brought up his stroke. If she investigated the real Finn, she'd see that his parents are crop farmers. I have to remember to remain in character at all times.

"Hi Finn," one of the little girls says, and offers me a big smile.

"Hi there." Shite, am I supposed to know her? Obviously, I am, considering she knows me by name.

"Hey Finn," a woman standing behind the girls says and gives me a wave, and I assume she's one of their mothers.

"Hey," I say back.

"It's that time of year," she alerts me with a laugh. That's when I notice the girls holding boxes of mint cookies and cue in.

"We weren't going to come by until tonight, but we saw the cars in the driveway and the girls insisted we try," the woman explains. "I hope we didn't catch you at a bad time."

"Not at all. Now what do we have here." I squat down to their height, and one of the girls holds a box out to me and shakes it enticingly, like she knows resistance is futile, and let's face it, it is. These mint cookies are like crack cocaine. I reach into my back pocket and pull out my wallet. "I'll be happy to take a box off yer hands."

"Just one?" one of the girls says, looking at me like Finn was right and I might have taken one too many hits on the pitch.

"Do I normally buy more than one?" I ask. "I can't remember." I tap my head. "Too many cracks to the head playing football."

They all laugh at my attempted cover up. "It's called soccer here, Finn. How many times do I have to tell you that?"

"A lot, apparently."

"You usually buy a dozen," the little blonde says, and I eye her, not sure if she's pulling a fast one or not, but then again, Finn always did have a sweet tooth. I do too.

"Well then, how about I take a dozen off yer hands."

One of the girls opens a pouch filled with money and holds her hand out to me. "That will be forty-eight dollars, please."

Forty-eight dollars? Christ, they're as expensive as crack cocaine too, not that I really know or buy the stuff. I don't. But good for her for having manners as she robs me blind.

I pull out a fifty and hand it over. "Keep the change."

"Thanks, Finn," they all say in unison and I stand as they hand me box after box, which I set on the table beside the door.

"We still on for next Saturday night?" the woman asks.

"You bet," I say, trying not to panic because I have no idea what she's talking about. As I plot the torturous ways to kill my cousin for only giving me enough information to hang myself with, Luce steps up behind me, and I open the door wider. "I hope you like cookies," I whisper to her. "If I eat all of these, I won't fit into my kilt."

She laughs. "They're only my favorite." She glances at the little girls. "Can I buy some too?"

The girls all light up and one claps her hands.

I arch a brow. "I think I've bought enough for both of us."

"Finn," one of them admonishes. "If she wants to buy cookies, she can buy cookies. She has a mind of her own, you know."

I hold my hands up palms out. "You're right. She certainly does." I bite back a grin. I'm not sure what they teach the young girls in the organization today, but I like the confidence and no-nonsense attitude. Go feminism. These little girls are going to be powerhouses in the business world someday.

"I think these would go over well in the break room at the office," Luce says.

"How many?" the little blond haired girl asks.

"I'll take a dozen too."

From the sidewalk, I can feel the woman's eyes drilling into me, and I lift my head to catch her little grin. Shite, I'd like to be polite and introduce her to Luce but I don't know who she is.

"I'm Lucille Johnson," Luce finally says, clearly picking up on the woman's curiosity. "My friends call me Luce."

"Nice to meet you, Luce. I'm Delilah Frasier." She gestures with a nod toward the house beside me. "Finn's neighbor."

Ah, my neighbor, which is probably why I'm invited over next weekend. Obviously, I'll have to find an excuse and get out of it. I'm not sure how close they are to Finn. If they know him well, there's a good chance I'll set off alarm bells.

"So nice to meet you, Delilah." Luce reaches into her purse and pulls out a fifty as she looks at the girls' empty hands. "Wait, do you have another twelve boxes?"

"Be right back." They run back to Delilah, who is dragging a wagon full of cookies behind her and they load up their little arms. "That's nice of you, Luce," I say.

"Just thought I could help out. I was a girl scout back in the day, and hey, maybe we can convince Sarah to give out cookies at her wedding instead of cake. That would save us time." She touches her flat stomach. "And save me from tasting all that cake."

I hold my arms out and stand guard over my boxes. "No way. I'm eating mine, and cake tasting is only my favorite thing to do."

Her little laugh curls around me and loosens something tight in my chest. "Didn't you just say you were worried about fitting into your kilt?"

"I'll let the waist out." I wink at her. "I learned that trick in boy scouts." She grins and my heart stalls. My God, she's gorgeous. I could stand here and stare at her all day, and I have no idea why Finn called her a ball buster. She's organized, smart as hell, and driven. Those traits on a man would be called assertive.

She arches a dubious brow. "You were a boy scout?"

"Why do you say it like that? Why can't I be a boy scout?"

"You don't strike me as the type."

"Judgy much?"

She grins. "Were you?"

"Well, ah, yes." Finn was the boy scout, I wasn't, so since I'm pretending to be him, I'm not really telling a lie, right? Yeah, I know it's a fine line.

She gathers up her boxes and I'm about to wave them off when Delilah calls out. "Luce, if you're around next Saturday night, we'd love to have you come to the barbecue too. Any friend of Finn's is a friend of ours."

Luce's eyes go wide and her gaze goes from Delilah to me. "I...uh..."

"Come," I say without thinking. Hell, what am I doing? I'd planned on finding an excuse, and the less time I spend with this woman, the less I'll be fantasizing about her, and possibly ruining this ruse. But I don't know, I kind of like being around her, too.

"Are you sure?" She leans in, her words for my ears only. "I don't want to give your friends the wrong idea about us, or start any rumors."

My mind instantly goes back to the way she hid her face when she nearly faceplanted. Have horrible things been written about Lucille Johnson? "We're friends. I have girl-friends, Luce, and I'm pretty sure there won't be any paparazzi or media leaks at my neighbors' barbecue."

She nibbles her lip, in deep thought, and I'm about to reas-sure her again when a smile lights up her beautiful face. "I'd have to get someone to cover me at work," she says under her breath.

"What?" Why the hell would she be working on a Saturday evening?

"Nothing, um, if you're sure."

"Positive."

She turns back to Delilah. "I'd love to come." I don't miss the happiness in her eyes or the smile that she's trying to control. Why is this woman still single...so lonely? I guess one could ask the same things of me. "What can I bring?"

Delilah waves her hand. "No need to bring anything. It's just a small gathering of friends and neighbors for my husband Jacob's birthday."

"She makes a mean grilled cheese," I say and the little girls light up.

"I love grilled cheese," one of them says.

"Mom, can we have grilled cheese?"

"We'll see," she says.

"I want one too," the third girl says.

"I also do great desserts," Luce says. "I'll whip up something you girls will love."

"Sure, sounds great," Delilah says. "But no need to go through the trouble, and the girls will be with their babysitters."

"No trouble at all." She winks at the girls. "I'll make a couple of cupcakes for you girls."

We wave them off and I shut the door. "No trouble at all?"

"I don't mind."

"You don't have enough to do?" Does she ever stop?

"She was nice enough to invite me. Are you sure I should go?"

"If you don't want to—"

She touches my arm, and my pulse jumps in my throat. "No, I do. It will...actually be nice to get out."

Why does a beautiful woman like Luce not get out? "Then it's settled, you're coming." Now I just have to figure out who these neighbors are, and what they know about me. I make a mental note to call my soon to be dead cousin. "Sorry I didn't introduce you. Sometimes I'm socially inept."

"You're the best event planner in the city, Finn. You're hardly inept. I think you were just a little focused on getting your hands on the cookies," she adds with a chuckle.

I turn and stare at the twenty-four boxes of cookies. "Probably, and we might as well get started." I open a box, rip the plastic open and hold it out to her. I'm sure she's about to say no, but I say, "Girl scout cookies, Luce. Resistance is futile."

She laughs and takes one from the box. I do the same, but don't moan quite as loudly as she does and that's problematic for my dick again. I start back down the hall to the kitchen, and when I turn back, notice she's nowhere to be found. I retrace my steps and spot her in the living room, looking at the pictures on the wall, and the framed photo of Finn and me fishing back in Glasgow.

Shite.

She picks it up, and examines it closely. "Is this your brother?"

"My cousin, Finn," I say, and try not to choke on cookie crumbs. Okay well that's a wrap. I just messed everything up for Finn, so I might as well throw in the towel, or rather the kilt.

She shakes her head. "Your cousin Finn? You guys have the same name?"

"Ah, no sometimes I like to refer to myself in first person." I take the picture from her and set it down. "I'm Finn and that's Gavan."

She eyes me. "He still lives in Scotland?"

"Yeah."

"You two are close?"

"Sometimes."

She crinkles up her nose. "This is the cousin you went to university with?"

"Aye."

"He's cute. What's he like?"

"He's a great guy. Would give you the shirt off his back if you were cold. One of the nicest guys you could ever meet," I say, building myself up. Not that she'll ever meet *me*. "Much nicer than Finn, and better looking too."

She angles her head. "Referring to yourself in first person again?"

Shite, she's really throwing me off my game. *Get it together, Gavan.* "It's a Scottish thing," I fib.

She grins. "If Gavan is that great, it's too bad he lives in Glasgow. We could use more guys like him in Boston and I could use a guy like that in my life." Under her breath she adds, "If I wasn't off guys, that is."

"What?"

Her blue eyes go wide and she tucks a strand of shiny black hair behind her ear, showcasing diamond earrings. "Nothing. I'm just not dating right now."

She turns and I follow her back to the kitchen. She picks up her lemonade and takes a big drink.

I toss the last triangle of sandwich into my mouth. "Dated a few frogs, have you?" I ask, even though it seems like she doesn't want to continue the conversation, but I am curious.

She laughs. "Frogs? No, not frogs. The guys I dated can't come out until after dark."

I laugh at that, even though it's not funny. "Vamps huh?"

"Something like that. Are you seeing anyone, Finn? Not that it's any of my business, but for the life of me, I can't find a good guy in Boston. Just wondering if you could."

I consider all my cousin's partners. Not all of them were decent, either. Always playing with his mind and heart. I hope things work out for him and Alistair. I only briefly met him before he whisked Finn off to the airport the other day, but I did like the way he looked at my cousin. I wonder if I'll ever look at a woman like that. Doubtful. Having lacked any nurturing women in my life, I don't even know the first thing about women—what they need, what they want to hear, what I'm supposed to do—other than the ones who hang out at Da's bar, and if that environment taught me anything, it's that I'm good for sex and not much more. Heck, I barely know how to do or say the right things around women. It was less than an hour ago that I told Luce to have a look at my balls. I'm lucky I didn't scare her off and lose the account.

"Still working through the frogs," I tell her.

"Sorry to hear that." I pick the plates up from the table and set them in the sink. "I guess we'd better get at the contract."

She pulls a pen from her purse, and while I know little—okay, let's face it, I know nothing—about contracts, I pretend to read it. "Everything look good?" I glance at her, and her brow is arched because yes, I posed that as a question.

"I've read through it and everything is in order."

I sign Finn's name and have a brief moment of panic. If it ever comes to light that I'm not Finn, does this mean the contract is null and void? I'm not sure, but I guess I'd better be careful not to ever let my real identity slip. I don't need any legal troubles.

She takes the paper, and looks over my signature. "I'll drop this off on my way home. I'd like to take a look at the venue again anyway. Sarah wants everything white, and I want to see the space again so I can think about the best way to decorate it." Her eyes light up. "If you're not busy, I'd love to have your thoughts and opinions. This is definitely out of my wheelhouse, so if you're free..."

"Sure. It's not like I'm doing anything other than trying to heal a nasty rash beneath the blazing sun."

A smile reaches her eyes, and she looks like she's trying hard not to laugh. "You'll come?"

"Aye. I'll come."

She crinkles her nose again, and I notice the cute freckles as she playfully crooks her finger and points it toward my nether regions. "Maybe we can stop at the drug store and get you a better ointment."

I stand and consider the kilt. Will Finn kill me if I don't wear it? Will it affect his reputation? I did make a promise and I am a man of my word, but I swear I'll sob like a wee baby if that wool brushes against my tadger one more time. How the hell does Finn do it? Have his parts become so weathered and battered, desensitized from years of wool abuse? I don't want any part of that.

"I'll be right back." I head upstairs to the master suite and tug my kilt back on, leaving my boxer shorts on. Back downstairs, Luce is putting the food away. She turns to me, her gaze dropping to my kilt and points.

"If you must present an authentic Scot in public, please tell me you're wearing something under that."

"I'm wearing my heritage and pride," I tell her as I lift my chin an inch. I grip the hem and lift it. "And my undershorts."

"Finn," she yells and puts her hand up to block me from her sight, but her voice is light and full of laughter and that's what I was going for. This woman has a lot on her shoulders, and even though she brushes it off, it's there. One just has to look to see it. "What are you doing?" With her other hand, she reaches out and tries to whack me. I drop my kilt and laugh.

"It's not like you haven't seen it."

"I didn't see anything," she says.

"The water was cold, lassie!"

6

LUCE

As my sister and her fiancé stand beneath a gorgeous cherry blossom tree, I glance around Boston Common in search of Finn. He doesn't have to be here for this, but he's a guy who likes to oversee every aspect of an event, and I find myself anxious to see him. It's odd, but I really enjoyed hanging out with him on Friday and he had great insight into how we should decorate the country club. It might be Sunday, but after this shoot, we have to head back to his office and pick out invitations—time is of essence—and I'm looking forward to spending more time with him.

I spent yesterday catching up on work at the office and last night busting my ass at the restaurant. I got yelled at by Chef more than once. Probably because I was in my head so much, reliving the moment I found Finn naked in his pool. OMG, the salve. Did he jump into a bucket of it? Just thinking about it now brings on a chuckle that I quickly stifle as my mother turns her head and looks at me like I had to be adopted.

How is it, with a simple look, she can make me feel like an outcast in my own family? As a socialite herself, image and the way we present ourselves to the world is everything. It's not my fault that they saved the long legs and beauty for their second daughter. I work hard at the firm, but without a powerful man on my arm, I'll never be whole in my mother's eyes. That reminds me, I have to work tomorrow night at the restaurant. I messaged a co-worker and she agreed to take next Saturday's shift, but asked me to fill in for her tomorrow night. I can't see it being a problem. I have to say, I am kind of looking forward to going to Delilah's barbecue.

"Such a beautiful bride to be," my mother says, and folds her hands and holds them over her heart.

"She really is," I say and smile at my mom, although her smile falters a bit as she looks back at me, and I brace myself for the lecture.

Breathe, Luce, breathe.

"Lucille, are you sure you and Ryland can't work things out?"

"Mom," I groan, as every muscle in my body tightens. "It's been over two years, and he's with my best friend." I nod my head toward Ryland and Chloe.

"Yes, well, he was one of the good guys."

I clench down so hard, I'm sure I'll need dental work next week. I get she's referring to Mr. Embezzlement, my mistake after Ryland, but come on, Ryland was sleeping with my best friend. How the hell does that make him one of the good guys?

Her gaze moves over me, takes in my blouse, dress pants, and heels. "If you gave it more effort, maybe he wouldn't have strayed."

I'm about to lose it, throw myself on the ground and start kicking and screaming, but from the corner of my eye, I catch Finn coming our way. Relief moves through me. His simple presence relaxes my tight body.

"It would be wonderful to have both my girls married into the same family," my mother adds.

"Not going to happen."

Her brow furrows, but not a wrinkle or line appears. "I just want you to be happy."

"I don't need a man to make me happy." I bite my tongue, and stop myself from telling her what I really think. God, I do so much to please them. Getting back together with one of my exes because they think it would be wonderful to have their two girls married to brothers is not going to happen.

"Darling, it doesn't look good that—"

"Finn," I yell out as he saunters toward us, in a different kilt today and I really hope he's wearing his boxers underneath. "Excuse me, Mom."

I hurry off in his direction, and I'm a bit breathless as I reach him. He dips his head, a strand of orange hair falling over his forehead as he looks at me through dark sunglasses.

"Are you okay?"

I exhale and work to pull myself together. I've always been good at letting Mom's barbed wire jabs slide off me. Today, for some reason, I'm feeling the sting. Maybe it's seeing my sister so happy, and knowing I'll never find what she's found.

"I'm fine," I say.

"No, you're not. Your face is red and fine is what someone says when they're not fine. What's going on, Luce?"

I love his genuine concern, but he's the wedding planner. My family troubles are not his concern. "It's hot out."

He lifts his head and looks over mine. "Are things not going well?" He stares a little longer, and I angle my head as the photographer takes pictures of my sister. "Do you need me to talk to the photographer?"

"No, I need you to talk to my parents," I blurt out without thinking.

"What?" His gaze jerks back to mine.

"I'm kidding." I let go a sigh. "Sort of. You're an only child, you wouldn't get it."

His brow narrows as his gaze goes from me, to my sister, back to me. "Let me take a stab at it. Your younger sister is getting married, and..."

"And I'm not. So you do get it. I have no problem with it. It's my mother who does."

He shakes his head. "I'd offer to be your pretend boyfriend, but well..."

I laugh and it comes out rough and...needy. "I get it, and no worries."

"I might not have siblings, but mothers..."

I angle my head and take in his pained expression. "What do you mean?"

"We're never good enough, are we? Fuck, I was a wee baby and could never do anything right." He snorts and looks off in the distance like he's a million miles away. "I tried to be good and not mess up, but I was never good…"

Whoa what did his mother do to him?

He shakes his head like he's trying to break the trance. "Yeah, it's fine. Let's get on with this."

"Come on. I'll introduce you." I slide my arm into his and we walk across the grass to where my parents are standing.

"Mom, Dad, this is Finn. Finn, this is my mother Fiona, and my father, Clive."

"Finn," Mom says. "It's so nice to meet you. We've heard so many great things about you."

"Aye, the pleasure is all mine, Mrs. Johnson." He takes Mom's hand and kisses the back. He turns to my father and shakes his hand. "Mr. Johnson." With his gaze going back and forth between them both, he adds in a thick Scottish accent, "I can see where your daughter gets her good looks. She's stunning."

"Yes, she is lovely, isn't she?" Mom says as she beams at Sarah. Mom's hand lands on Finn's arm. "I can't thank you enough for securing Cypress Country Club. Sarah is over the moon."

"Aye, but the thank you goes to Luce. She's the one who swayed them."

Mom blinks at me. "Oh, I didn't realize."

Finn moves in closer to me, his body strong and hard next to mine, and he gives me a little wink as the two of us stand together like a united force. The photographer continues to take pictures of my sister and her fiancé, and I don't miss the odd way Ryland is looking at me as I stand next to the big, handsome Scot whose arm keeps brushing mine and sending shivers through my body. At least I can blame the new rush of heat on my face to this heatwave we're having.

I go up on my tiptoes to whisper in his ear, but even in my heels, I can't quite reach. "Is it too early for a drink?"

"It's six in Scotland, and we never did care much about the time of day." He goes quiet for a second. "Luce?"

"Yeah?"

He inches ever so closer and angles his head toward me. "Why is that guy staring at you?"

I follow his gaze, until it settles on Ryland. "So it's not my imagination?" I've been imagining a lot of things lately, but they mainly evolve around Finn.

"Not." He takes his sunglasses off, and his eyes are the most glorious green under the early afternoon sun. "I thought you said your exes can't come out until after midnight."

I laugh. "How did you know?"

"Let's just say I have a knack for such things."

"He's Glen's brother. We dated for a while, and the girl he's with is my former best friend, Chloe."

"Jesus."

"Yeah."

"Do you still..."

"Hell no." Shit, I shouldn't have put so much emphasis on those words. Now it might seem like I do care. "I'm over him. In fact, I'm over all men."

"All men?"

"Let's just put it this way. My radar doesn't work, and like I said, I'm no longer dating, or putting myself out there." He eyes me. "Emotionally," I explain, because yeah, I definitely wouldn't mind putting my body out there for him.

"Let me just say this, Luce. It's him, not you. None of this is on you."

I swallow the lump in my throat and just smile at him. While I'd like to believe that, I don't. I mean seriously, how can it not be me? I'm the common denominator here—the person who gets dumped or used and left with nothing but bad memories and a cold bed.

His green eyes narrow in on me and I think he's going to press, but instead says, "We're definitely getting a drink."

While I like that idea, it's not a good one. "We have to work on invitations." I don't want to do anything to mess this up for my sister.

"I don't see why we can't kill two birds with one stone." I arch a brow, and try to understand what he's getting at. "That means—"

I laugh and put my hand on his chest, instantly wishing I hadn't as his hard muscles bunch against my fingers. I snatch my hand back and busy it with the straps on my purse. "I know what it means."

"You have to pick out the perfect wines, don't you? We'll do that as we go over the invitation books."

I nudge him but he doesn't move an inch. "I can't pick out the perfect poetic saying for my sister if I'm tipsy."

"You won't be tipsy, Luce. You'll be oot yer tree, and you canna and ya will."

I laugh at that as he throws his arm around my shoulder like we're the best of friends, and I don't miss the look it conjures in my sister, who is suddenly calling for a break. She hikes up the hem of her pretty blue dress and leaves Glen behind to come our way.

"Finn," she says. "It's nice to meet you. I've heard so much about you."

"Have ye now?"

My sister looks at me like I've been keeping a big secret and how dare I keep it from her. "Yes." She flashes him her winning smile. "My sister kept a few details to herself. I want to thank you for taking us on last minute and for all you've done so far."

"Not a problem, lassie. Luce has been great to work with. She's no bridezilla."

My sister laughs. "That's because she's not going to be the bride." She puts her arm in Finn's and begins to lead him to the pond, leaving me standing there. My God, is she flirting with Finn, in front of the bridal party? I shake my head, and now suddenly that drink is sounding better and better.

I have no idea what my sister is saying to Finn, or what he's saying to her, but she's laughing and touching him an awful lot. My phone pings, and I reach into my purse to grab it, and nearly bite off my tongue when I see the message is from Ryland. Didn't I block him?

Ryland: New boyfriend?

My head lifts and I search the grounds for Ryland, and find him standing in a circle with my former best friend Chloe, his brother and their parents. I'd like to tell him it's none of his fucking business but because I'm a damn lady, I text back.

Me: Wedding planner.

Ryland: Oh, I get it.

What, does he not think I could get a guy as hot as Finn?

Ryland: Nice skirt.

My anger flares. How dare he say anything derogatory about Finn. Finn has more integrity in his pinky finger than Ryland has in his whole body. And how dare he assume Finn is gay simply because he's a wedding planner. That's so damn cliché, it might be true in this case but still... I text back.

Me: I think so too.

Ryland: You like him, huh?

Me: He's the nicest guy I've ever met.

Ryland: Too bad he likes...(eggplant emoji)

"Oh my God," I mutter under my breath, and drop my phone back into my bag. I glance up and find him smirking at me. I resist the urge to cross the field and kick him in the shins. That would make him think I still cared. I don't. But I do care about how he talks about Finn. I turn and find Finn staring at me over my sister's head. His eyes are narrowed, as if he can see the irritation radiating off me. He takes my sister's hand off his chest and puts it by her side. A moment later, Sarah heads back to her fiancé for more pictures, and Finn talks to the photographer for a second before coming back to me.

"Want to get out of here?"

"More than life." I turn to my mother, who is not going to be pleased if I take off. "Mom, we have to go."

Her brow furrows. "You're not waiting until the end of the shoot?"

"We have to work on the invitations." I give her a bright smile.

"Oh, right of course." Before we can make our great escape, my mother glances at Finn. "Finn, darling, we're having an engagement party for Sarah and Glen. I'll be planning this one myself. You'll come, of course."

"I wouldn't miss it for the world," he says quickly.

"Lucille will fill you in on the details."

"I look forward to it. Now if you'll excuse us, we need to pick the perfect invitations for the perfect bride."

Mom beams and I bite back a grin. Finn is definitely a charmer. We turn and walk away, and once we're out of earshot, I glance at him, dying to know what he and my sister talked about. If I ask will I sound needy, or jealous?

He casts me a quick glance, and a cheeky grin pulls at his lips. I arch a brow and he says, "No, she did not ask what I wore under my kilt."

How can this man read me so easily?

I start laughing. "I wasn't thinking that at all."

"No, but you were wondering what we talked about."

I nibble my lip playfully, and don't miss the way his gaze drops to take it in. "Maybe, a little..."

"She simply thanked me for taking her on as a client." A moment of silence and then, "With her hands."

I start laughing. "What?"

He brushes at his chest, like she gave him the cooties or something. "She kept touching me."

"I noticed that." I say and work to keep the envy from my voice. Envy? Okay, yeah, maybe I want to be the one touching him, which is insane. "Most guys like it when she touches them, but…" He arches a brow. "Right." I laugh at the reminder that he's not most guys. If he was, he'd no doubt be all over my sister.

"Hot dog?" he asks as his stomach grumbles.

"You really need to eat better, Finn, and yes, with mustard." We head toward the hot dog cart, and the delicious smells make my stomach grumble. I steal a glance at Finn as he checks a message on his phone. "Ryland asked about you." His head lifts and he looks confused for a second. "He texted me when you were talking to Sarah." I pucker up my lips. "I thought I'd blocked him." I pull my phone from my purse about to do just that when I notice the strange look on Finn's face.

"What?"

He glances over his shoulder, toward the crowd gathered around my sister. "What did he want?"

I laugh like it's nothing when I say, "He asked if you were my new boyfriend."

"Oh yeah?" It doesn't seem to faze him at all, which surprises me a little. "Why would he ask that."

"No idea." Okay, maybe I have a little bit of an idea and it's that we were standing so close, sharing a secret smile, and probably giving off vibes that might be in my own head.

"Sounds like he's jealous."

I give an unladylike snort. "Hardly." I shake my head. "Wait, that came out all wrong. I mean, any guy would be jealous and intimidated by you. Look at you. I don't know any man who can pull off a kilt quite like you do, except of course for Jamie Fraser." He arches a brow. "Outlander. Only my favorite show. But anyway, Ryland is not into me, not anymore anyway." I'm not even sure he ever was. He was probably trying to get to my sister, but his younger brother got to her first, so he settled for my best friend.

Always the bridesmaid...

"It's his loss, Luce."

I glance down. "Honestly, I don't know what I ever did to him."

"Hey, what do you mean?"

I shrug. "I'm probably reading too much into it, but I think he was implying that a guy like you would never be interested in a girl like me."

"A guy like me?"

"You know...hot."

"You think I'm hot?" he teases with a wink.

"Well, yeah." No sense in lying. "I told him you were the wedding planner, and then he automatically assumed you were gay."

"He's kind of a dick."

"That's one of the nicer names I called him."

He smiles at me. "I'm glad you're over him."

He has a disgruntled look on his face as we get in line at the hotdog cart. He puts his hands on my shoulder. His lips slightly part, and my heart jumps into my throat. Is he going to kiss me?

"You can get any guy you want, Luce, and just so you know, when I told your mom her daughter was stunning, I was talking about you."

He lowers his head a bit more, and I instantly forget how to breathe. OMG, he *is* going to kiss me. Why would he do that?

"Really?" I ask breathless.

"Yeah, and I meant it." His head lifts, and he searches the gardens behind me. "Ryland is watching us right now."

"He is?"

"Maybe we should give them all something to talk about."

Oh, God, as much as I want him to kiss me, everything about this is wrong. I put my hand on his chest, and his powerful heartbeat pulses against my palm. "We can't...you're not into..."

"Gavan, is that you?"

7

GAVAN

I spin fast at the sound of my name, and nearly swallow my tongue when I spot Spencer Kane, a football team-mate from uni bouncing a ball on his knee as he comes my way. My first instinct is to pull him in for a hug and ask how the hell he's been, but I quickly stop myself. He was *my* friend, not Finn's.

"Ah, Spencer?" I say, like I'm trying to place him.

"Yeah, it's me, dude." He laughs, drops his ball to the ground and steps on it as he pats me on the shoulder. "Hasn't been that long. What are you doing back in town? Last I heard, you went back to Scotland to help your father. Sorry to hear about his stroke."

I clear my throat and straighten to my full height. Of course, he thinks I'm Gavan and not Finn. I was about two seconds from kissing Luce and killing my cousin's career. He laughs as he looks at my kilt. "What the hell are you doing in a kilt, bro?"

"You're mistaking me for my cousin," I say. "It's me, Finn." Fuck, lying is exhausting.

He grins and smacks my back. "Finn, my ass." He touches my hair. "This is new." Okay, he's going to blow my cover, and I need to do something fast. Before I get a chance, he turns to Luce, and his eyes widen. "Aren't you...Lucille Johnson?" he asks.

"Yes, nice to meet you, Spencer."

She shakes his hand. A grin on his face as his gaze goes back and forth between the two of us. "Are you two—"

"We're friends," I say quickly.

"Yeah right." He laughs. "You were seconds from kissing her." He nudges me. "She's way out of your league, dude."

I glance at Luce as she falters back a bit, and she turns her gaze downward, staring at her shoes like his words hurt, and while I don't know much about her, I get that he hit a sore spot.

"We were talking," I explain.

He rakes damp hair from his head and eyes me like he's in on the joke. Finn and I were never ones to pretend to be one another, so I'm sure he has no idea what the hell I'm doing.

"Could have fooled me," he responds with a smirk. "Drop the act, Gavan. You were seconds from tangling tongues."

Fuck.

"I'm planning Sarah Johnson's wedding, and Luce is her sister," I say in my best Finn voice. "She's assisting me."

He narrows his eyes and scratches his head. "Finn? Really?" He asks, skepticism, and confusion moving over his face. No, my friend, you are not losing your mind. It's me, Gavan.

"Aye," I say. "I'll tell Gavan you said hello." I stare at him, a pleading look in my eyes. He's a smart guy. If he knows who I really am, and I get I'm not fooling him, I need him to play along. I'll message him tonight and tell him the truth, but for now...

"Yeah, you do that." He bends and picks up the soccer ball. "The guys and I were just kicking it around." Back at uni, Spencer was our best striker, behind me of course. "A new league is starting and we play Wednesday nights at Madison field, just for fun and exercise. Love to have you join."

I nod. "Yeah, sounds like a great time. I'll check on my schedule."

He stares at me for a moment longer, until a dog comes dashing toward us, determined to catch the frisbee. Spencer backs up as the dog slows, turning its attention to me. Its owner calls him and he goes after the frisbee. "Yeah, okay. Nice to meet you, Luce. Hope to see you on the field, *Finn*."

Okay, so he clearly knows it's me, and my hair isn't about to fool anyone from my past. Which brings me to the upcoming barbecue at my neighbors. How well do they know Finn? Dammit, I need to talk to him. I can't do that with Luce standing next to me.

She glances up at me. "That was strange."

"We look alike," I say with a shrug. "You've seen the pictures."

"You play soccer?"

"Not anymore." At least that's not a lie.

She grins as I pull my wallet out and ask for two hotdogs. "I'd love to see you play."

"It's been so long, I'd probably injure something, and with this rash…" The rash is gone, but I'm looking for an excuse.

She laughs as I take the mustard-covered hotdogs and hand one to her. She peels back the foil and takes a big bite and I wish to fuck she wouldn't moan like that when sliding a big thick hotdog into her mouth. My dick thickens and there isn't a damn thing I can do about it. I'm a fucking dead man, but at least I'm a dead man in boxer shorts.

"So good," she says, and wipes the mustard from the corner of her mouth and slides her finger between her lips to lick it off.

Not helping.

"Speaking of food, we need to put a menu together for Sarah."

"What does she have in mind?" I ask and take a big bite of my own hot dog. My God, I forgot how good they were.

"You know the usual. A choice of fish, chicken or beef."

"No grilled cheese?"

She laughs. "No grilled cheese, and I'm not good enough to cater her wedding."

"Sure you are," I say and nudge her. Problem is, sometimes I don't know my own strength and she's so damn tiny, I nudge too hard and with high heels on, she loses her balance on the grass. This time I'm too slow to react and she falls on her ass, her hot dog landing on her blouse.

"Finn," she yelps.

Some guy pulls out his phone and laughs as he snaps a picture, and before I can stop myself, I toss the remains of my hot dog into the trash and step up to him. I snatch his phone from his hand, and quickly delete the photo. "Do it again, and you'll be eating this phone." I shove it into his chest, and help Luce to her feet.

"I'm really sorry about that, Luce. I didn't realize how hard I nudged you."

"These shoes weren't made for grass."

"Come on, let's get you out of here and cleaned up."

I put my arm around her back and brace her to me. She glances way up at me and says, "Thanks for deleting that picture."

"Not a problem. Did you drive here?"

"I came with my parents."

I guide her to my car and open the passenger side door for her. I scan the area to make sure no one else is taking any pictures before I cross the front and slide into the driver's seat. She pulls a few tissues from her purse and begins to dab at the mustard.

"I'll replace that."

"No, it's fine. A little soap will take it out."

I nod, but don't believe her. "Where do you live?"

"If you have something I can tug on, we can just go to your place. I'm a little further out, and I want to get the invitations done."

"Yeah, I do."

I turn the car around and head back to Finn's place. By the time I pull into the driveway, the stain has spread, and her shirt is completely ruined.

"Come on." I circle the car and open her door for her, and wave to our neighbor as she fusses with her flowerbeds.

"Hey Finn, Luce," she calls out and we both wave back.

"I think we might be giving her the wrong idea."

I laugh. "Maybe we should give her something to talk about too."

I guide her to my front door, and now, since I know which key to use, I easily open up. Inside, she drops her bag and tugs her shirt away from her body, and because she's tiny and I'm tall, it gives me an unobstructed view of her cleavage.

I clear my throat. "Follow me."

We head upstairs, and I go into Finn's room, the master bedroom that I've claimed. It's big and spacious, and decorated in light blue.

"Nice room."

I head to the dresser, and tug out a T-shirt. "This okay?"

She nods and I toss it to her. "Where can I get changed?"

"Bathroom, right there. If you want to give me your clothes, I can put them in the washing machine."

"It's worth a try, I guess."

She disappears into the bathroom, leaving the door cracked a bit, and I pace my room and try to tell myself I'm a gentleman, but that would be a lie. I really don't know much about women other than how to shag them. But I want to give Luce respect and privacy, and she's making it hard—and by it, I mean my tadger—by not closing and locking the door.

"Finn?"

"Yes?"

"Can I borrow a pair of sweats too? My skirt is a bit dirty, and would you mind if I jumped into the shower really quickly?"

"Ah, no problem at all. Let me grab you a pair of sweats." By the time I get back to the cracked door, her arm holding her clothes, is poking out, and I nearly swallow my tongue when my gaze lands on her lacy black bra.

I gather the clothes and push the pants into her hands. I note the skirt, blouse and bra. "No panties?" Shite, maybe she doesn't wear any, and fuck, I can't be thinking about that right now. It's bad enough she's in my bathroom naked, about to climb in the shower and put the scent of my soap all over her.

Wait, no she said she wore panties beneath her skirts.

"Ah, no. They didn't get dirty."

Fuck. Now I'm thinking about all the dirty things I can do to her in her panties.

"I uh...okay, I'll put these in the wash."

I stand there for a second, and suspect she's standing as perfectly still behind the door as well. I reach for the knob, and catch myself before I tug it open and ask if I can scrub her back. Her footsteps sound on the floor and I can finally breathe again as she turns the shower on and the sound of the spray reaches my ears.

I hurry out of the room, and go in search of the washing machine. I find it hidden behind closet doors and drop her clothes inside. I add half a bottle of detergent and set it to a delicate cycle.

I pace around the kitchen, working to dispel the image of her naked in the shower. My phone pings, and I'm grateful for the distraction. I tug it from my pouch, and see it's Finn calling.

"You're a dead man," I say when I answer.

"Nice to hear from you too, cousin," he says.

"The neighbors..." Shite, what was her name?

"Delilah?"

"Yes, did you forget to tell me about the barbecue next weekend."

"Oh, shoot. I did. Listen, it will be easy, a—"

"Monkey can do it. I get it. I'm not a monkey and I need to make a good excuse." Although Luce really seemed excited to go and I don't want to disappoint her. I listen to make sure the shower is still running and lower my voice. "I ran into Spencer Kane today, from uni. He recognized me, and called me out in front of Luce."

"Oh, no. That's not good."

I take a deep breath and let it out. "I covered. Luce isn't any the wiser."

"Look at you, thinking on your feet. Well done, Gavan."

"I don't need compliments. I need to know how to get out of the barbecue. Delilah invited Luce. I almost blew it yesterday."

"Blew what?" he asks in a teasing voice full of sexual innu-endo. Is that all he thinks about? Hell, who am I to pass judg-ment? Ever since setting eyes on the bonnie lass, I've been walking around half mast.

"Three kids showed up to sell cookies." I walk to the fridge and pull it open. "They knew me by name, and it really threw me off."

"Did you buy a dozen?"

I curse under my breath. "Not the point, but yes, and you're paying me back."

"Save a few for me."

"Finn!" I shout and check to make sure Luce isn't in ear shot. "Fill me in, or I swear I'm leaving."

"Okay, so Delilah's daughter is Maya, and her friends are Sasha and Bailey. Her husband's name is Jacob. He's a huge soccer fan, so we all have that in common. It's his thirty-fifth birthday, and you will go, eat some meat and enjoy yourself."

I brush my hair back, and numerous strands break free. I don't know if I'm going bald from the dye or the stress of this charade. "They're going to know something is off."

"I don't spend that much time with them, so don't worry. Talk sports, and call it soccer, not football."

"No."

"Coming, darling," Finn says, his voice a bit distant. "You've got this cousin."

I growl under my breath, my grip so tight on my phone, I'm sure I'm going to snap it. "I don't got anything."

I turn at the sound of footsteps, my gaze landing on Luce as she goes still at the doorway. She mouths the word *sorry*.

Okay, I was wrong. I might have something.

And that something is a goddamn boner.

I end the call, and drop the phone onto the counter as Luce smiles up at me. I knew she was petite, but without heels, she's just a mite of a thing, and for some unknown reason, it brings out the protector in me. Although, the second I saw the worry on her face at the gardens, and the disapproving stare of her mother, I went a little caveman inside.

"Everything okay?" she asks, a perfectly manicured brow arched.

Fuck, no. Nothing is okay. How can anything be okay with her standing there in a T-shirt that does nothing to hide her nipples and baggy sweatpants tied low on her hips. Without those heels, she has to look up even higher to meet my gaze. It does the weirdest things to me.

"Ah, no," I say, the first truthful thing coming out of my mouth since I met her. Before I can stop myself, I twist my kilt, trying to hide my growing erection. She crinkles her nose.

"It's just the two of us now. Why don't you get out of that, and into something more comfortable? I won't tell anyone." She winks at me. "Our little secret."

The only thing I want to get into that would be more comfortable is her.... I'm two seconds from tossing the charade out the window and asking if she'd like a little more Scottish in her when a beeping sound cuts through my thoughts. I stand there and stare at her, wondering if it's alarm bells in my head warning me to abort, and she laughs.

"The fridge is yelling at you."

"Shite, right."

I close the door, and my mouth waters as her hair drips, wetting the front of her T-shirt. My gaze goes to her nipples, and my entire body grows harder. If I took those perky buds into my mouth and sucked on them, could that be our little secret too?

Damned if I wouldn't like to find out.

"Are you sure everything is okay?" I shove my cell phone into the pocket of the oversized sweats, and the weight pulls them a little lower on my hips.

"Ah, what?" he asks, his gaze dipping.

I take in the tension in his body. I'm not sure who he was talking to, but he was doing a lot of grumbling. "You seemed a little upset on the phone. I...uh...didn't mean to overhear..."

His eyes dart back to mine and he shrugs one broad shoulder, but the ease doesn't reach his face. "No worries. It was just work stuff."

It didn't sound like work stuff, but why on earth would he lie to me? I glance around the kitchen. I guess we should get down to business. He probably has something better to do on a Sunday afternoon than go over invitations with me.

"Do you have the invitation books here, or do we need to go into your office?"

His gaze darts around his kitchen, his brows knitted together. "I...I don't know."

I laugh. "You don't know?" Sometimes he acts like he has no idea what's going on. I blame it on the artist in him, but I honestly find it quite adorable.

"Ah, wait yes, I remember Stefanie saying I brought some home."

"You don't remember?"

"I remember," he says, although he looks a bit confused and I'm a bit skeptical. "Let me get changed and look around." He pulls a bottle of wine from a wine chiller. "Why don't you open this and pour a glass."

I step up to the counter, and read the label. "What about you?"

"I'll have a scotch."

"Of course, you will." I lift my chin. When in Scotland. Not that I'm in Scotland... "I'll have a scotch too."

Surprise registers in his eyes. "You like scotch?"

"I guess we're soon going to find out."

He laughs. "The bar is in here." I admire the way his muscles move in his back as he leads me into another room, which is decorated in rich, dark leather furniture and a floor to ceiling bookshelf. I walk up to it and run my hand over the books.

"Wow, have you read all these?"

"Not yet. Do you like to read?"

"I do." I take in the books on fashion and design and decorating. "I just don't have much time for it anymore."

"What do you like to read?"

"I love romance books," I say and expect some kind of backlash. Men are so damn intimidated by romance books. Like the stories are some kind of fantasy they can't live up to. I guess they're afraid they can't live up to the expectations of a man being nice to a woman.

"Sorry, I'm not sure we'll find any on the shelf here. Maybe I'll have to restock," he says, and I smile at him. "What?"

"Nothing. What was the last book you read?"

"It's really been a long time since I've picked up a book."

"I used to like thrillers, and mystery."

"What was the last book that made you cry?" I ask.

"Microeconomics."

I laugh so hard at his answer, and his smirk does the most glorious things to the needy spot between my legs. Honestly, I love spending time with him like this, getting to know him. It loosens the weight on my shoulders just a little bit. I take a deep breath. "I think Sundays should be about reading, and long naps."

He kicks off his boots and stretches his arms over his head. "I can get behind that."

I frown as his body relaxes. "I'm sorry, Finn. That's exactly what you should be doing today. I shouldn't be invading your Sunday afternoon. You probably have things you want to do, other people you'd rather be with."

"The only thing I want to do is get out of this kilt, have a glass of scotch with you, and find the perfect invitation for your sister."

"You're sweet." As soon as those words leave my mouth he shakes his head. "What?"

"I'm not sweet, Luce. I'm not…I'm not anything you think I am…I'm…" His words fall off as he frowns.

I'm about to protest—I don't think Finn hides anything and I have a pretty good idea who he is—but he lifts his head and glances at the stocked bar. "Grab the top shelf Johnny Walker." He gives me a wink, like he's up to something, although I have no idea what. "Let's drink all the expensive stuff."

"If you say so." I turn and step behind the gorgeous, rich mahogany wet bar, and reach up. "Did you know this brand became famous after Winston Churchill declared that it was the only whiskey he drank." I go higher on my tiptoes and struggle to reach the bottle.

"You know a lot of trivia—"

"Useless trivia," I say with a very unladylike snort, that my mother would give me a disapproving look for. I glance over my shoulder, but Finn is smiling at me.

"Knowledge is never useless. We should hit up trivia night at a bar sometime. That'd be fun. I used to do that at uni. I wasn't very good though."

"Is that what you do for fun?" I ask.

He grumbles something about not knowing what fun is anymore, and I can totally understand that. "What do you do for fun, Luce?"

"Plan my sister's wedding, work, eat, sleep, rinse repeat." Sarcasm drips from my voice and his chuckle curls around me. "Honestly, Finn. Adulting is overrated. When I was a teen, before my driver's license, my friends and I would dream about all the places we'd go, and how we'd never be bored again."

"Where did you talk about going?"

"Museums, and bars, and dances...I can't remember the last time I danced. We used to dream of faraway places too."

"Like Scotland?"

"Aye, like Scotland," I say.

I stretch a little more, and as I consider grabbing my heels, big strong hands land on either side of my ribcage, and a warm breath washes over the side of my neck as he lifts me. A quiver goes through me as he braces me against his rock-hard body. I snatch the bottle from the top shelf, and work to cover the tremble he must feel by chuckling.

"You're so tiny, Luce." There's nothing in his voice to suggest he doesn't like that. In fact, there's a warmth, maybe even a need, and maybe I need to have my brain scanned for a tumor.

"Vertically challenged," I say as I work to control the want rising in me. "I don't have my sister's or my mother's long legs." *Stop rambling, Luce.*

"Like adulting, long legs are overrated," he murmurs.

"Did you know short people are always overlooked?" I laugh at my own ridiculous joke, as his green eyes turn dead serious and zero in on me.

"Are you always overlooked, Luce?" he asks, and ohmigod, I'm pretty sure I'm going to need a change of panties, because mine are getting damp.

"It's a joke...things I've heard people say."

He brushes the back of his knuckles over my cheek. "Any guy that overlooks you must be a total eegit."

My face warms from his touch, and my heart beats a little bit faster as my mind goes back to when I found him in the office calling himself that same name. "Are you an eegit?" I ask. I wish I didn't sound so breathless, but how can't I help it as he stands over me in the tight space, his body looming, crowding, an aching reminder that I want to be touched by him—even though he'd be another mistake on the long rung leading to spinsterhood. Wouldn't my family have a field day with this one.

"Aye lassie, most times I am." His head drops and he takes a step back, and dammit, I instantly miss his powerful body meshed against mine. "Pour us a stiff one."

My stupid gaze drops, and I don't miss the way his kilt is tenting. Speaking of stiff...is he? I tear my gaze away, and reach under the bar for two glasses as he disappears from the room, his footsteps heavy on the stairs as he races to his room.

What the hell is going on between us?

I give my head a good hard shake to clear it and pour a generous amount of scotch into the glass and take a big swig. I gasp as it steals my breath. Holy burn. But if I'm going to sit close to him for the next hour or so, I'm going to need something to numb my senses. Otherwise I might do something I can only regret later. I add more to my glass and pour some into his.

"Ice?" I call out.

"In the bar fridge, and yes." Drawers open and close from upstairs as I drop ice into the glasses. By the time I lift my head, Finn is standing before me, dressed in shorts and a T-shirt looking like he just fell from the Scottish heavens. "Better?" I ask as soon as I find my voice.

"Much." I step out from behind the bar and hand him the glass of scotch. He holds it up in salute. "To boxer shorts," he says and I laugh, even though the toast reminds me how damp my panties are.

"I'll drink to that."

He gestures with a nod of his head. "I found the invitation books in the office."

I glance at the sofa. "Maybe we'll be more comfortable in here."

"Aye, and it's closer to the scotch."

He disappears and comes back with a couple of large books and drops them onto the coffee table. "Your sister really wants you to pick out the invitations for her?"

"Yeah, why?"

"Seems odd, I guess. But what do I know?"

"You know everything." The more I think about it, the more I realize how right he is. Why isn't my sister doing any of this herself? "If I were getting married, and that's not happening, I'd want a say in everything."

He drops down onto the sofa and pulls the coffee table close. He puts his feet onto it, and goes still for a second, like maybe he shouldn't be doing that. "Fuck that," he murmurs under his breath and stretches out. His big hand pats the seat beside him and I drop down into the buttery soft leather.

"Why do you say you're never getting married?" He snatches up one of the books.

"Ah, vampires." He smirks at the reminder. "What about you, Finn? Do you see marriage in your future?"

"You know," he begins, seriously. "Over the years I learned that I might be good for only one thing."

"What's that?" I ask and take a drink of my scotch.

"Sex," he says honestly and I nearly choke on my drink.

"Come on, Finn. You have a lot to offer. You have a beautiful home, a successful business and a great reputation. If some guy can't see that, then he's an eegit." His grin is so cute it wraps around me and squeezes tight.

"Well thanks, but you know...I just...I grew up without a ma, you know."

Ah, the question I was wondering, but didn't want to ask.

"She fucked off on Da and me when I was a wee lad. Wasn't happy I could never do anything right. I guess my failures were a reflection on her. Seriously, Luce, what kid doesn't come home with ripped clothes. Try as I might...but I couldn't be the proper boy she wanted." He goes quiet for a second, like he's remembering something painful from his past. Does he think his mother left because of him, because he wasn't good enough...wasn't enough? "I don't know much about relationships, other than people can't seem to be faithful."

I exhale with a sigh. "I know."

He frowns. "Sorry."

"No need." I hold my glass up. "Go on."

"At the bar Da owns in Scotland, lots of cheating going on. I've witnessed it since I was a laddie. I'm not even sure fidelity is a thing."

"I'm sorry, Finn." I exhale slowly. "Ryland and Chloe...yeah, I get cheating and now I have to stand next to her at the wedding. She's the maid of honor, and I'm a bridesmaid. Apparently, she's grown quite close to Sarah, and the couples double date a lot." I take a big drink of whiskey to wash that slap in the face down.

"Unbelievable, and yet you're still so good to your sister."

"She's the golden child, you know. I love her, though." I twirl the melting ice. "You know, I like to think I'd be faithful. I never cheated on any guy. What about you?"

"I've never been in a serious relationship." I stare at him, noting his dodgy answer. "I have no doubt you'd be faithful, Luce, but now you're off guys."

"Totally."

Although I'd like to be 'on' Finn.

He goes quiet for a bit, and starts flipping through one of the books. "You know, I think it's kind of shitty."

I finish the whiskey in my glass, and Finn takes it from me. He goes back to the bar and refills us both, but my head is a bit lightheaded, so I'm not sure I should drink it. "What?"

"Your sister asking your former best friend to be in her wedding party. I don't think that's fair to you."

"She's Ryland's fiancée. What can I do?"

"I don't care. Is she the monkey that went to Mars?"

"A monkey went to Mars?" Okay, maybe we've had too much to drink, and that doesn't bode well for me. I have work tomorrow, and tomorrow night I'm covering at the restaurant, and I also have to get my sister to nail down her menu.

He laughs. "A monkey went somewhere, but that's not the point. The point is...and I mean no disrespect, Luce, but you're blood. That cunt isn't."

"Ohmigod," I say. "Did you just use the c-word?"

"Ah, sorry. Was that offensive?" He shakes his head. "I grew up in a pub in Scotland. Sometimes I don't know the right things to say, especially to women."

I snicker, but do wonder if that's because he likes guys, or grew up without a mother's influence. Although I suspect he was better off without her in his life. Maybe the emotional damage would have been worse had she stuck around. "It's fine, and it's accurate."

He sits next to me, a little closer this time. "It's awkward for you." I fall toward him as he adjusts his big body. "Your sister shouldn't be putting you in that situation."

He hands me my glass. "Why are you so intuitive, Finn?"

Why must you be gay?

"Years of bartending and listening to people, I guess." He puts the invitation book back on his lap. "How about this one?" He laughs as he points to a ridiculous but funny invitation that would no doubt give my mother a heart attack.

"And that, my friend, is why we should be doing this sober." He grins and flips the page.

"Probably."

I start laughing almost uncontrollably, and he looks at me like I suddenly lost my mind and it's possible he's right. "Do it again, and you'll be eating this phone." Finn starts laughing as I mimic what he said to that guy taking pictures of me after I faceplanted. "I can't believe you said that to that guy." No one has ever protected me like that or stood up to someone—threatened them, even.

"What can I say, I don't like anyone messing with my friends."

We laugh some more, and I like the idea of being his friend. I try not to let my gaze stray to his impressive bicep muscles.

"Tough guy. I like it."

"Oh, is that what you like?" he asks, and my spinning head comes to a resounding halt. Did things just turn sexual...intimate? "Then I should probably tell you I had to break up many drunken brawls at Da's pub."

"I thought Scots had a high tolerance for alcohol," I say, as my body warms from the inside out, and I'm pretty sure something else is going on to make that happen.

"Aye, we do, lassie." His gaze moves over my face, lingering on my lips after I dampen them. I take a breath and hold it for a second. Is he going to kiss me? He stares a moment longer, and I sit up a bit straighter.

He turns back to the book on his lap and studies the RSVP invites like they might be the key to solving world hunger.

"Aren't we supposed to include a menu so the guests can check off what they want to eat?" he asks, his voice an octave lower, and a bit rougher. The deep sound rakes over my skin, and I work to find my voice.

"You're asking me? Aren't you the wedding planner?"

He looks almost horrified for a moment. "And yet another reason we shouldn't be drinking." He takes a big swig and I cross my legs and let my thigh rest against his.

"We have to set the menu, then we can get the invitations mailed. My sister still hasn't decided on which restaurant she wants to cater the event."

"Maybe she's leaving that to you."

"Wouldn't surprise me." Just then, my phone pings and I pull it from my pocket. I read my sister's text and nearly swallow my tongue.

Sarah: *No way is Finn gay!*

GAVAN

"What the hell?" I ask as Luce goes pale beside me. She hides her phone—clearly she doesn't want me to see—as dark lashes blink rapidly over her big blue eyes. "Luce?"

"Oh, nothing," she answers. But as I stare at her, take in the way she's staring back, her chest rising and falling a little quicker, she says, "Ah, my sister. Speak of the devil." She laughs and it sounds strained and uneasy.

"What did she want? Is everything okay?"

She blinks once, twice, like she's thinking something through and then she snorts a little and shakes her head. "Um...nothing. Sarah being Sarah. Sister stuff. You wouldn't understand."

"You're right, I wouldn't." I don't know Sarah at all, but I am getting to know her sister, and what I'm getting to know, I like. My gaze moves over her flushed face, and I'm guessing she's not a girl who can hold her scotch. At least I think she's flushed from the drink, or maybe it was from her sister's text, not that she wants to share it with me. "I think we should eat something."

"I can cook," she says.

"No, I think we'll just order in, if that's okay. Then maybe we'll go for a swim." Christ, the last thing I should be doing is feeding her alcohol, especially on an empty stomach. She tossed her hot dog after she fell. "What do you like?"

She crinkles up her cute little nose and thinks about it. "How about Thai?"

I nod in agreement. "Do you know any good Thai restaurants? Oh wait, there was this place near campus that I used to love."

"You haven't had Thai since university?"

"Been busy."

She starts laughing. "You're kind of a strange guy, Finn. Just when I think I've started figuring you out, you surprise me again."

She doesn't know the half of it. "Do you like surprises?"

"Not really."

This time I chuckle. I pull out my phone and do a search. "Found it. Anything special you'd like?"

"I want those little ball things."

Jesus.

"You know..." She uses both hands and makes a circle and I quickly check the menu. "Balls. Like they're balls."

"You should probably stop saying balls."

"Why?"

I arch a brow and her mouth forms a little O.

"Yeah, oh. Okay deep fried chicken balls. Is that what you mean?"

"Chicken balls, that's it. Oops, I mean chicken...circles?" She puts her hand over her mouth to stifle a giggle and dammit all I want to do is tear it away and kiss her. She's so freaking cute right now.

"Chicken circles. Got it."

"Oh, and those other things. You know." She forms her fingers into rectangle.

I scan the menu and add a bunch of dishes. "Other things, got it and added," I say and she grins. "Let me place this order." I run my fingers over the phone and she takes the invitation book from me. She sobers quickly as she flips the pages, an almost forlorn look on her face. It punches me in the stomach, and a part of me wants to pick up the phone and call her sister, but I can't blow this account for my cousin. Seriously though, I hate everyone in her life right now.

"All done," I say. "It should be here in about thirty minutes."

"How about this one here?"

I lean into her. "Luce, that's beautiful."

"This is the one I would have."

"You have good taste. Classic and beautiful, just like you."

She puts the book on the coffee table and stands, walking back to the bookshelf. She looks like she's a million miles away, lost in her own thoughts as she examines them again.

"Want to take a dip in the pool before the food gets here, or maybe a lazy Sunday afternoon nap?"

She spins and grins. "A nap does sound kind of good."

"Come on."

I take her hand and lead her up the stairs. I guide her into the master suite, and she looks at my bed. "What about you?" she asks, and my heart squeezes as I take in the lost and lonely look on her pretty face.

"I'll tuck you in."

Don't do it, Gavan.

She gives an adorable snort. "It's been a long time since someone's tucked me in." She walks across the room in clothes that are far too big, but look so sexy on her. Damned if I don't want to take them off and discover all the sweetness underneath—with my tongue.

She tugs the bedding down, and I step up to her, pulling it down even more. "In," I command in a soft voice and don't miss the ever so slight tremble moving through her body. What, does this take-charge woman—ball buster, as my cousin declared—like the tough guy in me as well as my take charge attitude? Maybe she does. Maybe there is a part of her that's damn tired of taking care of everyone else, and always being the responsible one. Maybe what Luce needs is a little irresponsible fun and maybe I'm the guy to give it to her.

She climbs between the sheets, and moans as she snuggles into my bedding. "Tuck me in," she whispers. I pull the blankets up and she slides to the middle of the bed, making room for me.

"Luce?"

"Yeah."

"Do you want me to..."

"Friends nap together."

I'm not so sure about that. There is one thing I'm sure about though and that's my growing erection.

Abort.

As my brain screams for me to leave, she whispers, "Just for a second." Dammit, she sounds cozy, warm...vulnerable, and I don't have the heart to walk out on her. I slide into the bed, and keep to my side, and she rolls toward me, her body soft, and warm and goddammit, she smells so good. Her eyes are closed and I take the covers and pull them up to her chin. When I do, her eyes slowly open and my dick jumps to attention.

"Sleep," I command in a soft voice and once again her body reacts, and this time a little moan catches in her throat.

She inches closer, her groin aligned with mine, and before I can help myself, I brush her hair from her face, take in the need in her eyes.

Don't do it, Gavan. Do not fucking do it.

Her sweet lips part and common sense packs a bag and heads to Siberia, leaving only primal instinct to rule. I slide my hand around her head, and growl as I bring her mouth to mine. So fucking sweet. I kiss her like a man starved, and she kisses me back and grips the front of my shirt, holding me tight like she fears I might spontaneously combust any second, and she could be right. Maybe she's worried I'll bail.

She moves, and there is nothing I can do to stop my dick from swelling and pressing against her hot, writhing body. She is so goddamn needy and it's messing with me big time.

"Finn," she murmurs into my mouth and my one working brains cell kicks back in, reminding me this is a bad fucking idea. I'm about to pull back, grab my luggage and head back to Scotland, or maybe Canada where it's colder—maybe that will freeze the fire in my veins—but she says one word to me that stops me dead and makes me forget why this is wrong. "Please."

Fuck me.

I roll on top of her, take her arms and pin them above her head. Her chest rises and falls as I hold her down with my body weight, and her lids are barely open as I bury my face in her neck, breathing in the delicious scent of her fragrant skin, so soft and sweet I could lose myself in her. I move my body over hers. My God, she is so fucking tiny and delicate, I'm afraid I might crush her, but she doesn't seem bothered by my weight at all.

I shift to the side, and her hips lift, her body beckoning my touch. Her soft, needy moans curl around me, and my lips leave her neck to travel downward. My heart pummels my chest as I tug the T-shirt up and expose her beautiful breasts. Her hands go around my head, her eyes locking with mine. She links her hands, and guides me to her body, and moans as I lick one perfect bud, and I can't help but think every Sunday afternoon should be spent with Luce in my bed, my tongue on her. At least for the next month, while I'm here. Maybe if I make this really good for her, she'll be game.

"So fucking perfect," I whisper, my breath fluttering against her skin and pulling a quake from her. I lick her nipples, alternating between breasts, unable to get enough. My cock thickens against her leg, and I growl, wanting to free it from the confines of my shorts.

I suck on her nipple, and lightly bite down until she's squirming, her hips moving, her body desperate for so much more. When was the last time she's been touched? I don't know, and frankly I don't care, because I'm touching her now and that's all that matters.

I slide a hand down her body and find the string on her sweatpants. I release it and dip my hand inside.

"Yes..." she cries as I part her nether lips and a growl rumbles in my throat as I discover her wetness. I run my finger along her crevice, and circle her swollen clit, and her breathing changes, becomes a little more frantic. I love seeing her like this. She claws at my shirt, and tugs it over my head. I pull my hand from her pants, and help her get it off me. Big eyes roam my body and from the pleasure in her eyes, it's clear she likes what she sees. I like what I see too, I just need to see more of it.

I shift positions, and move between her legs. Her chest rises and falls, her sweet nipples hard as granite as she watches my every movement. I tug on the waist band and lower her pants just enough to expose the trim hair of her pubis. I go slow, even though I want to ravage her, but I don't want to rush this. I want to get to know her body, intimately. More importantly, I want to give this woman what she needs.

Her hips come off the bed, and I arch a brow. "Need something, babe?" I ask.

She nods, and wets her lips, her hands going to her breasts. I nearly shoot off in my pants as she rubs her nipples between her fingers. "Please touch me."

Wanting to end her torment and get my mouth on her, I tug her pants down her legs and remove them. I toss them away, flatten myself on the bed, and push her thighs wide open, so I can feast on her gorgeous pussy.

I lick from bottom to top and a keening cry catches in her throat. Yeah, she likes that. I do it again, and this time I swirl my tongue around her clit, coming close but never touching. She lifts, and bumps her pussy against my chin, and a tremble moves through her. I tease her a bit more, until she's chanting something incoherent, before I take her clit into my mouth.

"Finn," she yells, and goddammit, I want to hear my name on her lips, not my cousin's. But there's no time to think about that, not when her body is heating up, her orgasm so close. I suck on her clit, roll my tongue over it and slide a thick finger into her core. She reaches down and grabs two fistfuls of my hair and holds me to her and I kind of love that she's not being shy, and that she's taking what she needs. Way to be assertive, Luce.

"That's it," I murmur from between her legs. I work my finger inside her, lightly brushing the bundle of nerves that starts her chanting again, and she's so damn wet, my finger so slick, I keep sliding out. I put another finger in, and as small quakes begin in her core, I apply more pressure to her clit.

"Ohmigod," she whimpers, and I glance up to see her head rolling from side to side. This, right here, is exactly what I want from her—every day. I finger fuck her, changing the pace and rhythm until she's tugging on my hair so hard, I'm sure she's going to come back with a fistful.

"Come for me, Luce. Come all over my fingers and mouth."

"Yes," she cries, her body letting go, her liquid release scorching my fingers and mouth and dripping down my arm.

How long has this been building for her? As she comes and comes and comes some more, I swear, for as long as I'm here, I'm going to give her an orgasm or two every single day. She gasps for air, and her throat sounds tortured and dry as she swallows. I lap at her, drink her all in and coat my parched mouth.

The spasms around my fingers slow, and I stay between her legs, encouraging her to take all she wants and come back down slowly. She gives a low, contented sigh, her hands loosening in my hair. I stare at her, take in the small smile on her mouth, as well as the dazed gratified look in her eyes as she sinks deeper into the mattress.

The doorbell rings, the chime shattering the quiet, intimate moment between us and I slowly ease my fingers out of her. My chest swells as I take in the flush on her cheeks as her body slowly comes back from her high. I lightly rub her sex, and shift, moving upward until we're face to face. I tuck her damp hair behind her ear, and lightly brush my lips over hers, my cock aching to be inside her. Her eyes are dazed unfocused as she searches my face.

"Finn..." Her voice is breathless, and sated, and I can't even begin to explain how happy that makes me. I loved everything about pleasuring her. "What...what was that?"

"Doorbell, our food is here."

She goes up on her elbows and understanding moves into her eyes. "Finn..." she whispers, her eyes widening as she takes in the mussed sheets, like she can't quite figure out what happened.

"I'm sorry," I say quietly, and she swallows hard and scrambles to pull the blankets up. "No," I hurry out, to ease her sudden worries. "I'm not sorry about any of this." I run my hand from her neck, and along her outer breast. "I'm sorry, because you wanted to take a nap and I sort of distracted you."

She draws her bottom lip between her teeth, a smile forming. "Naps are overrated."

"No, they're not. We can take one after we eat." I hold my hands up, palms out. "I promise to keep these to myself."

She frowns, confusion moving into her eyes and why wouldn't she be baffled? I'm supposed to be Finn, and Finn would not be ravaging a client, especially a female one.

"What did we do?" she asks quietly as her gaze searches my face for answers.

We crossed a line, one there really isn't any coming back from, and while I'd like to blame it on the alcohol, that's a copout. I'm Scottish. I can hold my liquor. Luce is more of a lightweight and maybe it loosened her inhibitions, but she wanted this as much as I did. I brush her hair from her face, and hope for the best when I say, "What we did was something I hope we can do more of."

"Finn," she says, as the doorbell rings again. "But...I don't understand."

"You're good at secrets, right?" She nods. "I am too, so maybe this can be our little secret. Just something for us." She blinks once, then twice and nods slowly, and while she's clearly confused, there's no denying the fire in her eyes, or that she wants my hands and mouth on her again. I want that too, even though it's a very bad idea. A very bad idea, indeed.

Yeah, I know...I get it. I should run the fuck away. But what I should do, and what I'm going to do are probably two different things.

LUCE

As Finn pulls himself together, looking calm and handsome, like he didn't just give me the best orgasm of my life, he walks toward the open door. "I better get that before the delivery driver leaves. I want to give him a tip." He flashes me a panty-melting smile before he disappears and rushes down the stairs to get our food.

I take one deep breath and then another, my gaze going to the ceiling. I go perfectly still. Heck, I'm not even sure I can move as my brain bounces off the sides of my head like I've taken an egg beater to it.

He wants to do this again?

I mean, yeah, I do too, but he's gay, and I didn't even touch him in return. Did he not want me to put my hands on him... my mouth? Do I want to do that? Uh, yeah!

How the heck did an afternoon nap turn into me laying here naked, the burning imprint of his hands still marring my flesh? Maybe I shouldn't overthink this, maybe I should accept it for what it was, two adults engaging in a little afternoon delight, and leaving it at that.

No way is Finn gay!

Why would my sister text that? What does she know that I don't? Okay, well yeah, I'm lying in his bed, my body tingling from head to toe, so I guess I know more. But Finn dates guys. Everyone knows that. While I've not seen him out with a man, his reputation precedes him. Everyone in my social circle who uses his services knows he's not into women. But there's no denying he was into me today, and I damn well loved it.

Voices from downstairs reach my ears and I sit up as the door shuts, the lock clicking into place. Where the hell are my clothes? I search the bed frantically and tug them on, leaving off my damp panties. Once I'm covered neck to toe in his oversized clothes, I dart to the bathroom.

"Food's ready, Luce."

"I'll be right there," I croak out and glance at my flushed face in the mirror, and while I still have no idea what just happened—correction, I know what happened, I just don't know why—I can't wipe the smirk off my face. Maybe it was the alcohol. I can't hold mine well, but I was only tipsy enough to loosen my inhibitions. I knew exactly what I was doing. Maybe those drinks loosened Finn enough to forget that he wasn't into women. If he's not into women, how did he know exactly how to touch my body?

Honestly, is there anything wrong with two consenting adults having a little fun?

Wait.

Did I beg?

Oh my God, I think I did. Did Finn give into me because I was so pathetic and needy and he felt sorry for me? I briefly close my eyes to calm myself, and recall his moans. If this was all about me, if he was just helping a girl out, he wouldn't have been moaning and growling, right? I don't know. All I know is it's time to pull on my big girl panties—figuratively speaking, of course. I don't have any clean panties to pull on, but nevertheless, it's time to face the music.

I finish up in the bathroom and head to the stairs. I stand at the top for a second and listen as Finn takes plates out of the cupboard. At least he knew where to find them. I walk quietly, tentatively. I'm not even sure how I'm supposed to act after what we just did. I'm not great with morning-after conversation, or rather nap-after. Is there such a thing?

His smile is wide and easy as I enter the kitchen and it eases the tension inside me. Okay, so we're going to act casual, like he didn't just put his fingers in me, his mouth all over my body and that I didn't do anything to him at all. Maybe he didn't want me to do anything. No, that can't be right. His erection was hard against my body. We were just interrupted by the food delivery.

Ohmigod girl, stop overthinking everything.

I take a peek at the numerous containers. Did he order one of everything? "This looks great," I say, trying for casual, even though I sound like I might be a chipmunk with a cheek full of nuts.

Nuts....

Do not think about nuts of any sorts.

He opens containers and lays out spoons. "Dig in?" He gives me a playful wink." I got your chicken balls and those other things."

"Fresh spring rolls," I say, now trying not to think about balls. "That's what I was talking about. How did you know?"

"I didn't really." He laughs and shoves a spoon into the rice container. "I just ordered what I thought was rectangular."

"They're my favorite so thanks for getting..." I count. "Twelve!" I laugh at that.

My stomach grumbles and he laughs. "Worked up an appetite, huh?" Heat moves into my face. Now I'm blushing. Great. "Not so funny now that I got twelve, is it?" He picks up a spring roll and bites into it. His moan of pleasure moves through my blood, and arouses me all over again as it settles between my legs.

Alrighty then.

I grab the spoons and start scooping food onto my plate, and he picks up the containers and does the same. Once I have more than I can possibly eat, I carry it to the table and he joins me.

"Sarah should have Thai food for her wedding," he says. "This is so good."

"Nope, it's traditional all the way for her. Now that we have the invitations picked out, I should text her to see if she's decided on who she wants to cater. We need to get them in the mail asap." I glance around for my phone but have no idea where it is.

He tosses a chicken ball into his mouth and moans as he chews. He licks his lips afterwards and I try not to stare.

"What are some traditional Scottish foods that you like?" I ask, wanting to keep the conversation neutral. "Wait, you don't eat haggis, do you?"

"Hey, don't knock it until you try it."

I cringe. "Sorry, I never plan to try it."

"Maybe I'll make it for you, tie you down and force you to eat it."

The sudden image of him tying me down sends shards of need through me. What is happening to me? "I'm tougher than I look, you know."

"Doubtful."

I lift my chin, offended. He grins and his big warm hand closes over mine for a second. "I said doubtful, because I don't think you could be any tougher, Luce."

"Oh...okay." I think. I take a big bite of my spring roll, and moan.

I don't miss the way Finn's throat works as he swallows, although I don't think he has any food in his mouth. Was it because of my moan?

"You take everything the wrong way," he says, and digs into the beef noodle dish.

"No, I don't." He arches a brow in challenge and I shrug. "Okay, maybe I do. So, you do eat haggis?" Smooth, Luce, real smooth.

He wags his brows. "I eat it with neeps and tatties."

"That sounds...dirty," I say and grin. I lean into him, less self-conscious about what we just did. Hey if he's going to brush it off, I can too. "Tell me more."

"Not as exciting as it sounds." He laughs. "Basically, they're root vegetables."

Forget nuts and balls, now I have root on the brain.

"Potato and turnip," he finally explains. "When you have it with haggis, it's called a Burns Supper."

I pound my fist to my chest, indigestion flaring just from thinking about it. "I can imagine." I've never tried traditional Scottish food. Maybe I could make that for him. Just to experiment, and grow as a chef. "Do you miss Scotland and your traditional foods?"

He hesitates for a second and drags his fork through his rice. "Aye, I do."

"You like Boston, though?" I fork a steamy pile of rice into my mouth and take in the way his head is bobbing enthusiastically.

"I love Boston." He forks a big piece of beef into his mouth. "Scotland is beautiful, but I fell in love with this place when I went to uni."

I'm not sure what it is, but there's something in his eyes, a longing maybe. "Do you miss bartending?"

His head lifts and he stares at me with those gorgeous eyes. I don't know what it is, but being the sole focus of his attention fills my stomach with butterflies.

"I didn't know Thai food came with a Spanish inquisition."

I have no idea why I find that so funny, but I laugh so hard, the rice I just swallowed gets stuck in my throat. I choke and cough, and Finn jumps up to grab me a glass of water. He kneels in front of me and holds it out. Green eyes move over my face with fierce concern.

I cough some more, clear the food and take a big swallow. "I'm okay," I assure him, my voice high-pitched, no doubt from straining my vocal cords.

"You sure?"

"I'm sure."

Concern still dances in his eyes as he asks, "You don't need mouth to mouth?"

"I wasn't drowning. I was choking." *What are you saying, girl? Of course, you want mouth to mouth.*

Once he's sure I'm okay, he sits across from me again, and this time I eat slower and don't ask more questions.

"I do like bartending," he says breaking the quiet. "I like the people, the comradery." He smiles like he has fond memories. "I want to open a public house in Boston someday." Not only does my head rear back in surprise, but so does his. "I mean... never mind. Forget I said that."

"No, it's okay. We have our secrets, and nothing you say to me is going to leave this room."

"There's not too many people I trust." Fine lines crinkle around his eyes as he says that, and I take it this man has seen things I haven't. I also take it, that's not something he talks about a lot.

"I guess working the bar wasn't all comradery, huh?"

He gives a humorless laugh. "Something like that." He glances outside at the late afternoon sun, his thoughts a million miles away.

"What's stopping you from opening a bar, Finn, if that's what you want to do? You're obviously a great business guy. Look what you did with Finn-tastic Affairs. I think a Scottish bar would be a big hit. Just no...haggis."

He smiles but it's forced. "It's not the right time. It's never been the right time, and it's a big investment," he says, and there's something in his voice, the hint of pain in his eyes that says so much more. There's something holding him back, something other than time and money. Is it worry for his father? It's not my place to ask, and I think there are only so many secrets he wants to share with me. But I want the playful Finn back, and I'm the one who gave the inquisition, so I say. "How about a swim?"

He turns back to me, his smile reaching his eyes this time. "Great idea."

"Wait, you're not going to go in your birthday suit again, are you?" I move my hand around my groin region. "With all that..."

He laughs. "I'm healed, and I have a suit. I can probably find shorts for you, or you could go in your birthday suit. It's not like I haven't seen you naked."

"I didn't see anything," I blurt out as I blush at the comment.

"Aye, lassie, the water was cold. How many times do I have to tell you?" I chuckle and he shakes his head. "You've seen me naked too, so maybe we should just forget about suits."

"I think we should wear suits." The sudden image of my sister barging into the backyard looking for me because I didn't respond to her text—and I always immediately respond—plays out in my head. "Yeah, suits. Definitely suits."

"Whatever you say. I'll be right back." He disappears and when he comes back he's wearing a bathing suit and has a pair of running shorts for me. They're big but they tie at the waist.

I dart to the bathroom to change, which might be silly, but I do it anyway. I come back to Finn putting the leftovers in the fridge. His gaze moves over me as I tie the shorts, and I'm very aware that I don't have a bra on.

I walk to the back door and open it. Finn follows me out and my legs are shaky. Everything about me becomes completely aware of his close proximity. I turn to see him, but he walks around me and cannonballs into the water. I shriek as he soaks me and he comes up laughing.

"You're going to pay for that."

"You'll have to catch me first."

He swims to the shallow end and eyes me. I slowly slide in, and wince as the cold water penetrates my clothes and bones, but it is rather refreshing. Finn ducks back under the water, and I tread in the deep end. He surfaces in front of me.

I splash him. "You're not so hard to catch."

"I know." He exhales and looks down in shame, and I can't help but love his self-deprecating jokes. "I'm so damn easy."

He's not the only one who's easy...

I laugh. "Close your eyes." He angles his head, and gives me a suspicious look. "Just do it."

"Fine."

He closes his eyes and I call out, "Marco."

His laugh is deep and joyous and my belly flutters in response. "Polo."

He comes toward me, and I dive, swimming around him. My goodness, when was the last time I had so much fun? I honestly can't remember. My childhood was spent playing sports and music and studying and trying to please my parents. It wasn't until I excelled at finance in Harvard that they really stood up and took notice. I remember Dad's smile. He was so proud of my grades, and that's when we talked about me joining the family business.

I break the surface, and that's when I find Finn standing there, smiling at me, his eyes wide open. "Hey, that's cheating."

"What are you going to do about it?" Heat dances in his eyes as his gaze drops to take in my breasts, my nipples puckered and hard and clearly begging for his mouth again. I push away from him, and dip below the surface. I rise, and start choking, pretending I took in water.

For a brief second concern dances in his eyes, but it morphs to understanding as I back up and lift myself from the pool, sitting on the edge.

He comes toward me, hunger on his face as he growls, and there is no doubt he's thinking the same thing I am. He moves between my dangling legs, and cups the back of my head.

"Mouth to mouth requires you flat on your back," he says. I pat the spot beside me, and curiosity moves over his face as he hoists himself out and takes a seat. I slide into the pool. "Hey," he says. "Where do you think you're going?"

Feeling naughty and brave and adventurous—it's crazy what this man brings out in me—I move between his legs and he arches a brow.

He groans and grabs a fistful of my wet hair. "What are you doing, lassie?"

I run my finger along the band of his bathing suit and pull on the strings holding it around his hips. "I'm curious."

"Curious about what?"

I bite back a grin. "If you found the water too cold today." Heat brews in his eyes as he gazes at me, and it damn near boils the water around me. I tug on his shorts and he growls as I free his cock.

Hello, Loch Ness monster.

GAVAN

As I put my boots on Finn's desk and try not to think about yesterday and how much I liked having Luce in my bed, and her taking me with that sweet mouth of hers by the side of the pool, I go through the day's planner—anything to stop me from beating myself up. Everything about yesterday was mind blowing, and wrong in every possible way.

I exhaled sharply and glance around the wide expanse of showroom. My gaze goes to the table full of magazines and books, and the big bouquets of flowers that I have no idea how to fluff. What was that Finn said about my sex appeal on flowers? Eegit.

I've wasted the entire morning doing nothing but floating around and checking social media. Luce has a couple of accounts, but she doesn't post much. Jesus, am I stalking her now? Honestly, I should be back in Glasgow helping out my father. A measure of guilt floods me, and my chest tightens. Despite the situation Finn left me in, I can't deny that I'm enjoying myself here. While I'm no wedding planner, I have been having fun helping Luce, and I can't believe she liked my decorating ideas for the venue. Maybe I know more about decorating than I think. I'd given a lot of thought on how I'd lay out a bar if I ever opened one. I even talked to an architect friend back in Scotland. Then again, maybe Luce was just humoring me, and I should stick to bartending.

I pick my phone up and consider shooting off a text to her, but decide against it. She's busy with work, and probably has to get caught up after taking last Friday off. I drop my phone and glance around.

I don't have much to do, other than wait to find out what Sarah wants for her menu. For a girl who insisted on a fast ceremony, she has no problem taking her time in choosing a restaurant and leaving her sister in the hot seat. I can't get the invitations sent out without her menu. I guess at the end of the day, she figures her sister will come through for her, with or without a stress ulcer. The pressure they put on Luce, the way they don't seem to care that she has other responsibilities really pisses me off, and don't even get me started on ex-best friend being in the bridal party. How fucking awkward for her.

The bell over the door jingles and a young man dressed in a pair of shorts, a button-down pink shirt and a bright green bowtie that clashes with well, everything, walks in. I'm about to stand, to see if he needs anything, but he waves to me and heads into one of the offices. Okay, that could have been awkward. I crane my neck to see Stefanie, and she whispers, "That's Nathan." I nod. Christ, I can hardly believe I pulled this charade off this long. I'm sure come this weekend's barbecue, my cover will be busted, and what about the engagement party Luce's mother invited me to? I just hope no one there recognizes me, and I'll have to remember to be showy and flamboyant, à la Finn.

Speaking of Finn. I haven't heard from him in a while, and I hope everything is going okay. I grab my phone, ready to shoot off a text, but stop and sit up a bit straighter when a message from Luce comes in.

Luce: Sarah picked her restaurant.

A text is a text. You can't read emotions, but something seems off... I could be reading this wrong and maybe that's because I haven't heard a word from Luce since she left yesterday. Not that I expected to hear from her, but dammit, she must be wondering why a guy like Finn would be all over her. I want to tell her who I really am, and she's good with secrets but what if it slips. Besides, it's not like this relationship is going anywhere. I'm not the kind of guy she'd bring home to her parents—not to mention the fact that I need to get back to Glasgow. But her parents want her back with her ex, who, in my humble opinion, is a total douche bag. They all piss me off. But as Finn would say, it doesn't take much.

Me: Which one?

Luce: Prime.

Me: The steakhouse? I hear it's great.

Luce: Would you be free to help me pick out a menu? I can't tonight, but maybe tomorrow after work, and we can finally get those invitations planned.

Me: I'll pick you up.

Christ, I'm far more anxious to see her than I should be. I stare at my phone. Three dots appear, and I wait. Her message must be a long one. Her text finally comes through and it's simply her address. I wait for more to come in, and when my phone goes silent, I decide I need to get the hell out of the office before any of Finn's staff start asking questions. I should probably think about picking up another box of hair dye. I'm starting to get a skunk line and I don't want Luce to think I color my hair.

I tuck my phone into my pouch, and let Stefanie know I'm headed out for the day. At least I only have one client, which allows me to have a lot of free time. I make my way out into the late afternoon sunshine and jump into Finn's vehicle. Out of sheer curiosity, I punch in Luce's address, and make my way to her place. I drive for a few miles until I come to a big house, which is behind a gated fence with a monitoring system. This is all a very different world from the one I still live in.

I make my way downtown and park. I'm wasting time, but I suddenly find myself meandering into different bars to check them out. I have no idea if there's any retail space in Boston's downtown core, or even if that pipe dream will ever come true. I walk around, and eventually find myself standing outside a Boston real estate agency. I scan the posters they have on the window, and see plenty of houses for sale.

My da's words come back. "At least take a look around."

I guess there's no harm in seeing if there's space available. I have no idea why I have such a huge knot in my stomach as I pull open the door and step inside. It's actually a mixture of unease and excitement. I'm instantly greeted with a very cheerful realtor, young and blonde with a megawatt smile that probably sells a shit ton of property. She'd probably be someone I'd take to my bed in the past, but I have a little brunette invading my thoughts. Just thinking about Luce has me smiling and the realtor must think it's for her. She flips her hair, a little flirtatious, and as her gaze drops to take in my clothes, a smirk pulls at her lips.

"Nice kilt."

"Thanks."

"I'm Tamara." Her dark eyes narrow in on me. "Wait, you're the event planner." She goes quiet for a second, like she's searching her thoughts. "Finn-tastic Affairs."

"How did you know, lassie?"

She laughs. "We don't have too many Scots walking around in kilts here in Boston, and I knew your cousin Gavan from university."

I give her a once over again, trying to place her. "Aye, it is me, Finn," I fib. "Did you and Gavan have a class together?"

"No, I dated Caleb. He and Gavan were on the soccer team together."

Recognition hits. "How is Caleb?" I ask my mind going back to my football days. I miss the guys. Maybe I will join them on the pitch.

"He's my husband." She holds out her ring finger to showcase her band.

"Congratulations." My world is getting smaller and smaller and sooner rather than later someone is going to put this shit show together.

She smiles, her gaze going over my face and I try not to fidget. "I forgot how much you and Gavan look alike. How is he?"

"Good. Back in Glasgow working at his da's pub."

She stands there and smiles at me, like she's remembering old times, and I look past her shoulders to the files on her desk, indicating I'd like to get down to business. She straightens and returns to professional mode. "What can I help you with today, Finn?"

"Retail space," I say. "I was thinking about something downtown, suitable for a Scottish pub."

"What fun," she says and claps her hands. "Wait, now that I think of it, that's something Gavan used to talk about."

Before I can answer, and really, I have no idea what I'm about to say, a yappy little rodent comes running from the backroom and skids around the corner to come my way when he sees me.

"What the fuck is that?" Tamara's eyes open wide. Shit, did I say that out loud? The rodent comes close to me, and lunges at my kilt. It latches on and drags it low on my hips and Tamara yelps. I'm not much into yappy dogs and clearly, they're not much into me. She bends and scoops up the toothy animal.

"I'm so sorry. He never acts like this. I don't think he likes… your kilt."

That makes two of us. "What kind of dog is it?"

She pats its fluffy head. "His name is Chester. He's a Glenn of Imaal terrier. A rare breed around here. We got him on our honeymoon in Ireland."

I laugh. "That makes sense. He's Irish. I'm Scottish. We dinna get along, you know."

She chuckles at that, the mood lightening, and gives her dog a pat on the nose, warning it to behave, but it simply barks at me. "Let me put him in the break room." She disappears and hurries back and waves me over to her desk. As she sits, I cross the room and the reality of what I'm doing comes crashing over me. Christ, I can't move to Boston and leave Da in Scotland. He needs me.

He didn't sound like he needed you when you called...

Shite, where did that thought come from. Sure, he might be having fun with Freya but that doesn't mean he's tossing his only son to the curb. For as long as I can remember, it's always been Da and me, two peas in a pod. I had Finn and Da had his brother (Finn's father), and sister-in-law but the two of us are as close as any father and son can be. We swore never to fuck off on each other like Ma.

With that uneasy thought careening around in my brain, Tamara wakes her computer and does a quick search. "Are you thinking downtown core?"

"Aye."

She hits a button and from behind me, a printer starts spitting out cuts. "There's a space for lease not too far from here. It's new on the market and I don't expect it to last long. You'd have to act fast."

That's the problem. I can't act fast. I have savings—heck, I've put away every dime for as long as I can remember, and even worked during uni. But fast decisions aren't my thing. The last time I made one, I landed in Boston, with my cousin telling me I had to be him, so yeah, thinking through decisions is in my best interest.

What's the time limit on thinking, Gavan?

Maybe I'm wasting her time with all this. I'm seconds from standing and telling her I made a mistake when she pulls her purse from her desk drawer and says, "Come on. Let me show it to you."

"I don't want to waste your time. You probably want to get home to Caleb."

"You are not wasting my time at all. Caleb is actually out of town on a meeting, and I'm yours for as long as you need me."

I follow her up, and we head outside. She hands me a sheet of paper with all the information on it, to look over as she locks up behind us. My brain buzzes with ideas as I examine the space.

"Nice, isn't it?"

I look up. "It's not far from here. Should we walk?"

"I don't see why not!"

We head down the sidewalk, and it's so weird to be back in my old stomping grounds. How many nights did Finn and I walk out of one of these bars drunk? I chuckle to myself and Tamara eyes me.

"How's the event planning business?" She gives me an apologetic smile. "Sorry we didn't hire your company. We had a destination wedding. It was glorious."

A part of me regrets not staying in touch with the guys. I miss them. I miss the pitch and the friendship, and clearly, I missed Tamara and Caleb's wedding.

"No worries. I'm currently planning Sarah Johnson's wedding." I glance at her to see if recognition hits and it does.

"Oh wow, I bet that's going to be spectacular."

"I've been working closely with Sarah's sister, Luce. Do you know her?"

Okay, what are you doing, Gavan?

The answer is simple. I like thinking and talking about Luce.

"Not personally." She crinkles her nose. "I did hear what happened to her, though. You know about her fiancé leaving her for her best friend."

"Fiancé? I didn't realize they were engaged."

"I thought they were. I could be wrong." She cringes again. "The guy she dated after him." She glances around to see if anyone is within earshot. "Embezzlement," she whispers. "She actually hired him, or so I heard. She doesn't have much luck in the guy department." I nod as I consider that. Is it any wonder Luce is off guys, or says she has no radar? At least she knows what we're doing is just about sex and she already told me she doesn't get involved emotionally. Which is perfect. She takes a turn when we reach the corner and I pivot to follow her. "Why are you working with Luce if it's Sarah's wedding?"

"Your guess is as good as mine." I wait to see if she has a guess, but she doesn't. Her heels tap on the sidewalk and I look ahead and see the sign for Prime. What a coincidence. My stomach grumbles. I guess it is getting close to feeding time. Maybe I should check out the restaurant and taste their offerings before tomorrow night.

I slow as we walk by the window, and glance into the upscale steak house. From the corner of my eye, I catch movement. I zero in on a petite woman in a white apron, and a hat pulled low on her face. She's speaking to a man behind the bar, but there's something about her petite frame and the way she moves that...

Is that...Luce?

I am not good. I am so not good at all.

I take deep breaths as I pace around my house and try not to chew on my fingernails. I nixed that habit years ago, and I'm not about to start again, but Finn will be here in minutes, and I have to figure out a way to get out of tonight's menu sampling. I can't believe my sister chose Prime to cater her event. Of all the places in Boston, why did it have to be the upscale steakhouse where I'm secretly working? My God, what if someone recognizes me? How stupid will I look, and will my coworkers hate me because I haven't told them who I really am?

The intercom pings and I hurry to it. I press a button to open the front gates and try to get my heartbeat under control as I peek out the window to see him drive up to my front door. I back up, take a quick glance at myself in the mirror and note the dark smudges under my eyes. It's no wonder I'm tired. I've between working at the firm and the restaurant and planning a wedding, not to mention the stress of trying to get out of tonight. It's all taken its toll on me.

The doorbell rings and I pull it open, and my tongue nearly rolls out when I spot Finn standing there, looking so damn handsome I'm sure I won the main lottery. My gaze leaves his face and takes in the kilt. It instantly reminds me that this isn't a date and I have no idea why my thoughts would even stray down that path.

Oh, probably because of what you guys did Sunday afternoon during nappy time.

"Hi," I blurt out trying not to sound short of breath...aroused.

His grin is slow and sexy as he takes in my short, tight black dress. "You look amazing, Luce."

"You do too."

He snorts. "I look like Finn."

I angle my head and laugh. Sometimes he says the strangest things. Catching me off guard, he leans in and kisses me on the cheek. Maybe it's a Scottish greeting or something.

"Mmm, you smell good too," he murmurs.

"Thanks," I say for lack of anything else. "It's my bodywash." *Shut up, Luce, he doesn't need to know that.*

"Vanilla?"

"It is."

"Now I'm going to be thinking about dessert all night."

Is he talking about me being dessert, or is he thinking about something decadent like a cream puff with vanilla pudding? We serve that at Prime.

"Are you ready?" he asks, his body still close to mine, his scent teasing my senses.

"You know," I begin. "I've eaten at Prime before. Maybe we can just stay in and go over the menu online."

He eyes me, and a beat passes. I'm about to twitch, uncomfortable under his scrutiny. "When was the last time you've eaten there?" he asks.

Oh, I get it. He must be worried about a menu change. "Oh, it's been quite some time." It's not a lie. I sample every item I make, but it's been years since I sat at a table myself. I can't very well dine at a restaurant where I'm secretly working. Honestly, I'm sick of people treating me with kid gloves once they discover who I am.

Finn didn't treat me with a kid glove when he pleasured me in his bed. Oh my, I can't think about that right now. Not while he's standing before me, looking far better than any prime rib I plated up last night.

"What about you?" I ask. "When was the last time you've eaten there?"

"Last evening, actually."

My entire body stiffens. Finn was at the restaurant yesterday? I was working. Did he see me? Even if he did would he care? I suppose not, but it's best to keep it a secret. I wouldn't want it to slip out. My relationship with my parents is strained enough as it is. I do my best to remain calm and relaxed. "So you know the menu well."

"Not that well." He reaches out, his fingers grazing mine. "If you don't want to go, we don't have to."

"Really?" I say, my entire body releasing, so happy that he's not pushing it.

"Whatever you want."

"You're so accommodating," I say, and drop my bag. "I guess that's what makes you the best event planner in town."

He nods and eyes me, his mouth tight. I get the sense he wants to tell me something, but isn't sure how to say it. Or maybe he's waiting for me to confess. "Everything okay?"

He scrubs his palm over his freshly shaved face. "Yeah, sure."

I don't want to push, but I'm about to question him, but stop when he gestures toward my buzzing handbag.

"I think your purse is ringing."

"Oh, right." I tug my phone from my purse and groan as I read the message from my sister.

"What's wrong?"

I exaggerate an exhale. "My sister decided she's joining us for menu tasting. I have no idea why. She hasn't seemed interested in anything to do with her wedding—"

"Other than to pose for the camera. Shite. Sorry, I shouldn't have said that." I grin at his bang-on observations. "Look, just text her back and tell her I'll meet her. You don't have to go if you don't want to. You must be exhausted."

I turn to the mirror, and examine my face. "What a nice way to tell me I look like a zombie."

His soft chuckle curls around me. "No, you look beautiful like you always do, but if you're not up to going tonight, kick your shoes off, get out of that dress and pour a glass of wine."

While that all sounds amazing, and it's probably crazy, I have the worst feeling in my stomach. If he goes, will my sister quiz him on his sexual preference? What he does and who he does it with is none of her business.

Will he fall for her charm and begin to overlook you like every other guy?

He steps up to me, and slides an arm around my back and pulls me hard against him. "Although I really would love it if you joined us."

His words reassure me and I shake my head to get it on right. Finn is gay and he isn't going to fall for my sister, and what we're doing is simply scratching an itch. He hasn't been with anyone in a while and neither have I.

I nibble my lips. "I should probably go. Sarah's expecting both of us."

He dips his head, his eyes full of concern. "Are you sure?"

"Yeah."

His fingers play with a strand of my hair. "You know I can handle your sister, right? I grew up in Glasgow, in a bar. She doesn't scare me."

I smile at that. "You don't know her."

"No?" He arches a brow. "Daddy's little girl. Has everyone wrapped around her finger? Always gets what she wants. Has her big sister to take care of her, and—"

I hold my hand up to stop him. "Okay, you know her."

"I'm not saying those things to be mean, Luce."

"I know."

He cups my chin and lifts it. "How about this. Tonight, after dinner, you let me take care of you." I have no idea what he has in mind, but my entire body quakes, eager to find out. "We can come back here, get you out of these shoes and I'll pour the wine."

I exhale, liking the sound of that. "Sounds heavenly."

Will he make me scream for God?

"Hang on, I'll be right back." I leave him standing in the foyer as I dash up my stairs and head to my closet. I grab a scarf and wrap it around my neck. If only I could cover my entire face. I hurry back downstairs and find him in the living room, looking at photos on the wall.

"You know, you and your sister look nothing alike."

"I take after my father's side of the family." He picks up one of the photos, a family trip to Greece when I was a teen. "My mother was a model," I tell him.

"She's beautiful." He sets the picture down. "She must be so proud of you, Luce."

"She is, actually. I worked my way up in the firm, and I'm the youngest financial advisor. I even have a corner office." I hold my index finger up. "Yes, I earned it."

"I never said you didn't. I'd love to see this office someday. Wait, did someone say you didn't earn it?" He cracks his knuckles. "Point the way and I'll go straighten them out."

"Stop." I laugh and put my small hand over his fist.

"You're right. What am I saying? You're a girl who can fight her own battles." Appreciating his faith in me, I put my arm in his and guide him toward the front door. "This is a pretty big house for one person," he says as I set the alarm before we step outside.

"It's an investment."

"Ah, smart. Now I get it." He taps his brain. "Always thinking. I guess that's what makes you good at what you do."

I nod in agreement as he walks me to his car and opens the passenger side. I slide in. I usually drive myself and I have to say it's kind of nice to have someone else taking care of me for a change, even if it is the wedding planner. Wait, I don't mean it like that, that he's less than me. I just mean... well, I shouldn't get used to it. When the wedding is over, so are we.

"Finn?" I ask, and nibble my lips.

He puts the vehicle in drive and heads toward my gates. "Something on your mind, Luce?"

"Just...the sex."

"You want to have sex!" He slows the car, his jaw practically on the steering wheel, and his over-the-top antics make me laugh. "Okay, but I'm not sure I can do my best work in a car, with..." He glances at the clock. "Fifteen minutes to spare."

I shake my head and whack him. My hand connects with his hard chest and he lets loose a big oomph. "That's not what I mean." Although, I bet he can do just about the most amazing things with his tongue in the back seat in fifteen minutes. My body warms and my panties grow damp. Great, that is so not what I need right now.

"You said you wanted to, you know..."

He casts me a quick glance. "Do it again?"

"What exactly are we doing?"

His hands tighten on the steering wheel, and the muscles in his jaw clench. "Do we need to give it a name?"

"No, I guess not." I know better than to let my heart get involved, and it's not, but I'm really enjoying this time with him.

"But if you need to, we could say two consenting adults having fun, you know just...kidding around." I go quiet and he turns in his seat to see me. "You don't like that?"

"No, it's not that. I was thinking we were just...kilting around."

He stares at me for a second, and as understanding dawns a wide smile turns up his lips. "You're kind of funny.'"

"Says the guy wearing a kilt that leaves a nasty rash."

"There you go with the balls again."

"I never said balls, you said balls."

"You just said it, twice."

"Ohmigod," I say and sink into the seat, all worry ebbing from my body. What is it about this guy, who can be pretty inappropriate at times, that puts me at ease? I pull my phone from my purse and let my sister know we're on our way. Should I tell her not to bring up his sexual preferences? She knows better, and if I do, that might just entice her. I do worry, that one look at me and she'll know I've had sex. Technically I didn't have sex, if one considers intercourse sex.

Okay, Luce, get your mind off sex already. I cast a glance at Finn and take in his handsome features as the setting sun shines the last rays of light into his car. I blame my thoughts on him. He's the one who keeps talking about his damn balls.

Yeah, Luce, but you're the one who keeps thinking about them.

GAVAN

I pull open the door for Luce and she adjusts her scarf around her neck, covering half her mouth as we enter. Is she cold? I realize the heat wave is over, but it's still really warm. She gives the hostess her name, letting her know two more will be joining us and she seems a bit relieved when we're given a table in a dark, intimate corner. I'd have to say it might be the best table in the place and I'm not surprised. The Johnson name holds a punch.

I might not have grown up with a mother, or know all the right things to say to a woman, but I'm enough of a gentleman to pull her chair out for her. She smiles at me, and my dick swells and once again I'm grateful that I'm wearing boxers. I take the seat with my back to the wall, and Luce is to my right. The table is small, and my knee bumps hers as she fidgets with the wine glass on our table. Is she nervous about dining with her sister and fiancé, or is it something else? We cleared the air about sex and she seemed on board. She even made a joke. Maybe she's simply exhausted and I plan to make sure she gets a long nap after I take her home.

"What did you have when you were here yesterday?" she asks as she glances at the menu.

"Meat."

She laughs at that. "Not a surprise. This is a steakhouse." She arches a brow, her pretty blue eyes lifting to mine. "What do you recommend?"

I recommend her in my bed, beneath me, but decide to save that suggestion for later. Before I can answer, in walks her sister and her fiancé Glen. "They're here."

Pulling her scarf up a bit again, Luce turns and waves her sister over. I stand and shake Glenn's hand and give Sarah a small kiss on the cheek before they take their seats.

"What fun to have us all together," she says and gives her sister's hand a squeeze. "Luce, you look different. Did you do something with your hair?"

Sarah flips her long blonde hair over her shoulder as she sizes up Luce. "Nope, just tried a new shampoo."

"Well, whatever it is, it looks good on you."

Luce keeps her attention on her menu like she doesn't want to have this conversation. She's either not used to being complimented, which is crazy, or Sarah might be referring to something else. My bartending days have left me with a good intuition.

"Thanks," Luce mumbles.

"You should keep doing it." Sarah cocks her head, a small smirk curling her lips like she has a secret. "You even have a glow on your face."

Luce gives her sister the death glare and Sarah laughs. "I don't use it on my face, and there is nothing different about me." What is going on between the two of them? Siblings. I wouldn't know any about that. Although Finn and I are close enough we could be considered brothers.

"Glen," I say and turn to him as the sisters spare off in some battle I know nothing about. "Luce tells me your uncle owns the New England Patriots. Do you play football?"

He lights up, and lifts his head. "Played in college. Star running back. Couldn't go professional. Banged up my knee, and went to law school. Do you play football?"

"Aye," I say, half my attention on Sarah as she leans in and whispers something about Sarah's radar being off, and her gaydar being on. "I do. But you call it soccer in America."

He laughs at that. "Heard you grew up in Glasgow."

"Aye, my da is still there."

"Not the nicest place in the UK," he says, his lips puckered like he just tasted something sour. That's fucking rude. He does a quick check on his cell phone. Again, rude.

"You been to Glasgow?"

"God, no." He shakes his head and looks at me like I might be insane. "I've been to Europe of course, but never to Glasgow."

I take a deep breath and unclench my hands. Knocking his teeth out might not be good for Finn's business, but how does he put up with assholes like this? I already hate his brother for what he did to Luce, and I guess a part of me hoped Glen was one of the good guys, but it doesn't appear that way.

"Don't knock it until you try it. There are lots of great things about Glasgow."

He snorts. "Yeah, and that's why you're here in Boston instead of Glasgow."

Fucking rich asshole. They all think they're better than everyone else. I catch the way Luce's gaze flickers to mine, and I take a deep breath and let the comment go. What was that saying Da had when we were kids? No sense in arguing with a pig. You both crawl in the mud and get dirty, but the pig likes it.

The server comes and I don't miss the way Luce shrinks a bit in her seat. "Can I start you all off with a drink?"

"I'd like a scotch," Glen says, as he glances over the menu. His head lifts and asks, "What do you suggest, Finn?"

Is he testing me? Jesus, I'm from Scotland. I know all about scotch. Hell, I could drink him under the table, but I'm a grown-ass man, far beyond that ridiculousness now. Unless of course he challenges me, then I'm not beyond anything.

I turn to Luce, who doesn't at all seem surprised by Glen's rudeness, and maybe he isn't being rude. Maybe I'm just sensitive in defending my hometown.

Nah, he's rude.

"What would you like, Luce?"

She keeps her head down, buried in her menu. "I'm going to have a glass of merlot."

"I'll have the same," Sarah says.

Since I was here yesterday and know what they serve, I say, "I'll have Johnnie Walker Gold Label Reserve on the rocks."

Glenn nods, like I passed some test. "I'll have the same."

The server smiles at me and he pauses for a second as his glance goes to Luce. "Great choice. I'll be right back with your drinks and bread for the table."

"Uh, bread. I know how much you love bread, Luce, so you can have my share," Sarah says with a wave of her hand. "I want to fit into my wedding dress."

"We should talk about the menu." Luce is clearly anxious to eat and get out of here. I can't blame her. I'd rather be anywhere else myself.

Sarah grins. "I'd rather talk about my bachelorette party."

Luce goes pale. "Oh, right. The bachelorette party." She swallows, and it goes unnoticed by her sister, but I don't miss it. Luce forgot all about planning the party.

Sarah wags her perfectly manicured eyebrows. "What surprises do you have up your sleeve?"

"It's short notice, Sarah. So, it's not going to be Fiji or anything."

I nearly swallow my tongue at the mention of Fiji. All I need is for them to run into the real Finn. "I was thinking something local."

Sarah frowns. "But extravagant, right?"

"Of course, but the big stuff will be for the wedding."

Sarah's eyes go big. "Did you book Harry Styles?" she asks, excitedly. "You know he's my favorite."

Luce looks like she's about to swallow her tongue. "Harry isn't available on such short notice."

Sarah pouts. "Glen, can you do anything?"

"Sorry, babe," he says, half his attention on Sarah, the other half on his phone.

Under the table, I give Luce's knee a squeeze. "Didn't you know that's the wedding planner's job, and I have someone brilliant in mind."

"Tell me," she says anxiously as Luce gives me a grateful smile, and dammit, while I don't have anyone brilliant in mind, I'd do just about anything to see her smile at me like that again. I'm going to have to call Finn and see if he has anything up his sleeve.

I wave my finger back and forth. "Some things need to be a surprise, Sarah. You put this wedding in Luce's and my hands, so let us work our magic. Unless of course, you want a say in something that's important to you."

She puckers her lips like I've seen Luce do, and thinks about it. "No, I trust Luce and I don't really have the time with that fashion shoot coming up." She taps Luce on the nose. "Plus, this will be good practice for Luce when she finally walks down the aisle."

Luce pales a bit and her sister pisses me off. "If she wants to," I say. "Marriage isn't for everyone." From beneath the table, Luce clasps onto my knee and gives it a squeeze. I like the reassuring messages between us, and hate the way her family takes advantage of her. But I bite my tongue. Their family dynamic is not my business, right?

The server comes back with our drinks, and someone else brings the bread, which I'm happy to gorge on. I look up to see a woman around my age at a nearby table staring at me, wide-eyed. I'm guessing she knows me.

Shite.

Who the fuck is she, and does she think she's waving to Finn or me? Either way, I can't see this going down in my favor. I take a fast sip of my drink, and shift in my chair and pretend not to see her, and focus on Glen. "What are the plans for the bachelor party?"

"There better not be any strippers," Sarah says coyly.

"Of course not, babe. We're civilized men and I only have eyes for you."

She glows under his praise, and I can't help but think if he only has eyes for her, why hasn't he taken them off his phone? Do these two even like each other, or was this a match approved by the parents?

"Glen, you should invite Finn to your bachelor party," Sarah shrieks like she just had the idea of the century as she wags her brows at me. "Quinn will be there."

"Who's Quinn?" I automatically ask, and judging by the cringe that just crossed Luce's face, I wish I hadn't.

"He's a family friend. He's gay, like you," she blurts out.

Okay, then.

Is this the kind of bullshit Finn has to put up with? On the streets of Glasgow, kids teased him and I beat the hell out of them. Life was simpler then. Just assuming two men will be attracted to one another because they're gay is ridiculous. Back home, no one ever tried to set me up. Everyone knew I was good for a fuck and nothing else. I assume it's the same for Luce here. We're different people from different worlds, and she doesn't even really know who I am. But sex, that's where we have common ground.

Sarah eyes me, a smirk on her face like she's challenging me in some way. I'm about to decline, and tell her I'm not into fix-ups, when Glen speaks.

"If you think that's a good idea, so do I." He sets his phone aside. "We'd love to have you join us, Finn."

"I uh…I'm pretty busy with work."

"Of course, you'll go," Sarah announces. "I'll make sure Ryland adds you to the list."

I want to say don't bother, but I'm Finn, and Finn wouldn't be rude.

But the last person I want to hear from is Ryland. Luce's ex that I hate. Wow, the bachelor party that he's planning and attending is sounding better and better. What would Finn do to get out of this? I'm about to excuse myself, go to the bathroom and shoot him off a text when the woman who'd been staring at me is suddenly at my table.

"Finn, I thought that was you."

Okay, so at least she thinks I'm Finn. "I wasn't sure at first. You look a bit different."

"It's been years," I say, praying I'm right. "I lost my charming boy looks."

She laughs at that. "You'll always be charming." She looks around the table. "I hope I'm not interrupting. I wanted to say hello. Finn planned our wedding a few years ago, and everything was perfect."

I do a quick introduction of the table, and let her know—whoever she is—that I'm currently planning Sarah's wedding. The woman smiles at Sarah and proceeds to reassure her that it will be a dream wedding and that she hired the best planner in town. While I'm still going to kill my cousin, I make a note to pass that compliment on to him. It's something he'd like to hear, and hell, I am proud of what he's built here.

After the woman leaves, Sarah smiles at me. "You have quite the fan base."

"I aim to please."

"Yes, I bet you do," she says, her brow arched as she runs her fingers around the rim of her cup like she can see right through me. Shite, I'd better be careful around her. I don't want to fuck this up for Finn or her sister.

"Okay," Luce says, pulling the attention back to her and I'm grateful. "I think we should order a chicken, fish and steak, and see if they're suitable for your menu choices." I smile at her. I do love her take charge attitude, but I'm really going to enjoy stripping her of it later. "Have you decided on desserts, we can order them here, or—"

"I'm getting the cream puff with the vanilla pudding," I interrupt and I'm not sure why I wanted to point that out. Maybe I want to see Luce blush again. Maybe I want her thinking about the last time I had my mouth on her. I sure as hell can't get it out of my brain. "I'm craving something vanilla." I watch Luce carefully, take in the rise and fall of her chest, and the delicious way she takes her bottom lip between her teeth, like she's remembering the taste of me. My cock twitches.

"Have you had it before?" Sarah asks, and I slowly pull my gaze from Luce and meet her gaze.

"Once, and I'm dying for it again."

Luce doesn't look at me. Instead, she picks up her glass of wine and downs almost half the glass. I hope it doesn't make her tipsy. When I took her in my bed the other day, she was feeling no pain, but tonight, I want her feeling everything I do to her, and dammit, I plan to do everything and then some, over and over. My cock throbs just thinking about it, and my mind drifts. Maybe she opted for no panties underneath that tight dress.

Sarah moans. "That sounds delicious. Maybe we can have a vanilla wedding cake."

"Babe, you know I want chocolate."

"Different layers can have different flavors," I say and surprise myself. Where the hell did that come from? I haven't been to a wedding in years. The last one was my buddy Noah's in Glasgow after uni. That ended in divorce.

"Finn, what a great idea."

"That's why he's the wedding planner," Luce says, and when she smiles at me, I grin back and bump my leg against hers under the table. I like the secrets we share. Soon enough we put in our food orders, and conversation centers around Sarah as we taste the food and I make notes in my phone on what she'd like added to the menu. I'm no monkey, but maybe this wedding business isn't so hard after all.

By the time the meal is done, I'm so ready to be out of here. The server brings the dessert menu, and I'm glad when everyone declines. Luce leans in. "I thought you wanted something with vanilla?"

"Oh, I do," I say and enjoy the little blush that moves into her cheeks. I straighten as Sarah watches us. Quickly returning to professional mode, I clear my throat and direct my words at Sarah. "I'll get the invitations addressed and out in the morning."

We head outside and stars dot the night sky as we say our goodbyes. Luce has a grin on her face as she lifts her chin to see me.

"Sorry about that."

"What are you sorry for?"

"Sitting through a meal with my sister and Glen, and getting roped into the bachelor party. I'll get you out of it."

"And miss the chance to meet Quinn?" I wave my hands, mimicking Finn, and add, "Not a chance, darling."

She laughs, but there's confusion in her eyes. No wonder. She opens her mouth like she's about to ask something but stops when we come across a homeless person sitting on the sidewalk. Her gaze goes from me to the person back to me, and she looks worried, agitated about something.

"Hey, Jane."

Jane?

"Umm..." She turns from me and drops to her knees. "Hey, Kev."

She knows this person?

"I'm sorry I don't have any food for you..." She glances around. "Hang on. I'll be right back, okay. Just...a sec."

I stand there, having no idea what's going on as she darts across the street, moving as fast as those little legs will carry her and disappears inside a burger joint.

"Nice kilt."

I turn back to the guy with a dozen or so black garbage bags piled around him. "Thanks."

"Are you Jane's boyfriend?"

"I'm her friend."

He nods, and adjusts his ball cap. "That's good. She could use some friends."

Sounds like he knows her well. "How do you know...Jane?"

"She's one of the good ones," he says, his non-answer telling me something I already know.

"Aye, that she is." I rock on my feet. My kilt sways, the wool tickling my thighs. I adjust it and the phone in my pouch bounces off my nut sack. Goddamn. "She brings you food?"

"Are you Irish?"

"Scottish."

"Same thing."

I resist the urge to tell him he's wrong, and glance across the street and look for Luce.

He angles his head, like he's trying to get an up close and personal look at my balls. "What do you wear under that kilt?"

I laugh. "Usually nothing, until I got a nasty rash."

The guy laughs. "Had one myself not too long ago." He waves to someone behind me. I turn, and spot a man and his dog walking toward me. As they get closer the dog—a great big rottweiler—starts pulling and barking and I'm pretty sure I have something to do with it.

"Sorry that took so long," Luce apologizes as she drops to hand a bag to Kev. He tucks it into one of his bags.

"Thanks, Jane."

"There's enough there for you and Larry." She stands again. "What's gotten into Killer?"

The dog's name is Killer?

As the man and Killer get closer, I slowly start to back up. Are animals offended by my kilt or something? I stand there. Christ, I grew up on the streets of Glasgow, and fought the toughest of guys. I'm not afraid of a goddamn dog.

"You'd better run," Kev says in an easy nonchalant manner. "I don't think Killer likes you."

Okay, maybe I am a wee bit afraid. I back up as the dog lunges, nearly pulling the owner's arm from his socket.

"Finn..." Luce says and steps between me and the dog. "Go around the corner."

"But..."

"I've got this. Killer and I are friends. He won't hurt me."

I back up and Killer lunges again. "Run," Kev says casually, and I turn quickly and dash through a chain link fence, running straight into an alleyway. Only problem is, there's a loose wire and it catches on my kilt.

Ripping it clear off my arse.

"It's not funny," Finn grumbles, a growl rumbling from the depths of his throat. God, could he be any more adorable when he's grumpy.

I bite back a grin. "I'm not laughing."

"Like hell you're not."

"Finn," I yell loudly, partly to stifle a laugh because he's leaning against my bathroom vanity in my pink robe, that he ripped tugging on, and partly because well, I'm trying not to moan at the sight of him. My God, the look of horror that crossed his face when the fence snagged his kilt. Killer was after him for some reason, and nothing was stopping him from getting the hell out of Dodge. I don't blame him and that's not entirely true. A loose fence wire stopped him.

"Stay still." I resist the urge to smack his ass to stop the squirming, but it might just set me to squirming instead. Needing a distraction and fast, I wet the cloth under warm water, and press it against the long gash in his rear end. "At least it's not deep."

Deep.

Oh God, Luce, do not think about deep.

I catch his eyes in the mirror and he looks genuinely perplexed, sad, even. "What did that dog have against me?"

"No idea. Killer likes everyone."

"I like animals. We had sheep growing up. My cousin had a donkey who didn't like anyone but me. He even let me ride him."

"You rode a donkey?"

"Phil."

I can't help but laugh. "How did you not crush Phil? You're too big to get on a donkey."

"I wasn't always two hundred pounds, Luce. I was a scrawny kid."

"I'd love to see pictures. I bet you were adorable with your ginger hair."

He rubs his hair, and his fingers come away with strands wrapped around them. "You like ginger?"

"On you, it's cute."

"Yeah, well you're not seeing any pictures of me as a wee lad." I crinkle my nose and stick my tongue out at him, and he grins. "Unless you show me yours. Then it's tit for tat."

Is he talking about sex?

Do I want him to be talking about sex?

Why yes, yes, I do.

"You already saw that picture in the living room, and you're going to see more when you go to my parents' house for the engagement party." I cringe at the thoughts of that. I'm sure a bunch of uptight people all vying for center stage is not his thing.

"Is it going to be that bad?"

"Yes." I consider Ryland and Chloe and all the comments Mom is going to make about me still being single. Ugh. "I have to face—"

"Douche bag and douche baggess."

I stare at him for a second. "You mean Ryland and Chloe?"

"Who else could I mean?"

I can think of a few more people. I whack him. "That's not a word, but it is funny and now I'm going to think about that every time I see them and I'm not going to be able to stop myself from laughing."

His grin is cheeky and sexy. "Good, that was my goal."

Why is this guy so sweet?

His smile fades, and his eyes darken as I meet them in the mirror. "You bring food to the homeless?"

I glance away, not really wanting to talk about that. "Yeah. How does it feel now?"

He ignores my question and asks one of his own. "Why did he call you Jane?"

"It's my middle name." I snort. "Jane. Short, simple and boring. Like me."

"You might be short, but you're not simple or boring."

"I wasn't fishing, Finn."

"I know, but I happen to like the name Jane, and that's really nice of you." His eyes are still trained on me as I clean his cut. "You don't want Kev or Larry to know who you are?"

"There's no need for that." I grin. "Sometimes maybe I do like being overlooked." I sure do at the restaurant. It's the only way I can get treated like one of the staff.

"You're a good person, Luce."

I shrug. "Thanks."

He goes quiet for a long time, and when I meet his gaze, he's solemn. "Seriously though, what did Killer have against me, and yesterday Tamara's dog lunged too?"

"Tamara?"

"Oh, a friend," he says casually.

Wow, what is that careening through my blood? Jealousy? Oh hell no. I have no right to be jealous that he has other girl-friends.

Is he giving them awesome orgasms too?

"But her dog was Irish and I'm Scottish so that makes sense, but Killer..."

Ah, what? "Maybe he wasn't trying to hurt you. Maybe he was excited and wanted to get close, or something. Oh hey, maybe he wanted to see what you were wearing under your kilt."

"Yeah, with his teeth. He was going for my balls, Luce,"

This time I can't help but smile. He looks so forlorn and utterly confused. "I don't know about that."

"Did you see where his gaze was trained? Right here."

He points to his nether regions and I'm not sure what it is about this man and his balls and why they always seem to be the topic of our conversation. He winces as I press the warm water to his cut.

"Stupid fence," he says with a grin. "I might have fared better had I taken on Killer."

Chuckling, I finish cleaning his cut, and reach into my drawer and pull out some antibiotic ointment. "Do you think I need stitches?"

I whack his arm. Yes, anything to touch him. "Don't be such a baby."

"I'm not a baby. I've just been having a lot of trouble..." He pauses and waves his hand over his groin region. "...in this area lately."

"Yeah, it's true. You've been having a rough go."

"Well, there was a good time too."

My gaze lifts and I catch his in the mirror. Oh, God, he's talking about what happened at the pool. I have no idea why, but heat crawls into my neck and paints my cheeks. I gently rub the ointment on his butt, and try not to think about the way his muscles bunch and relax again beneath my touch.

"All better." I finish up with a bandage. "Feel good?"

"No, I feel like I was just torn a new one."

I laugh as he twists and tries to see the end results. He pushes off the counter and my robe falls over his ass. "How about a glass of scotch?"

"Fine," he grouches, and I grin as we step from the bathroom, head downstairs and walk to my spacious living room, overlooking my very unkept garden. I've had no time to weed, and it's a passtime I enjoy. I must say, I'm enjoying my time with Finn a lot more.

He walks up to the window and looks out at the private back yard. "You have a nice place."

"Thanks." I put a crystal glass on the bar and pour a generous amount of scotch into it.

"Big for just one person." He turns to me and leans on the wide window sill. "Since you're off men, I guess you have no plans to fill it with kids."

"No plans. What about you, Finn? Do you want kids? Do you see a bunch of little gingers running around in the future?"

"I don't know. I don't even know if I like kids. Most times I didn't even like myself when I was a kid."

"You were good with the girl scouts."

"They had cookies, Luce."

I laugh as he pushes off the window sill, but when he curses, I wince. "Here, drink this. Short of me kissing it better, this will help with the pain." I shake my head. What the hell. "I mean..."

"I didn't know that offer was on the table." He grins and takes a big swig of scotch. On that note, I uncork a bottle of wine and pour myself a big glass.

"Do I have to walk around in this all night?" he asks, tugging at the frilly robe that barely closes in the front.

"It's either that or naked?" Why on earth did I give him the choice? I don't know him well, but the man has no problem with naked. I have no problem with him naked either. "Do you want me to drive you home?" We came to my home because it was closer, and he was bleeding all over the place. He frowns, and glances down, like the idea of going back to his place holds zero appeal. It does to me too. I like his company.

"How about dessert?" I ask.

His mood changes. Fast. Heat flashes in his eyes as his gaze moves over my little black dress. "I'm up for dessert." I resist the urge to let my gaze fall from his eyes, but I really do want to see if he's *up*.

"I have cake," I tell him.

"Is it vanilla?"

"No," I croak out. "I can make one, though. I have a recipe for one with vanilla icing. You'd probably love it."

"I love everything vanilla." The air around us changes, going from playful to a full blown sexual charge as he takes a step closer, the slit on the robe widening to give me a glimpse of his hard chest and tight abs. "That seems like an awful lot of trouble, and you do enough for everyone else as it is."

"It's okay," I say quickly. "Let me get out of this dress first."

"Uh huh," he says as he brings his glass to his lips and I stare, mesmerized as he takes a big swallow. Wow, I'm in bad shape if watching a guy take a drink turns me on.

"I'll just be a second." I practically run from the room and dart up the stairs. In my bedroom, I reach behind my neck and I'm sure my movements would impress a contortionist as I search for my zipper. I finally find it, and I'm breathing like I just ran a marathon as I get it down to the small of my back. I'm about to let it fall to my feet when a groan curls around me and fills the air in my room. I don't need to turn to know Finn is standing in the doorway. Every nerve ending in my body jumps to life.

"Finn..." I angle my head and catch sight of his big body eating up the entire entranceway.

"Baking a cake at this time of night seems like an awful lot of trouble, Luce."

"I don't—"

"Especially when I can satisfy my sweet tooth and get my fill of vanilla by putting my mouth on you."

Oh my freaking God.

I swallow as heat pools between my thighs, encouraging me to go for it. "I guess when you put it that way."

Heavy footsteps sound on my wood floor as he takes three big steps to cross it, and his warm fingertips land on my back. A fine shiver goes through me, his heat searing my skin as he trails it over my flesh, and I don't even bother to hide what he does to me. "Finn..." I murmur.

He puts his mouth close to my ear and the warmth of his breath falls over my body, and tickles my nipples. My body shuts down, coherent thought gone as lust moves in to take its place.

"Luce," he murmurs, and the way he whispers my name lets me know he's going to devour me, and I'm going to let him.

I'm about to turn, but a ridiculous thought hits. "Your butt."

He chuckles and it rumbles through me. "I'd rather talk about your butt." He slides his hands down lower and cups my ass cheeks through my dress, giving a tight massage that travels all the way to my throbbing sex.

My dress tumbles off my left shoulder and he groans before he rakes his teeth over my flesh, and a part of me hopes he mars me. When did I ever want a man to mark my skin? I tremble, and he peppers hot, wet kisses to my neck. I swallow, and lean my head back, opening my body to him.

"Nice," he murmurs and slides my dress from my right shoulder. He steps back and I miss his heat as my dress slides down my body and pools at my feet. His growl of appreciation curls through me. I grin, never having felt so desired or cherished before. "All night I've been thinking about ways to get you out of this dress."

"All night I've been thinking about ways for you to get me out of it," I admit, my entire body throbbing now.

He laughs. "I like your honesty, Luce." He moves close again, his hands on my hips as he grazes his lips over my right shoulder.

"I like yours too," I say and for a brief moment his lips are still on my skin. I'm about to spin, to see if he's had a change of heart—maybe he's decided he's not happy with what he sees beneath the dress. He is, after all, gay. Then again, he liked me naked before and proved it with every touch, kiss, and moans. What we're doing is having fun...just kilting around, I quickly remind myself as I give myself over to the sensations coursing through my body.

I move my hips, encouraging him to touch me, and my backside connects with his hard erection. Yeah, he likes what he sees, and yeah, I like what I feel. With a bump of his body, I inch forward. He keeps doing it until my knees hit my bed. He turns me and I almost forget how to breathe as the heat reflecting in his eyes nearly burns my bra and panties from my body. Has any man ever looked at me with such hunger before?

"Finn..."

He cups my chin, his eyes on my mouth as he dips his head. "This mouth, do you have any idea what this mouth does to me?"

"No," I croak out.

Instead of answering, he shows me how much he wants my mouth by pressing his lips to mine and devouring me. His tongue slides in, and I melt against him as I wrap my arms around him and sink into the kiss. I close my eyes, and lose myself in what he's doing to me. I might regret this tomorrow, but tonight I'm just going to go with it.

I touch the robe, and say, "Pink really isn't your color."

"You're right." Lacking any sort of modesty—hey, it's just the two of us, not two guys and a dog—he shrugs in the manliest way and the robe falls off his hard body. A groan I have no control over crawls out of my throat and he grins. He likes what he does to me.

"Fun?" he asks, the question taking me by surprise.

"Fun," I say and put my hands on his body. I splay my fingers, and without any inhibition, I let myself explore him. His head falls back and he groans.

"Your hands are so little." I go still for a second, and his gaze meets mine. "Did I tell you little was my favorite?"

That brings a smile to my face and unable to help myself, I do something I never in a million years thought I'd do. I reach down, take his girth in my hand. "Did I tell you big was my favorite?" I'm not sure what this guy does to me, but I like it. A lot.

I love his reaction, the way his green eyes darken and his jaw clenches as he growls. I rub my hand along the length of him, enjoying the soft velvet stretched over steel.

His hand goes around my neck and he grips my hair, his lips falling over mine and devouring me with a new kind of hunger. I stroke him, long smooth caresses that have pre-come pooling on his tip and he growls into my mouth as I dip into it. His other hand unhooks my bra with a practiced ease that both excites and confuses me. My bra falls and he tears his mouth from mine to gaze at my bare breasts. My God, the way he admires me, studies my body, is like the first time he's looked at a woman, but it's not the first time he's looked at me. He just makes it seem that way, his eyes gleaming like I'm a prized possession.

"These," he murmurs, and cups my breasts, his thumbs going to my nipples. His green eyes meet mine. "Are perfect." I'm not big, and I'm not small. I'm average and no one has ever called my breasts perfect before.

He nudges me and my hand slips from his cock as I drop to the bed. He takes his cock into his hand as he stands before me, the hunger about him, the intensity radiating off his rock-hard body nearly frying my brain cells. I take a gasping breath, my heart racing, my lungs constricted in my chest. I love him like this. A wild animal, restrained by a tether.

I want him off that tether.

Without taking my eyes off his, I lean forward and lick his crown, and the resulting grumble fills me with joy. Nice. I do it again, and this time I swirl it around his swollen head. Poor baby is hurting, and he's had enough hurt in this...

general area...to last a lifetime. I plan to make him all better tonight.

"Luce," he murmurs, his voice deep and steeped in need.

"Yeah?"

"I want to take care of you." He touches my shoulders and eases me off his dick. It plops from my mouth and I groan in response. The groan is quickly replaced by a moan as he leans over me, slips his fingers into the band on my panties and drags them down my legs.

Yes, please.

His growl of appreciation curls through me, gives me the strangest kind of courage. I'm not sure why I always feel safe with Finn. Maybe it's the fact that he's gay, and this relationship can't go anywhere. I know what I'm getting into and I'm not setting myself up for any kind of failure.

He tosses my panties aside and my entire body quakes as his gaze slowly takes in my nakedness. I grin and shift to the middle of my big bed. This is so much fun. Feeling a little wild, and wanting to tease him, I part my legs, and lightly run my fingers over the inside of my thighs, moaning as my fingers tease my body. I have never, ever pleasured myself in front of a man before, but I guess I'm doing a lot of new things with Finn.

I brush my index finger over my swollen clit, and my hips come off the bed. The growl it pulls from him thrills me.

"What are ye doing, lassie?"

"You don't like this?"

He takes his cock into his hand. "Does it look like I don't like it?"

I laugh and it loosens everything inside me. Have I ever laughed like this during sex? Nope.

"Maybe you should come here and put that inside me."

"Oh, I plan to, but first this." He wets his lips, and I resist the urge to scream hallelujah as he climbs onto the bed and buries his face between my legs.

I grip his hair and tug as he eats at me, his tongue swirling and tasting and teasing.

"Yes, just like that," I cry out, and he rewards me with a thick finger. He fills me, stretches me and my body quakes aching for his big cock. I think he might destroy me with it, but I don't really care. I want his cock.

I want him.

Careful, Luce. You just said you weren't setting yourself up for failure.

My thoughts fade as he works his finger into me and adds a second. His talented tongue swirls over my clit, and I take my breasts into my hands and tease my nipples. Pleasure builds inside me, and I begin to pant, searching for air as he takes me to the highest mountain and leaves me hanging.

"Finn," I murmur...beg. "Please."

He changes the pace and rhythm, long, hard blunt strokes meant for release, and I tumble over the edge, my body pulsing and vibrating as pleasure centers in my core. His fingers slow, as my liquid heat coat them, and his moans of sheer pleasure curl around me, untie something inside— something that allows feelings in.

Oh boy.

He stays between my legs as I ride out the orgasm and as my body comes back to earth, he climbs up my body, pushes my damp hair from my face and kisses me deeply. His cock presses against my pubis and I lift to massage it.

"Condom," he murmurers into my mouth. "My shorts."

I put my arms around him to hold him close. "My night-stand," I tell him.

He reaches out, pulls out the drawer and after searching around, comes back with a condom. With an insane intensity about him, he goes back on his heels, and I admire his hard body as he quickly sheathes himself. His head lifts, vibrant green eyes on mine.

"Is this what you want, Luce?"

"Yes. Is it what you want?"

He grins and points to his hard dick. "Can't hide what you do to me."

Thrilled, I crook my finger and urge him back. He falls over my body, his weight nearly squeezing all the air from my lungs. I don't care. I spread for him, and offer myself up, and his crown slides in an inch. I've never shagged a Scot before. For some reason that thought makes me giddy.

But he devours my mouth and absorbs my chuckle as he pushes in deeper, and ohmigod, he's so gloriously big, filling me so deeply, I'm not sure I'll be able to walk tomorrow, or a week from now.

"Doing okay, Luce?" He breaks the kiss, and puts both hands on either side of my face.

"Never better." He smiles at that, and with a flick of his hips drives all the way inside, hitting my cervix so hard, it nearly brings on another orgasm. "That's so good."

"Yeah," is all he says as he buries his mouth in my neck and rocks his hips. I run my fingers over his hard back, his muscles rippling beneath my fingers and I kind of love it. He inches out, and drives back in again, taking my ability to speak with him. I moan and scratch at his back as his thick cock spreads me.

He braces his hands on either side of my bed, lifting himself to ease up on the weight holding me down, and his pubic bone grinds against my clit.

"Oh!"

He grins, but it's twisted from pleasure. "Like that, huh?"

"If you're asking if I like shagging you, the answer is yes."

"I like shagging you too, Luce."

I lift my hips to get him moving again, and he obliges. His big hard body rocks into mine, and I wrap my legs around him as each glorious stroke brushes over my G-spot before pressing against my cervix. Before long, a hard quake goes through me, and I'm honestly not sure what's happening. I open my mouth, but no words form as he grinds deep, his cock and body hitting every erogenous zone in my body.

I break around him, a hard shudder nearly stopping my racing heart as a full-body orgasm races through me. I've only ever read about them. Never in my life until now, until Finn, had I experienced one.

"You're so hot and wet, babe. You've got me right there."

I let my hands slide to his ass, being very careful not to touch his cut, and hold him to me. His cock swells inside me—he's so close—and he pulls out, driving back in again. Sweat breaks out on his brow, and I love the mess we're making of each other, and how it makes this that much more intimate.

He moves, harder, faster, every thrust for him now, and I stare at him, mesmerized as he closes his eyes, clenches down on his jaw and goes perfectly still inside of me as he reaches his own climax. It's a beautiful sight.

He collapses on top of me, his lips finding mine. "Luce," he murmurs into my mouth, our hearts crashing against each other. "You good?"

"Yes. I don't think I've ever come so hard in my life," I admit honestly, and that's a problem, because yeah, I'm going to need about one hundred more of these before this affair is over. Does he have a hundred to give, and better yet, how will I ever be with another man after mind-blowing sex with the hottest Scot on the planet?

15

GAVAN

I'm pretty sure I haven't stopped smiling since Luce and I shagged. She's been busy since, and tonight I'm playing football with the guys at Madison. I miss her. Yes, it's true, if I had it my way, I'd be spending every day with her before I go back home. Guilt hits that I'm here in Boston having myself a great time while Da is busting his hump back in Glasgow.

I park Finn's car at the field and pull my phone from my football shorts, about to call my father, when my phone rings.

"Cousin," I say as I answer. "I hope you're having a wonderful time in Fiji."

"Of course I am. It's Fiji. How's Boston?"

My lungs tighten, once again a measure of guilt goes through me. "It's not Glasgow." I don't think I'm ready to admit how much fun I'm actually having.

"No, you're right and thank God for that. Now, how is my favorite cousin making out with the Johnson wedding?"

I snort. I better be his favorite considering what I'm going through for him. "Everything is going great, actually. Glen even invited me to the bachelor party."

"Seems like you're getting along with the family."

I wish I could say I liked them, but I don't. "I don't think I give you enough credit for what you do, cousin."

"Ah, has bridezilla come out?"

"Something like that. Anyway, what did you want? I'm just about to join some old friends on the pitch. Wait, have you noticed dogs don't like kilts?"

He goes quiet and I can almost picture the line in his forehead. "Yer aff yer heid?"

I once asked him the same question. "No, seriously. I've had two dogs nearly attack me in two days. I don't think they like your kilts."

He starts laughing hysterically, but I find no humor in nearly getting mauled to death. "Pull it together, will ya."

"The treats," he says still laughing as I grab my water bottle from my sports bag. I use my teeth to open the lid and squeeze the water into my mouth. "Alistair has a dog and I make the most delicious homemade liver treats for him. Check the bottom of the pouch in the kilt."

I nearly choke on my water, as my gaze searches the field. "You've got to be kidding me?"

"Drives the dogs crazy."

That explains a lot.

"Wait, when was the last time you washed your kilts?"

"I take them to the dry cleaner the first of every month."

"Are you telling me I'm wearing dirty kilts that brushed up against your dangly parts?" A hard quiver goes through me. "There's a lot of things I'll do for you, Finn, but that's not one of them. I'm getting them all dry cleaned and you're paying."

"Aye, you do that, Gavan."

I shake my head, repulsed. "What did you want, anyway?"

"Just wanted to see how things were going, and if maybe you checked around to see if there was any great space to rent for your pub." I narrow my eyes and glance around his car. Is he tracking me in his car or something?

"Yeah, I checked out a place, but it's probably not going to happen. It won't be on the market long."

"Then maybe you should jump on it."

"You know I can't."

"Ah, but you can, cousin. Maybe my dangly parts aren't the ones you should be worried about."

"What the fuck is that supposed to mean?"

"Maybe you should stop being a wee baby."

"I'm not—"

"Oh, I have to go. Snorkeling awaits."

The call ends and I sit there. Is he telling me I need to grow a set? What the fuck? He knows I'm not about to just up and leave my father. I'm not Ma.

You're not Finn, either.

Okay, while I admire what he's done, he doesn't have a sick parent at home, one he nearly lost. I turn the car off, toss the keys into my bag, and decide a good hard game on the pitch is just what I need to work out my frustrations with my cousin, and maybe a few of my own. After I lock the car, I shoot a text off to my Da. It's late, but he's likely still at the bar. I wait for a response and when none comes, I walk to the field. I'm about to shove my phone away when it pings. Expecting it to be Da, I pull it out to see that it's a message from Tamara asking if I'm still interested in the space.

Maybe I should look at it again. I wonder what Luce would think of it. Christ, what am I doing? I can't plan a life here until I can get Da to agree to move, and the more I think about it, the more I realize he's probably never going to leave Glasgow. I text her back and let her know I need a bit more time. She reminds me that other people are looking at it. I toss my phone into my bag, and head to the bleachers, where the guys are all standing around and tugging on their shin pads and cleats. Their girlfriends and wives are chatting and laughing in the bleachers.

Luce would like to be a part of that. A longing fills me. I would like for her to be a part of it too—not just for her, but for me. I've never been envious before, until this moment.

"No fucking way," my old friend Luke says as I approach. "Look what the damn cat dragged in and why the hell is your hair orange?" He touches my hair and I swat his hand away.

"Piss off."

"You pretending to be Finn, or something?"

Before I can answer, Spencer comes over, and pats me on the back. "So glad you made it, *Finn*." He emphasizes the name and I cringe. "What the fuck is going on, buddy?"

I exhale and drop my bag. "I'm not sure you'd believe me if I told you."

"Spill," Trent says, and I laugh. Honestly, it's so good to be around the guys again. I've missed them. I've missed the pitch.

"Look, can we all just pretend I'm Finn for a bit. I'm doing him a favor, is all."

"Does that favor include banging Lucille Johnson?" Spencer asks as he makes two fists and pounds them together."

"No, it's not..." Okay, it is, but I don't want them talking about Luce like that. "She's a nice girl."

"Then what the hell is she doing with the likes of you?"

At the mention of Luce, I lift my head and spot her coming toward me. My heart leaps, and a smile I have no control over flits across my lips. "Look, she's here. Just pretend, okay?"

"Whatever you say, Finn," Trent says and slaps my back before running to the net.

Luce's smile does the weirdest things to my insides as I walk toward her. "Hey, what are you doing here?" I squeeze her arm, and resist the urge to go in for a kiss.

"You said you were going to play tonight, so I thought I'd come watch." My heart beats a little faster and my thoughts are so scattered, I don't respond. Her smile falters. "Oh, if you didn't—"

"I'm glad you're here, Luce."

She relaxes. "Okay."

"Now I have to try not to embarrass myself. It's been a while."

"I won't laugh."

"Yeah, right. You're still laughing from the fence incident." She takes her bottom lip between her teeth, and I growl, wanting to bite that lip myself. "Why don't you take a seat on the bleachers?"

I walk her over, and she sits, a little away from the group, and I get into my gear. I give her a wave as I run to the field, and start my warm-up. I keep casting fast glances her way, still finding it hard to believe, with all she has to do, that she took time out of her schedule to watch me play.

After we warm up, I'm given my old position as striker. I guess they want to see if I still have the magic touch. We take our positions and the ref blows his whistle, and just like old times, we all fall into place together. I run the field as our defense gets the ball and kicks it. It's a battle between me and the other team, both of us chasing the ball. I get there first, do a bit of footwork and get around him. The goalie spreads his arms as I take the ball down field and go for a corner kick. The ball flies into the net and the guys cheer.

"Guess you still got it, Gavan," Adam our defense player calls out, and my gaze flies to Luce to make sure she didn't hear. I find her clapping, and a few of the women are standing and moving closer to her. For the first time in a very long time, I'm feeling alive. I've missed this more than I realized and to have Luce standing there cheering me on... It's strange, I never really knew what I was missing until this moment.

"Lucky shot," someone on the other team calls out and one of my guys shoots an insult back. I laugh and fall back into formation as Luce begins chatting with the other women, and I smile. I think Kev was right and Luce could use a few good friends.

We play for the next ninety minutes, and the sky is dark as we all head back to the bleachers, spent, and wet and just happy. I only scored that one goal, and our team lost but I don't even care. I had a blast.

The men kiss their wives and girlfriends, and Luce gives me a sweet smile. "Nice moves," she says. "You didn't embarrass yourself at all."

"I scored."

"Yeah, you did." She leans into me, her words for my ears only. "If you play your cards right, you could score again later."

I growl back and my dick twitches. "You can't say stuff like that to me when I'm on the pitch with the guys."

She puts her hand over her mouth. "Oops."

"Finn," Spencer calls out. "We're hitting up the Crow for a cold one. You and Luce are joining us." I turn to Luce to see if she's up to it, although I'm sure Spencer was telling us, not asking us.

"Of course, you'll come," a pretty brunette says as she waves Luce over.

"That's Jess," she says. "She's sweet. She's married to Derek."

"We should go then."

"I'd like that, actually."

I kick off my cleats, and tug on my boots. At least I don't have to wear a damn kilt tonight. "Don't think this is getting you out of me getting another goal later." I wink at her and she laughs.

Everyone starts filing off the field. "Meet you guys there." I glance at Luce. "Did you drive?

She nods. "I parked over there."

"Do you want to meet me there, or do you want to go together?"

"I'll come with you."

I like the idea of driving my girl places. Technically, she's not my girl, but for the time being, that's what I'm going to call her. We make our way to Finn's vehicle, and I open her door for her and toss my stinky bag into the back. That smell is going to penetrate the upholstery and never come out. It brings a secret smile to my face.

"Something funny?" Luce asks.

"Nope." I squeeze her legs. "It's just really nice that you came to watch."

"I had nothing better to do."

"Wow, I feel so important," I joke.

She laughs. "Kidding. I have a ton to do, but I needed a break."

She does need a break and I am going to make sure she gets it. I back out of my spot. "You'd better give me directions. I'm not sure where we're going."

She points as we drive. "Finn?"

"Yeah?"

"Why did that guy call you Gavan?"

I try not to swallow my tongue. "They just keep getting us mixed up." Liar, liar.

"Did Gavan play soccer?"

"Yeah, he was damn good too."

"He doesn't play anymore?" We hit a red light. "Go left when it turns green."

"No, not anymore."

"That's too bad. You really came alive on that field. You were totally in your element. I loved watching you." I take a left on the green and she scans for parking spots. "Right here." I pull into a spot, not at all too far from Prime restaurant. "It's just around the corner, we can walk from here."

I lock up and we start down the sidewalk, and my steps slow as we walk in front of the retail space I viewed the other day.

"What's this?" She asks, and presses her nose to the glass.

"Just ah...space I looked at the other day."

She turns to me, her eyes wide. "Finn, really? You're really going to look for space for your pub idea?"

"Just looking. It might not be the right time and this place is going to move fast, and I can't make hasty decisions."

She takes my hand and gives it a squeeze. "Your dad?"

"Yeah."

I start walking and she keeps pace beside me, her hand still holding mine. I brush my fingers over her silky smoothness. I really like her company, and the easiness between us. I just wish I could tell her the truth about who I really am. Maybe I can. I don't think in the end she'll care and I'm sure it will clear up many of the questions undoubtedly racing around in her brain.

"I wonder if they'd hold it for you, you know, until you can be sure."

"I don't think it works that way."

"I know, you're right." She glances behind her. "It's a great location, though."

We reach the pub and I open the door for her. She walks in and the guys and girls are all at the pool tables. They wave us over and Brett tosses his arm around me as he gestures for the waitress to bring us a couple of beers. He makes a fist and nudges my chin.

"We'd choose Finn for our team over Gavan every day. Gavan sucked. Isn't that right guys?"

"Yeah," they all say. "Gavan sucked at soccer."

I shake my head at their razzing. I guess I deserved this. "Tell Luce how much Gavan sucked at soccer and everything he did," Spencer says, and I make a mental note to make his death slow and painful, like Finn's.

"Gavan sucked at soccer, and everything he did."

"I thought you said—"

"Don't believe anything I say," I tell her with a shake of my head. Our beers come, and I tap mine to hers. "To Gavan sucking."

She laughs, and we both take a swig from the bottle. How can I ever possibly tell her the truth now? I'm getting deeper and deeper into this lie, even bringing my buddies into it, and if she found out others knew and she didn't—she's not a girl who would like to have the wool, or the kilt, pulled over her eyes—she'd have every right to hate me.

LUCE

I glance at the clock as my staff file out of the boardroom, and not only is my stomach grumbling, I'm getting a headache from the morning's never ending business meetings. I gather up my files and glance outside, taking in the sun casting shadows on the street far below. I exhale, wishing I could go to lunch with Finn. He messaged me earlier, and I'm just too swamped with Friday meetings and getting everything in place before the close of the week. I have to say, I am looking forward to the barbecue at his neighbor's house tomorrow night.

A grin touches my lips as I step from the room, shut the door behind me and make a beeline to my gorgeous corner office, keeping my head down so I'm not pulled in a million different directions. I'm going to shove a salad into my face and over my lunch break make some calls about getting decorations for the country club, and try to find a venue for Sarah's bachelorette party.

She'll want it on a Saturday night, naturally, which means I'm going to have to ask for another weekend off. Chef wasn't happy with me last time, and if I keep it up, I'm going to end up fired. Honestly though, I'm shocked that the bachelorette party slipped my mind. I have been busy though, and there is a part of me that assumed it was the maid of honor's job. Hard to believe my sister picked my former best friend for that role and no, I'm not about to work with her to pull it off.

I love my sister, but there's a line I'm not about to cross. I suppose I'll have to send invitations to that, which means another afternoon at Finn's picking them out, and maybe I'll get lucky enough that we can do it on a Sunday and he'll want to have a nap in his bed. Thinking of Finn, and knowing we'll be hanging out again soon is always the bright spot in my day.

Careful, Luce.

I shut that inner voice down because I am being careful —sort of.

I spot a figure moving in my office as I approach and my stomach twists. I can't handle one more meeting. I'm getting hangry. Of course, that makes me smile too, as I remember when I cooked for Finn after finding him naked in his pool. Was that only a week ago? It was but I've had more fun than in the last two months...years...okay, maybe decades.

Yeah, I think the last time I had fun was when I was seven and went to see the Ice Capades with Chloe and her family. My chest suddenly squeezes so tight breathing hurts. Every now and then, the loss of my best friend rears up to kick me in the face. I take a breath as anger mingles with hurt and betrayal as I shove my door all the way open, about to tell whoever is inside to take a long walk off a short pier, but nearly bite my tongue off when my gaze lands on Finn leaning against my window ledge, looking like sex in a kilt.

Le sigh....

"What...are you doing here?" I ask, assuming he's on the clock since he's dressed professionally.

"Are you okay, Luce?" His body hardens as his gaze moves over my face, and I remind myself years of bartending made him great at reading others.

I shake off thoughts of Chloe, happy to see Finn. In fact, he makes the loss of our friendship, and the sight of her with my douche bag ex just a little easier to handle.

"I'm great now," I say, in no way hiding how happy I am he's here.

His smile is warm and slow—panty melting—as I glance behind me, and shut my door tight. For some reason, I even set the lock.

What, do you think he wants to have sex in your office, Luce?

A girl can hope, right?

"I always wanted to see where the important people work." He angles his head, and I almost forget how to breathe. "Love the corner office, Luce," he says quietly, his voice soft, his green eyes sincere. "It suits you, and you deserve it more than anyone I know, and I know a lot of people."

I laugh and while I appreciate his vote of confidence in me, I toss my files onto my desk. "I'm not sure how important I am."

"Hey, don't be modest. You're smart, successful and gorgeous." He waves his hands in a circular motion, first over me and then around my office. "All that, and wrapped up in a little package so sweet and small, it makes me want to put you in my pocket and take care of you."

I angle my head. "You want to put me in your pocket?"

He chuckles. "I once told you I wasn't great with words, especially around women. Half the time I don't know what to say, or even what to do. But you get it, right?"

"I get it." Truthfully, I don't know why he thinks he's bad around women. He seems to know all the right things to say to me.

"I'm just saying you should own that," he emphasizes.

"You should own all that, too. Minus the sweet and small package, that is," I say.

"Are you saying I'm not sweet?" he asks, his tone teasing at first.

"No—"

A change quickly comes over him. "Well, you should be, because I'm not sweet, Luce." There's a hitch in his voice, a stiffness in his jaw I don't understand.

"All I'm saying is that you own the number one event planning business in the city and that's no small feat." His frown deepens and I'm not sure what I said or did, but I think I hit a nerve. "Finn?" Is he not proud of his accomplishments? Is it going to take owning a pub before he's fulfilled? Deciding to change the subject, I say, "What do you think of the view?"

He offers me his back as he shifts to glance out the window, and the Finn I know and love is back as he turns toward me. Love? Okay, like. The Finn I know and *like* is back.

"I like it, but I like this view better."

"Wow, what a sweet talker," I tease. "Did we have business I forgot about?"

"Since you couldn't meet me for lunch, I brought lunch to you." He waves his hand to the paper bags sitting on the side table just inside my door. I hadn't noticed them earlier. How could I when Finn is eating up all the space in my office and turning me from an educated financial advisor to a dim-witted moth.

"No way." I walk toward the big paper bags and stop to eye him. "Homemade mac and cheese?" I ask, hopeful.

He laughs. "You wish. I do owe you that, though."

"You don't owe me anything. I don't know what I would have done if you hadn't taken us on as clients last minute. I owe you."

"Oh, I like that." He taps his chin. "Let me think of all the ways I can wring payment out of you."

Something in the way he says the word wring triggers a response from my body and it begins tingling, right at the apex of my legs. I turn back to the numerous containers inside the paper bag and pull out soup, salads and sandwiches. My stomach growls.

"This is from my favorite café. How did you know?"

He wags his eyebrows playfully. "I have my ways."

I laugh at that. "I thought we had no secrets."

His shoulders deflate. "Okay fine, I asked your assistant."

"Cherise sold me out," I say with a laugh. Her desk is right outside my door in the main area, and she doesn't usually let anyone in to see me without an appointment. "I'm surprised she let you into my office, actually. This is a secure building."

"It's the kilt." He shakes his head. "What can I say, it opens doors for me."

"It worked on Lester downstairs too?"

"It works on everyone, lassie."

Grinning, my gaze moves over his hard body. "Maybe I should wear one."

"I don't think it will work for you, lassie." Jokingly he lifts his kilt to showcase rock-hard thighs. "You don't have the legs for it, besides," he says, but then his smile drops, and he goes serious. "You can't tell me doors aren't always open for you, Luce."

"Everyone thinks I have it so easy."

"I never said that, but are you saying your name doesn't pave your way?" I realize he's thinking how easy it was for me to secure the country club once they knew who wanted it.

"No, it does." Which is why I work incognito at Prime. Switching gears, I say, "I guess I'm just worried about the bachelorette party and the wedding on such short notice, and I don't have Harry Styles."

He frowns. "I hate the pressure on you, and for what it's worth, I don't think you have it so easy. How about this," he says, as he gestures for my chair to sit. I do, and he opens the containers and sets them on my desk. He hands me a spoon and fork and pulls a chair closer to sit across from me. "Let me take that on."

"The bachelorette party isn't in your contract, Finn."

"No." He dips his spoon into the soup and moans as he takes a mouthful. I'm so glad he likes it. "But you're busy and I have some time. Just tell me what you have in mind."

"I don't have anything in mind, which is the problem." I take a mouthful of soup. "This is so good. I really appreciate you bringing me lunch." I take a big bite of my sandwich.

"Fancy hotel rooms?"

"Something like that."

"Okay, let me look into it." I crinkle up my nose, wanting to protest. "It's done, Luce. I'm taking it on, end of discussion. Now eat your lunch."

We both dig into our food for a moment. "Have you thought any more about the rental space?"

"Still thinking." He leans back in his chair, and bites into his sandwich and my phone pings. I decline the call and put on some music.

"Who's that?" he asks, and gestures to my phone.

"Vass and Clem. Do you know them? They're from Scotland."

"I said I know a lot of people, but that doesn't mean I know everyone," he says.

Everywhere we go, he runs into some old acquaintance or client. "You seem to know everyone."

"Finn knows everyone," he grumbles around a mouthful of soup.

Sometimes he's so strange, talking about himself like that. We go quiet again, and I finally break it and ask the question that has been on my mind. "You've never heard from your mother since you were a wee baby?"

He snorts at my language. "Nope, don't want to either."

Okay, when someone pisses him off, he stays pissed off. It's not my business, but I can't help but want to know more about Finn Duncan and what makes him tick. "That must have been hard, Finn. Growing up without a mother, just you and your father, working a pub together."

He smiles. "Da and I had some great times, Luce."

My heart beats faster. "I love how close you guys are. I'm not close with my parents." A tinge of envy at what he has grips my stomach. "I can't seem to do anything right in their eyes."

"They're proud of what you do here though, right?"

I snort. "They are and I guess that's why I do it. I don't love it. It's not my passion." I cover my face with my hands. "I'm a grown woman and still trying to please my parents. How pathetic is that?"

"Not pathetic at all. I am sorry that they're disappointed in your other life choices, but I don't think you should get back with Ryland to make them happy."

"He could be the last man on the earth and I'd still run the other way!" I profess, and his gaze holds mine for a second longer, his spoon halfway to his mouth. Crap, why do I always protest too loudly, too strongly when he asks about Ryland. He's going to start questioning my honesty.

"Do you think Sarah and Glen are happy?" he finally asks.

"I don't know. Are any married couples happy? I'm not even sure Mom and Dad are happy, but they'd never divorce because it would look bad."

"I don't know if married couples are happy, either. Ma left, so I guess she wasn't happy, and at Da's bar, everyone's shagging everyone. No one seems happy. People just shouldn't get married."

"Says the wedding planner."

"Okay, then maybe I shouldn't get married."

"You know I'm off guys." Yeah, I'm off guys, but I'm *on* a hot, kilted Scot. "I'm just glad I found out who my best friend and Ryland were before I walked down the aisle only to become another statistic, although that might have never happened because I'm sure Mom would have talked me out of divorce—especially if kids were involved."

"Kids should have two parents, but not if one of them isn't happy. I just wish..." He glances at his feet and goes quiet for so long, I can't help but wonder if he's asleep with his eyes open. "She never even said goodbye," he says softly, almost under his breath.

My heart jumps into my throat as it squeezes tight, and I fight the sudden prick of tears as I picture Finn as a wee boy, and waking up with no mother, no explanation. That had to have been devastating and have a long-term effect on him. My gaze moves over his tight face, and I have no doubt he's telling me something deeply private, something he's never told another soul and his faith in me means more than he could ever know.

"I'm sorry, Finn." I reach across the table and put my hand over his as my throat burns.

He gives a fast shake of his head. "I'm sorry, I shouldn't have—"

"What she did was wrong. You deserved an explanation."

"I just...I guess I wasn't enough for her to hang around."

I stand quickly, and circle my desk. "Finn," I say and push on his chair. Its wheels squeak as I move it away from the desk. "This isn't your fault. You were a child. It was never about you."

He puts his arms on my waist. Making light of the situation, he tugs me onto his lap. "Look at that. Got you right where I wanted you."

"Oh, is that what you were up to this whole time?" I ask and even though he's kidding, I get the sense that his mother leaving was pretty damn hard on the wee Scottish boy.

"Aye, that was my goal." He glances past my shoulders. "Is your door locked, Luce?"

17

GAVAN

As I wait for Luce to show up, I stand in my backyard and bounce a football off my knee. I might have scored first and fast at Wednesday night's game, but I'm rusty as hell, and ashamed to admit it. The rest of the game proved I wasn't in uni anymore, and maybe I need to hit the gym. I bounce the ball off my knee and catch it with my foot, bouncing it a few times before kicking it up and catching it between the back of my shoulder blades.

"Nice moves."

The ball slides down my back and I grin as Luce comes through the back gate. "Are you trying to throw me off my game?" My gaze races down the length of her petite body. This afternoon she's in tight yoga pants that instantly harden my dick, and a thin, V-neck T-shirt with The Rolling Stones emblazed across the front, and I can't seem to stop staring at the S in stones as it sits right over her nipple—which I suddenly want in my mouth. Suddenly? Who am I kidding? I always want her nipples in my mouth.

She shuffles numerous bags in her hands. "How am I throwing you off your game?"

I set the ball aside, and arch a brow as I take the bags from her. "You look good enough to eat."

She laughs. "I'm in my old yoga pants, and this T-shirt is a hundred years old."

"A hundred, huh?" I head toward the doors and she follows me. "I didn't know the Rolling Stones were around that long. Did you see them in concert?"

"I did." I turn and see her smile. "I wasn't always boring Luce the workaholic."

"You're anything but boring." In the kitchen, I stop and she bumps into me from behind. I turn to her. "Who called you boring?"

She snorts. "For one, my mother."

Anger flares in my stomach. "Are you serious?" What kind of a mother says that about her child—one who goes out of her way to impress her own parents? What kind of mother leaves her husband and wee boy, never to be heard from again? People suck.

"Yeah, I'm not my sister."

"Thank God for that." I shake my head and a few loose strands of hair fall free. By the time this gig is over, I'm going to be bald. "Shit, did I say that out loud?" I need to stop saying the wrong things around her, but it fucking kills me that she has to earn love from her parents. That's just shitty. If I ever had a kid—and I don't see that happening—I'd love them unconditionally.

She bites back a grin. "Ryland also told me I was boring. Growing up, Chloe was always the daring one, the fun one." She glances at her shirt. "I probably never would have gone to this concert if she hadn't begged me."

My heart squeezes. "That had to really hurt." I'm sure it still does.

"I miss her so much. We grew up together, shared everything. Even my fiancé, obviously," she says with a laugh that holds zero humor and one-hundred percent hurt. "She can have him. I just wish...I wish things were different."

"You dodged a bullet, and they don't deserve you." She is so much better than those eegits. I'm not sure whether to bring it up or not, but decide since we're being honest with each other, mostly, I say, "Kev said you needed good friends in your life."

She angles her head, like it's taking her a minute to figure out what I'm talking about. Either that or she's trying to figure out why my hair is an odd shade of orange today. She's too kind to point out the hack home dye job, though. I just wanted to make sure to take care of the skunk line before I went to the neighbors and they noticed the faded color. "He said that to you?" She seems genuinely surprised by Kev's observations.

I nod. "Do you two know each other well?"

"Not really. I bring him food when I can, and we chat. He's a good guy, just had some hard hits. If I could, I'd give him a job at the firm, but he's not qualified, unfortunately. I don't think he's the kind of guy to stab me in the back."

"You've given jobs before and that's happened, huh?"

"Bad judge of character," she says, an indirect answer to my question that tells me everything I need to know. "Also, I do have good friends." She nudges me with her shoulder. "One, anyway."

I wink at her. "Yeah, you do." She is my friend, and I like that. "Friends with benefits." Shit why did I say that? I hope I haven't offended her.

"Two consenting adults just...kilting around. Except today, you're in your soccer shorts, and I have to bake, so there's no time for anything else."

"There's always time for kilting," I counter loudly. "But I should be out there practicing my moves, so I don't make a fool of myself next week."

She nibbles her bottom lip, and her gaze is appreciative as she admires me. "You've got moves, Finn. On and off the field." She steps up to the counter. "It's great that you ran into Spencer and you're on the soccer team. I meant it when I said you were totally in your element on the field and I loved watching you."

I feign exasperation with her American lingo. "It's called football and I was on the pitch." She rolls her eyes at me. "Are you coming next Wednesday?" I love the idea of her being there. What is wrong with the men in this world? How can they not see how amazing this woman is? I guess if they had, I wouldn't be having such a great time with her. Still, I want Luce to find someone and be happy, although the thought of her with another man doesn't sit well in my gut and that's just not good, not good at all.

"The girls invited me." She beams. "They're so nice, Finn. Candace is in marketing. Emma is a nurse and Shyanne is a hair stylist. She owns her own salon." She glances at my hair and how nice of her not to comment that I should think about paying Shyanne a visit. "I really like them." Her smile curls around me and tugs at something deep. "But I'm not sure I can go Wednesday."

"What's up?"

She hesitates for a second, seems a bit cagey which is odd. "Work stuff," she says and turns her back to me. Why do I have the strangest feeling she's not telling me the truth? "Okay, can you put everything here." She taps the counter beside her.

I drop all the grocery bags onto the counter. "Are you feeding an army?" I pull out icing sugar, regular sugar, vanilla, chocolate chips, and more. "Why did you bring all this?"

"I had no idea what ingredients you had, so I brought everything I'd need for cupcakes." She holds up a big tote bag. "Plus my clothes and makeup for the party."

It's insane how much I like the idea of her getting ready at my place—or rather Finn's place. I wipe the moisture from my brow. "Okay, what can I do to help?"

"Probably stay out of the way."

"Hey," I say and step up behind her. I pull her hair to the side and press my lips to her neck. She moans and leans against me. Her body melts against mine as I lightly run my lips over her fragrant flesh.

"Vanilla...my favorite."

"This...this right here is why you need to stay out of the way. You're a distraction. Especially when you do that." My hands span her small waist and I rub my growing cock against her. "Finn," she warns as my brain rings with need. "Your phone."

I go still and listen. "Oh, right." I thought that ringing was coming from my head. Using a bag of chocolate chips, she points to my phone on the table.

"Don't go anywhere."

"I'll be right here, baking." I grab my phone and as I step from the room, I glance back to find her watching me, a small grin on her face. I love making her smile. I duck into Finn's office when I see that it's a long-distance call.

"What's up, cousin," I ask my mind still on Luce.

"Just checking in to see how things are going?"

"Good." I glance up to make sure Luce is still in the kitchen. "We're just making cupcakes to bring to the barbecue."

"We're?"

"Luce is here."

"Oh?"

Shit, I'm not about to tell him I'm shagging his best client. "We were going over the contract when your neighbor showed up and invited Luce." He makes a sound, like he's worried I'm fucking things up. "Listen, I wanted to ask you about music. Sarah Johnson wants someone special. Any idea?"

I hear a tapping sound. "Let me think on that, but it's such short notice."

Deciding to go for a long shot, I ask, "Do you know Vass and Clem?"

He gasps, and I pull the phone from my ear. "Gavan, you're brilliant."

"Yeah, I know, but do you know them?"

"Seriously, Gavan, you need to stay off the pitch." Once again, I glance around the room to see if he has cameras on me. "Vass…"

"Um, okay."

"Vass…" he says again, and I scratch my head. I dyed my hair this morning and even more is falling out. "Fergus Vass. Gavan, why do you not know these things?"

"Because these things aren't important to me."

"You need to get your head out of your arse. Fergus Vass. We went to school with his cousin, Bran."

"Holy shit."

"Yeah, holy shit."

"Do you have his contact information?" I laugh to myself. Luce assumed I knew him because he was from Scotland, and look at that, it turns out I do—through his cousin. If his cousin is as ornery and contentious as mine, I probably won't get anywhere, though.

Finn huffs. "Do I have to do everything?"

"Do I have to remind you that this is your business, not mine."

"That reminds me. When are you going to start your own, cousin?"

I wondered when he was going to bring this up. "You know, I looked at some space," I tell him to shut him up.

He gasps. "Did you lease it?"

The last time we talked about the space, he basically told me I needed to grow a set. "No, I can't just jump on it."

"Why not?"

"Da, the stroke, you know...I can't just leave him."

"Gavan," he admonished. "Your da is fine. I talked to him the other day and he was perfectly happy."

Okay, that takes me by surprise. My da is his uncle and I suppose they talk, but why would Finn call him when he was in Fiji? "Why did you call Da?" Unease works its way through my bones. "Is he okay?" Is there something Finn isn't telling me?

"Oh, just to say hello and tell him how fabulous Fiji was." I guess that's plausible, but it still sounds weird. "You should lease the space, Gavan."

"But—"

"You don't have to be afraid of new challenges because you don't have to live up to anyone else's expectations but your own. If you fail, you fail, but that doesn't make you a failure." His words bounce around my head. He was there in those early years when my mother ridiculed me because I didn't meet her expectations. "I totally understand how those early years shaped you, Gavan. But remember this, we learn by those mistakes—hell, I made a lot of them starting my own business—but those mistakes are stepping stones to teach us how to do better. If you fail, you learn, and I'll always be here for you no matter what," he says softly, his wise words hitting on something deep in me. "You'll always have your da too. You won't be alone, and you're not abandoning him, cousin."

I swallow the lump jumping into my throat. My cousin might be a lot of things, but in this moment, I'm pretty sure he's right about everything. I don't speak. I can't and I'm certain he knows it and is leaving me to my thoughts when he says, "Oh, I have to go. Cocktails are here."

With my heart beating a little too hard against my ribcage, I say, "Bye Finn."

"Bye Gavan."

I shake my head as a million thoughts ping off my brain, and walk over to Finn's surround sound system. I go through his selections and play Vass and Clem. The music spills from the speakers piped into every room of the house and I am a bit envious of his set-up. I nod to the beat as I head back to the kitchen and the second I set eyes on Luce, her hips swaying as she turns knobs on my stove, I nearly bite off my tongue.

"You should dance every day," I say and step up to her as she turns to me. I take her in my arms, and she giggles.

"Finn, I have work to do."

"First we dance."

She relaxes in my arms. "It's been so long since I've danced." Our bodies move together, a warmth and intimacy between us that I've never quite experience before. "I love this music." She sighs, and the warmth of her mouth falls over my neck.

Her hands link behind my back, and we create a rhythm, not at all unlike the way our bodies are in synch in the bedroom. The song ends and we don't break apart right away. I glance down at her and she tilts her face up, her eyes partially closed, her lips poised open, an offering I can't resist.

I press my mouth to hers and moan as her tongue finds mine. My heart beats just a little faster in my chest, as foreign feelings course through my veins. If this is so wrong, why the hell does it feel so right? I break the kiss and take in the want in her eyes. I understand that want.

"Finn," she murmurs and once again it's like a goddamn slap to the face. I want my name on her lips, and that can never happen. This is a fling, and we're friends with benefits. Even if I wanted more, and I'm goddamn worried that if I do, if I told her who I was now, she'd kick me right in the nuts. So many people have fucked her over and I don't want to be one of them. It's best when I leave here that she never knows who I am, and that way we both part with happy memories, and no one ends up with a battered heart hit with betrayal.

"I guess we should cook," I murmur.

She chuckles. "We were cooking and I think you mean bake."

"Right, what can I do to help?"

"You're doing enough for me as it is."

"That reminds me. I secured the Aria room at Four Seasons for Sarah's bachelorette party."

She turns to me wide eyed, her mouth agape. "No!"

"Yup, went there yesterday after lunch. I dropped—"

"Your kilt?"

Her grin is so wide and playful, I give a big belly laugh. "Do you really think that's something I'd do?"

"I don't know, Finn. You do seem to like to show off your... dangly bits."

"I like to show them to you. Wait, do they offend you?" I ask, dead sober.

She laughs and whacks me. "No."

"You want to see them now, then?"

"Ohmigod, are you fourteen? And while I do," she admits with a grin. "Cupcakes."

"Right, and no, I name dropped. The Johnson name opens doors, Luce, but you know that. They couldn't do enough for me. I even managed to book the spa for the night, where champagne will flow freely."

"I'm sure it had more to do with your charm, Finn, and less about the Johnson name." She goes up on her toes and kisses me. "Thank you so much though. I'll let Sarah and her maid of honor know."

"Maid of honor who should be doing the organizing for this, yes?"

"Right, but it is what it is." She smiles at me. "What would I do without you?"

"No idea," I tease as my brain races, wondering how the hell I'm going to go back to Glasgow because now I'm suddenly wondering what would I do without Luce.

This isn't good. This isn't good at all.

18

LUCE

"Do you think I made enough?" I ask as I count twenty-three cupcakes. Yes, Finn, unable to wait until later, gorged on one. At least I know they passed the delicious test, judging by the moans and groans and the amount of chocolate icing he got all over his face as he practically ate the entire cupcake in one bite.

"I have no idea how many people are going to be there."

I frown and look over the treats. "Maybe I should do another batch." I'm really looking forward to going, despite the fact that Finn seems less than enthused, but Delilah was so lovely, and it was sweet of her to invite me.

"Maybe we need to get cleaned up. We're supposed to be there in an hour."

"I thought you didn't want to go."

"I don't, but I like the idea of us getting cleaned up for the next hour."

"I can make another batch in a whole hour."

He shakes his head and sticks his tongue out, trying to lick the chocolate from his face, and once again, I picture a wee little Finn herding sheep. Someday, I'd love to see where he grew up, and what life was like for him in Scotland. He might have been raised by a single dad in a pub, but dammit, his dad did a fine job with him. I'm not sure Finn realizes what a catch he is, though. Always saying he's only good for sex and never knows how to say the right thing.

"You're missing the point."

"Which is?" I ask. I'm not missing the point at all. I'm just playing with him, and forcing him to tell me exactly what he has on his mind. Who knew I loved dirty talk?

His brows wag over those gorgeous green eyes of his. "We could get you out of these clothes and wash all the icing from your body." I glance down at my completely clean clothes.

"I don't have—" Before I can finish, Finn dips his finger into one of the cupcakes and smears the icing on my face and neck. "Finn."

"See? Dirty."

"You're going to pay for that," I yelp. He scoops me up, and I shriek as he carries me up his stairs and deposits me in his bedroom, where he dropped my travel bag earlier. I feel like I'm back in high school, getting ready for the dance at a friend's house. But we already danced, and I'm sleeping with this friend. "Now I only have twenty-two cupcakes."

"I won't eat one at the party," he says, his eyes dark and full of hunger. He grips the hem of my T-shirt and peels it over my head like it's the most natural thing in the world, and I have to say, everything in what we're doing does feel easy, comfortable...right.

"You already had your dessert."

He tosses my shirt away and drops to his knees. "I don't know about that."

"You have the evidence all over your face."

He peels my pants to my ankle and I lift my feet one at a time to aid him in undressing me. A fine shiver goes through me as he tugs my panties down and presses his mouth to my pussy. He parts me with his tongue and rubs his face all over my dampening sex. I moan and reach down and grip his bright orange hair to hang on. It seems a tad brighter than yesterday, but now is not the time to think about that.

His head lifts, and mischief dances in his eyes as he says, "Now I have dessert all over my face."

My legs nearly give at his playfully sexual joke. "Ohmigod, Finn. You did not just say that." I feign offense even though I love it. His grin widens as he peels off my panties and stretches to his full height to reach around my back to remove my bra. I stand before him completely naked, and completely comfortable in my own skin as he admires me with hungry eyes.

"We have a problem," I say, deadpan.

His smile falls. "What?"

"You're completely overdressed."

"Aye, I am." He makes quick work of his clothes, captures my hand and leads me into the bathroom. This time, I stand back and admire his back and backside as he reaches into the shower, and turns the water to hot. Steam begins to fill the room, as he steps in and gestures me over. I step in and he puts me under the spray.

"Feels good," I murmur, as he stands behind me, presses his hard body to mine, and cups my breasts as the spray pelts against my hardening nipples.

"Sure does." His mouth is close to my ear, his words vibrating through me and causing shivers. A girl could really get used to this. "In these romance books you read," he begins, and I brace myself. I really hope he doesn't diss something I enjoy immensely. "Is there a lot of shower sex?"

I laugh at that. "Yes, and they make it very romantic, but let me tell you, Finn. If you drop to your knees right now, you're going to drown."

His deep, guttural chuckle falls over my skin and my heart beats a little bit faster. I love being here with him. I love how we can talk and laugh while we're naked.

"How about maybe we don't try that."

"There are other things," I say seductively—or at least I think I sound seductive. It's possible I sound like that horned up donkey I once saw at the zoo. He trails one hand downward, pressing along my stomach. He stops at my sex, and his thick finger brushes over my swollen clit and I whimper in delight.

"Things like this?" he asks, and I move against his finger, wanting it inside me. But this man does not need instructions.

"Yes, things like that."

He slides a finger into my body and I lean forward and brace my hands on the wall. He slowly moves his finger in and out of me, and applies pressure to my clit with the butt of his palm.

"How are you so good at this?" I murmur, and for a brief moment his finger stills. I move my hips, wanting more, and he obliges.

He finger-fucks me and I rock my hips shamelessly, taking everything he's willing to give me and quickly reminding myself, he's only willing to give sex, even though there's a stupid part of me that might want more. I shouldn't be surprised, though. I do go for men who are completely wrong for me.

His breathing changes, becoming a little faster, his hard erection pressing against my back and my mouth waters for a taste.

I rock and groan and grind against him and he whispers encouraging words into my ear. I honestly love how I don't have to hold back with him, worrying I'm not coming off as a proper lady. I can be who I am, and he can be who he is too— a gay man who is attracted to a girl.

Could we have more?

Oh, God, what am I saying? He finger-fucks me a little faster, and I claw at the wall. "Please, Finn."

"I don't have a condom in here with me, otherwise, I'd put my cock in you, Luce."

Don't say it, Luce.

Don't.

"I'm on the pill and I'm clean."

He goes still again, and I curse under my breath. "I'm sorry. I shouldn't have—"

"I want that."

I steal a fast glance at him over my shoulder, and his eyes are burning hot, his muscles tight. "Do you trust me, Luce?"

"I do," I say, and I mean it. I don't trust a lot of people, but he knows that.

"I'm clean," he says. "I always have sex with a condom. I want to feel you. I want to fuck you with no barriers."

It could—probably will—be my undoing, but I nod. He lightly brushes his fingers over my back. "Only if you're sure, Luce. I can go get a condom."

My heart swells. I love his concern. "I'm sure."

He gives me a big hug, practically lifting me off the shower floor. Warm lips touch my back and he peppers kisses over my damp flesh, and each kiss curls around me and tugs at something deep inside. I can't let myself fall for this man. I just can't.

His hands trail down my back and he cups my ass and lightly squeezes. I moan and he puts one arm around me to hold me tight as he gently kicks my legs open a bit wider. It's so crazy how much I love it when he takes over and takes care of me.

"Bend a little more," he murmurs, his chest against my back as he guides me down, placing my hands a little lower on the tile wall as I present him with my backside.

He growls when he gets me into position, and I whimper as he positions his cock at my opening, sliding in a mere inch. I move and he races his fingers down my spine, sensations rocketing through me.

I angle my head to see him and find his eyes concentrated on his cock as he casts his hips forward and enters me with one fast thrust.

"Finn," I cry out as he hits my cervix, this angle giving him greater reach and creating different kinds of sensations inside me. Flesh meets flesh and creates friction as he pulls out, groans, and slides back in again. I scratch at the walls and gasp for air as he keeps one arm around me to hold me upright and fucks me hard.

"You are so beautiful," he murmurs, his words hugging my heart.

I push back, welcoming each hard thrust, and begging for more. We're going to look like we spent a week in bed by the time we go to the barbecue, but at the moment, I just don't care. My body burns as he pumps, and one hands slides around my body and between my legs to tease my clit

"Yes," I croak out and push forward and backward, wanting it all and no longer knowing how to move as pleasure takes over every cell in my body. His cock thickens inside of me, stealing my ability to talk. I shut down my brain, and focus on the amazing things we're doing to each other.

"Babe."

His other hand moves up to latch onto my shoulder, like he's using it for leverage as he pumps and rocks and brings me higher. I suck in air, and as I let it out, I give over to the pleasure and I come around his pistoning cock.

"I feel you," he murmurs, bending over my body, and pumping hard. He thrusts and grunts and just as my climax subsides he groans and lets go. I go still as he spurts, filling my body with his seed. He kisses my quivering flesh and stays inside me for a few more minutes as we both struggle to regulate our breathing. He finally pulls out, lifts me up and spins me around. There's a smile on his face, and I smile back.

"That was fun," I say.

He brushes my wet hair from my face. "And no one drowned."

I have no idea why, but I start giggling, and he pulls me to him and laughs. I revel in the way his heart pounds against my cheek, and he reaches up to adjust the spray, until the warm water falls over our bodies. He squirts soap into his hands and begins to clean my body and I just stand there on rubbery legs and let him take care of me.

After we're both cleaned, we dry off, a comfortable quiet between us. We drop our towels in the hamper and walk back to the bedroom. I open my bag, and turn to him as he heads to the closet.

"It's not fancy, right?"

"It's a barbecue. I'm thinking khaki shorts and a short sleeved dress shirt."

"Good. I brought a sundress. Something easy and simple." I tug it from my bag and shake it out.

"You'll be the sexiest woman there tonight."

"You know all the women there, do you?"

"No, and I don't need to."

His compliments always make me feel so important. "You don't have to sweet talk me. You've already gotten into my panties."

He laughs at my teasing and we both dress. I turn my attention to my hair as he grabs a comb and starts tugging on his. I resist the urge to ask him if he dyes it. I don't want to embarrass him.

Fifteen minutes later, Finn opens the front door, and I step out, the late day sun shining down on us. I admire him in his casual clothes as he locks up and he puts his hand on the small of my back as we head to Delilah's. I cast a quick glance his way, never having felt so close to any man in my entire life. My gaze lifts to his face and I take in the tension.

"Are you okay?"

He scrubs his face. "I'm not great with names. I tend to forget."

"That's okay. You see a lot of people in your business. It's not always easy to remember."

He gives me a grateful smile, and rings the bell when we reach Delilah's place. Voices sound from her backyard, and Finn grows antsier. I decide then and there not to leave his side.

Delilah swings the door open. "Finn, Luce, I'm so glad you could both come."

"I'm sorry if we're a bit late." Finn gives her a kiss on the cheek, and she takes the cupcakes from me. "Something came up."

Finn casts me a sheepish glance, and I turn from him. Way to give away what we were doing and raise questions.

"These cupcakes look amazing," Delilah says, her eyes wide.

Finn winks at me. "Luce is amazing in the kitchen."

Great, now I'm thinking about kitchen sex.

Delilah smiles at me. "All I've heard about are these cupcakes. The girls will be delighted."

"There's only twenty-two. Someone was anxious."

She laughs. "Twenty-two is plenty. Come on, we're all out back. I'll introduce you." Finn looks a bit relieved about that, as we walk through her lovely home and out into the sunshine. Her husband is at the barbecue, along with a bunch of other guys, and he waves Finn over. So much for staying by his side. He seems a bit reluctant, but when Jacob holds up a beer for him, he leaves me with Delilah.

"Happy birthday, Jacob," I call out and he lifts his beer in salute.

"Come on, I'll introduce you to the girls."

She walks me to a long table beside an in-ground pool, a group of six women seated around it. There are numerous wine bottles on the table, and what looks like a pitcher of some fruity drink with ice. I assume it's non-alcoholic, considering the woman with a belly swollen to twice its size is drinking it.

Delilah does the introductions, and pulls a chair out for me. Everyone says hello and they're all friendly and welcoming and no one asks me what I do for a living, or judges me on who I am or what I do. I like Finn's friends. These ladies, as well as the ones I met at his soccer game, are the kinds of women I'd like to surround myself with.

When the wedding is over, the relationship is over and this all goes away, Luce.

"Luce is Finn's..." She lets her words fall off, and it doesn't surprise me that she doesn't know how to classify my relationship with her neighbor, because yes, we likely do have sex written all over us.

"We're friends," I say. "I hired Finn-tastic Affairs to help with my sister's upcoming wedding."

"Oh, I do love a wedding," Olivia says. "Finn did mine years ago."

"I wouldn't mind him doing mine..." Blakely says as she admires him from head to toe.

"Oh, are you getting married?" I note her ring finger is bare, not even an engagement ring.

She snickers. "Nope."

I give her a confused look, and as a smirk crosses her face as she takes a drink of her wine, I get it. I laugh, but it comes out sounding nervous and edgy.

"He is one fine looking Scot." She takes another drink of her wine and sighs as Finn meets my gaze. He's checking in on me and I appreciate the concern. I smile at him and even though I think Blakely might have started on the wine early, it doesn't go over her head. "You're sure you're just friends?"

"We are," I say quickly, as Delilah points to the wine.

"Red or white?"

"White, please," I say and resist the urge to ask for the whole bottle. Honestly though, he can shag Blakely all he wants. We're friends with benefits, and I can't forget he once told me he doesn't think people can be faithful.

"How the hell could you be friends with that and not want to climb him like a tree?"

"He's—"

"Gay," Delilah whispers. "Isn't that right, Luce?" I meet Delilah's curious gaze; her eyes hold numerous questions about her neighbor.

"That's right."

"I do love a challenge," Blakely says, and stands. As she heads toward Finn, I take a big drink of my wine, but it does nothing at all to wash down the jealousy I have no right to feel.

How the hell did I get myself into this mess?

19

GAVAN

I stretch my body out and slowly open my eyes as memories of last night creep into my still tired brain. I smile, unable to help myself as I recall the way Luce's body moved beneath mine, the eager, responsive way she reacted to my every touch. The barbecue at my neighbor's house was fun, for the most part, but the party Luce and I had afterward in this bed was even better, despite the fact that we got such little sleep.

I roll to the side and slide my arm across to find the bed cold and empty. The happiness welling up inside me dies a slow and painful death as worry moves in to take its place. Had Luce figured out I wasn't who I'm claiming to be and bail under the cover of darkness? Had someone at the party tipped her off? One of the women, Blakely, kept flirting with me, like she was trying to get a reaction and prove I wasn't the gay neighbor Finn. I thought I pulled it off, but maybe I hadn't.

I sit up, and listen for sounds, and my smile reappears when I hear music and banging pots coming from downstairs. I kick the blankets off, eager to see Luce, and slide off the bed. I hope she's downstairs lounging instead of cooking, because I planned on making her breakfast. I'm also hoping she doesn't have plans for the rest of the day because it's Sunday, and like she once said, Sundays are made for napping, and reading, and any other activity that's relaxing and brings happiness. I can think of a couple.

I tug on a pair of sweats and a T-shirt and finger comb my mess of hair in the mirror before I head downstairs. At least the orange has faded a bit since yesterday and I don't look like a ridiculous clown. I stop at the doorway to the kitchen, and my throat tightens at the sight before me. I go quiet, not wanting to disturb Luce as her hips sway to the music of Vass and Clem, which sends sparks of reminders to my lust-imbued brain. Delicious smells reach my nose, and a moan I can't stifle crawls out of my throat and gains her attention.

"Hey," she says, her voice low and sleepy and so goddamn sexy, my heart swells.

Unable to help myself, I cross the room, slide my hand around her head and bring her mouth to mine for a deep, early morning kiss. Her hands snake around my body and she holds me tight and I swear to God my heart has never ever beat so fast. I could wake up to this every morning. Our lips linger for a moment, and when she smiles up at me, there's a part of me that thinks maybe I could be faithful. Lord knows since I met her, I've not wanted to look at another woman.

"What was that for?"

"I kiss all my friends like that in the morning," I say like a total arse, but holy hell, my brain is spinning at how happy I am to see her, and I want her again. Which is insane, considering how many times we shagged last night. I tried to go slow and gentle for the most part, but the more I had her the more I wanted her and I still couldn't seem to get enough.

"Wow, lucky friends."

"What are you doing up?"

"It's eleven." She snatches up her spatula and points to the clock. "I can't even remember the last time I slept this late."

"Is there somewhere you need to be?"

"No, but I'm sure you must have plans for today."

"I do, actually."

For the briefest of seconds, I spot disappointment in her eyes, but she recovers quickly and I fucking hate that she doesn't think my plans involve her. The men in her past—not to mention her own family—have done a number on her. "Yeah, of course you do." She's about to turn from me, but I stop her.

I capture her chin. "Those plans involve you, Luce. I have a surprise for later."

Her eyes widen, then dim. "I don't like surprises."

"You'll like this one."

She eyes me for a second, her lips pursed. "Tell me."

"No."

She points the spatula at me. "Tell me, or you get this."

"What are you planning on doing with that?" I ask with a laugh.

"I'll smack you with it." I easily take it from her hand. "Hey!"

"Maybe I'll smack you with it."

"You wouldn't."

"I might."

"Finn," she warns, but there's a fire in her eyes like she might actually like the idea of a whack to the arse. "I'm making you breakfast. You'd never smack someone making your breakfast, would you?"

I glance at the stove and spot a couple of Lorne sausages. "How the hell—"

"I went out this morning and made a trip to a market that specializes in international cuisine." I turn back to her and notice she's dressed in her yoga pants and T-shirt again.

"Are you kidding me?" I breathe in the scents and look at all the food on the counter. "You did this for me?"

"Sure, why not?"

"I just...I think I'm in love."

As soon as the L word leaves my mouth, she stiffens in my arms. "With Lorne sausage," I explain quickly.

"Of course. I've never had it, but this is what the guy recommended. Also, a tattie scone. I remember you saying something about tatties being root vegetable, but I'm not exactly sure what kind this is."

"Potato," I tell her, my heart a bit wobbly. "You didn't have to go through all this trouble, Luce."

She gives me a sexy grin. "After all the trouble you went through last night?"

"Babe, putting my mouth on you." I dip my head and kiss her again as I slide my hands around her back, grab her ass and pull her against my groin. "And my cock in you. The pleasure was all mine."

"It was mine too."

I love the sexy way she's swaying against me, her body warm and satiated, and the smile on her face curls around me. I love everything about her this morning.

"What can I do to help?"

"Grab us each a cup of coffee. I have everything under control here."

I reluctantly move away from her and drop a pod into the coffeemaker. I lean against the counter and admire her body as she goes back to swaying to the music. I could be in real trouble here.

She casts me a fast glance. "Something on your mind, Finn?"

"I just like watching."

"A voyeur. I had no idea."

I laugh at that. She's right, she has no idea and I feel like a goddamn turd for not telling her who I really am. She's going to hate me, and probably rank me right up there with every other asshole she's been with.

Her phone pings and she glances at it. Her demeanor changes after she reads the text message.

"Everything okay?

"Yeah, that's Ryland. He just sent details regarding the bachelor party."

"Fuck."

"You don't have to go."

What would Finn do?

"I'll think about it."

"I don't think you'll fit in." As soon as the words leave her mouth she says, "I just mean, they can all be a bit pretentious. I'm pretty sure Glen was trying to one up you at the restaurant. As if you didn't know your drinks. You want to open your own pub someday and you grew up bartending."

"He's kind of an ass, but I can hold my own against him."

"I know you can," she says. "But I wouldn't want you to. He's powerful, and God knows he could make trouble for you. With your business, word of mouth is everything, and he has a big mouth and a big reach."

She's right and I can't mess this up for Finn. "I'll play nice as long as he doesn't mess with you, Luce. Then nice is off the table."

"You're sweet."

"No, I'm not." I study her for a second. Is there something she's not telling me? "Is that all Ryland wanted?"

"Yup. How's that coffee coming?"

I turn back to the machine and remove her cup, adding a splash of milk before I hand it to her. She takes a big drink, and gets to work on cracking the eggs. I stand back, feeling rather useless, but there's no denying she's in her element in the kitchen. It's clearly her passion and it really sucks that her family doesn't support it.

"For what it's worth, you should have been a chef."

She glances at me and stares for a second. I get the sense she wants to tell me something. "Like I said, I like to fool around in the kitchen," she finally responds, but I get the sense that's not what she really wanted to say.

But today is Sunday and that means it's a day of fun, so I don't press. "Want to eat outside?"

She brightens up. "Sounds great. Why don't you set up? We're just about ready here."

I set two plates on the counter, and grab the orange juice from the fridge and utensils from the drawer. After setting up, I head back in just as she finishes plating our food.

She smiles up at me as I clear a path for her to carry our breakfast outside. She sits and I settle in across from her. She looks at the food with skepticism. "Should I ask what's in this sausage?"

"Nope, just eat and enjoy."

She cuts into it and examines it closely. "Here goes nothing." She tosses it into her mouth and I truly love her adventurous spirit as she chews. "This is delicious," she finally announces and I laugh.

"Of course it is."

She dances a little in her seat and digs into the tatties. "Mmm," she murmurs and my dick stands up and takes notice.

I bite into my own food and moan. "You keep cooking for me, Luce, and I might tie you to my bed and keep you hostage." I'm joking, but her chest rises as she sucks in a fast breath. She's either excited by the idea of being tied to my bed, or appalled at the idea of me wanting to keep her.

"Tell me more about this pub you want to open," she says, changing the subject, and okay, maybe she doesn't like either of my ideas.

Because I've spent years dreaming of owning my own place, I burst into sharing details and talk and talk and talk, long after our breakfast is gone. She sits there aptly listening and when a bird flies overhead and squawks loudly, like it's sick to death of listening to me, I hang my head.

"I'm sorry."

"For what?"

"For hogging the entire conversation."

"No, Finn. I love it. I love the passion in your voice. You're good at event planning, but obviously owning your own pub, and showcasing your Scottish heritage is what you really should be doing."

"I want a fun place where everyone can relax, but I want to be known for great drinks and great food. Not just Scottish cuisine, but upscale local food, market fresh every day."

"No mac and cheese?"

I laugh. "No mac and cheese." I nod to my plate. "But this kind of breakfast for sure. I think breakfast should be served all day long, too. What a team we'd make, Luce. You cooking and me serving up the drinks."

She smiles at me, clearly humoring me. Why on earth would she want to quit her high paying job and come work with me? Oh, maybe because she hates what she does. She's happiest when she's creating in the kitchen and there's no disputing that. But change is scary. I know that.

Instead of answering me one way or another, she says, "You sound like you have it all figured out. What's been holding you back?" The question is so innocuous, and asked with genuine curiosity, but for some reason it really gets under my skin. Could it be because maybe Finn was right and I need to grow a set? That I'm using my da as an excuse because I'm worried I'll fail? Christ knows before my ma left, she reminded me I wasn't good at anything—that I wasn't enough to keep her around. Am I really afraid of failing, of being alone?

Shite.

"It's a big investment, and a tough business." It's not a lie. "Lots of pubs don't make it past their first year."

She nods and I sense she wants to say more, and I'm not sure I want to hear more, so I push my plate away and stand. I hold my hand out to her. "Come on?"

"Am I getting my surprise now?"

Her adorable smile lightens my mood. "Maybe."

"Are you sure I'm going to like it?"

"I'm sure. Come on."

She eyes me because I'm grinning like the village idiot and I know it. I take her hand and lead her into the library, and take her up to the shelves. She scans them, and after a few minutes a gasp fills the room.

"Finn!" she yells. "What did you do?"

She snatches one of the many romance books off the shelf. "I can't believe you bought all these romance books...for me." There's warmth, and genuine appreciation in her eyes when they meet mine and my heart fills with foreign emotions.

"I was thinking that you can read me all the good parts and then maybe we can act them out."

She laughs and I can't help but gather her into my arms. "If there's a shower scene, we'll have to improvise, like last time."

She moves against me, rubbing her body on mine, letting me know exactly what she has in mind for the afternoon. "I do love a good improvisation."

"Good," I say and snatch a random thriller book off the shelf. "Let's get to bed so we can get to the good parts."

20

LUCE

I stare at the spreadsheet on my computer screen and the numbers blur before my tired eyes. I pinch the bridge of my nose and blink rapidly, but can't seem to keep my focus. Nor can I keep the ridiculous smile from my face. Yesterday I spent the day with Finn, reading, napping, sex...rinse and repeat. I can't even believe that he stocked his bookshelf with romance novels. We laughed so hard acting out the bedroom scenes. Everything about the day was fun and entertaining, and deeply satisfying and not something I could ever see myself doing with anyone but him. Maybe the fact that I know we can't go anywhere in this relationship has given me the freedom to simply enjoy.

Ah, but you're thinking you want more, aren't you, Luce?

I shut down that disheartening thought and instead concentrate on my body and all the glorious ways it hurts with each movement. Even reaching for a pen takes my mind back to yesterday. My goodness, muscles I never knew existed still hurt, but we did do some contortionist twisting that would make any acrobat proud—or not.

I shake my head, desperate to get my mind on the task at hand and off Finn, but there's a part of me that wonders—hopes—he's going to show up with lunch and a little office quickie. Although it's nearly two, so that's doubtful, and we have the appointment for cake tasting at three and no, I'm not counting down the minutes like a ridiculous, giddy teenager about to see her crush. Liar. A movement at my door catches my attention and I lift my eyes to find my father standing there looking ever so handsome in his designer suit.

"Hey, Dad," I say, and quickly pull myself together and get my mind on work as I push from my chair, cross the room and give him a hug. God, I hope he can't see the stupid smile still lingering.

"How's it going, kiddo?"

"Monday, what can I say," I joke. "Come in, sit down."

"Can't, I have a meeting in five." He frowns as he perches on my desk. "We haven't seen much of you, lately. I just wanted to pop in to make sure everything is okay."

Everything is perfect, better than okay. I've been having the best sex of my life with a man who is gay. Honest to God, that doesn't even make sense. Obviously, there's a part of him that's attracted to women, and I can't forget that we're just kilting around. Besides that, I've been working at the restaurant to make up for missing my weekend shift, and planning a big-ass wedding.

"Been so busy, Dad." Not a lie. "I want Sarah to have the perfect wedding."

"Everything is coming together?"

"Everything is falling into place." I hold my fingers out and start ticking off all the things we've accomplished in such a short period of time. "I couldn't have done it without Finn." Dear God, just look at me. I'd do anything to work his name into a sentence simply because I like hearing it on my tongue.

Oh God, I cannot think about tongues and what he did with his yesterday.

Dad produces an envelope from his suit pocket and waves it. "I have tickets to the Red Sox game this weekend. Interested?"

My heart leaps. The last time Dad and I went to a game...I think I was about twelve. "No way," I exclaim. "I'd love to go, Dad."

"Oh, sorry. I didn't mean the two of us. I can't make it. The dates conflict with Danica's art show. We certainly can't miss that." Danica is Mom's best friend, and they absolutely have to go to the opening of her new gallery. "I thought maybe you could use them. Go with a friend?"

Friend. Doesn't he know I'm in short supply of those these days? Between everything I'm doing, I have no time to make new friends. Although the women at soccer were lovely and inclusive and I really like Finn's neighbor and her friends— with the exception of the one who'd spent the night trying to get into Finn's pants. Thank God he wasn't wearing his kilt. Lord knows what she would have done to get a glimpse underneath.

My phone pings and I glance down. My stomach twists as a message from Ryland flashes across my screen. What the hell does he want? I make a mental note to delete him after the wedding.

Dad arches a brow over eyes as blue as mine. "Everything okay?"

"Yeah, it's just Ryland. He's probably giving me more details about the bachelor party or something." My dad angles his head, intrigue all over his face. I quickly explain, "Glen invited Finn when we were picking the wedding menu."

"You and Ryland still text?" There's a measure of hope in his tone that I don't miss.

"Not really. I've heard from him lately because he's in the wedding party."

A small chuckle rumbles in his throat. "What fun it would have been if it was a double wedding. The Johnson girls and the Baxter boys."

"Dad—"

"I'd think if he and Chloe were going to get married, they'd at least be engaged. Maybe it's not working out. It's been what, two years."

"I have no idea." It's a lie, I do know, and yes it's been two years since my fiancé and best friend stabbed me in the back. But I don't want Dad to think I'm still pining for Ryland. Although, I'm pretty sure both of my parents still think I'm hung up on him and hold out hope that I'll marry into his wealthy family. Dammit, I'm educated, have a great job and I'm wealthy in my own right, on my own terms. I don't need a man for that and neither does my sister. But it's how things are done in my circle. We marry within our social status and it's all ridiculous to me and it's starting to feel a little incestuous. "So the tickets," I say, getting back on track. "Red Sox at Fenway?"

"You can use them?"

"I'm sure I can." A little bubble of excitement wells up inside me. Finn thinks the only game worth playing is soccer, or rather football, and maybe I can open his eyes to baseball and how great it is. I grin, because I can actually hear him now. "Bunch of men running around in a circle for no good reason." It's crazy, because I'm really getting to know him and how he thinks, rather well. Dad hands me the tickets. "What day did you say they were playing?"

"Saturday night." My shoulders sag. Shoot, I really want to go, but I have to work Saturday night. "Is there a problem?"

"No problem." I plaster on a smile. Every time I ask for one Saturday night off, I usually end up working two through the week to make up for it. I can understand it. The regular staff don't want to have to cover Saturdays for me. With the upcoming bachelorette party, engagement party, and wedding itself, I'm going to end up missing a lot of weekends. My boss is only so tolerant. But how can I not do this with Finn? I only have so much more time with him, and while it might kill me in the end, I want to spend as much time with him as possible before this wedding is over. "Thanks so much for these."

My dad's cell pings and he fishes it from his pocket. "Have to take this."

"Bye, Dad."

I drop back down into my chair and reach for my own phone. I swipe my finger across the screen and my stomach tightens as I read the text from Ryland.

Ryland: What's going on with you and Finn?

I stare at the text as anger floods my body. Of all the freaking nerve, thinking he has a right to know what's going on in my life. I should simply delete his contact now, and be done with it. But unfortunately, curiosity has gotten the better of me—what would make him ask that—so I shoot a text back.

Me: I have no idea what you're talking about. The wedding planner is helping me plan your brother's and my sister's wedding.

Ryland: I heard you all went to dinner the other night.

Me: To pick the menu for the wedding.

Ryland: Your sister said he isn't gay.

Ohmigod, I'm going to kill Sarah. Why on earth would she tell Ryland that? Although she probably told Glen and Glen told Ryland. There are no secrets between them—just like there are no secrets between Finn and me, besides my side gig at the restaurant—but the Baxter brothers definitely had secrets they kept from me a couple years ago.

Me: What Finn is or isn't is none of your business.

Ryland: Are you two, as they say in Scotland, shagging?

I toss my phone like it's diseased and spew a few curse words that would put an entire ship full of sailors to shame. What Finn and I are doing is no one's business, and Ryland's the least. I just hope he doesn't go around spreading rumors that could affect Finn's business, and I don't need to hear from Mom or Dad about my bad choices in men. Not that Finn is a bad choice. He's the best guy I know, but when this is over—and if Mom and Dad ever found out what was going on behind closed doors—they'd remind me that I once again went for the wrong kind of guy. Why they can't see that Ryland also fits into that category is beyond me.

Honestly, I couldn't hate Ryland any more than I do right now and I wish I didn't. Hate denotes emotion and I don't want to have any kind of feeling, good or bad, when it comes to the douche bag and douche baggess.

Simply calling them that makes me smile—and juvenile. But I'll take it. I really wish I could walk into a room on Finn's arm, but what we're doing is a secret. Another thought hits like a slap. I'm Finn's dirty little secret—he's mine—and I'm not exactly sure that sits well with me.

Just enjoy it for what it is, Luce.

Pushing down the unease rising up inside me, I pull the tickets from the envelope and look at them. I reach for my phone again, closing Ryland's message and calling Chelsea from work. She answers on the third ring and I go straight to begging. After agreeing to work three shifts for my one Saturday, I sigh and hang up. Maybe it would be easier to run my own place.

I'm sure Finn wasn't just being cheeky when he talked about the two of us working together as partners. I can't do that. I have a full-time job here—that I hate—and I don't have any experience running a Scottish bar. Finn does, though. God, am I just considering this to find a way to be around him after the wedding, or is this something the two of us could pull off? Working closely with him though, and him never really being mine, I might as well just cut my heart out and hand it over now. I shoot Finn a text.

Me: We still on for Sweet Dreams at three?

Three dots appear fast and it's insane how my insides are all warm and fluttery.

Finn: I had lots of Sweet Dreams yesterday.

Heat barrels through me at the reminder, and I'd like nothing more than to crawl back into his bed and do a repeat of Sunday.

Me: So did I, but at least we'll get to eat vanilla cake today.

Finn: No other vanilla will taste as good as you.

I stifle a laugh and glance up at my open door when someone walks by. I can't believe I'm sexting Finn. It's highly inappropriate from work and I think that's what makes it so much fun.

Me: You can't say things like that to me when I'm at work.

Finn: Fine, I'll whisper them in your ear at the bakery.

Me: See you soon, oh and I have a surprise for you.

Finn: Does this surprise mean I'm going to see you tonight?

Dammit, I wish I could, but I have to cover a shift tonight and Wednesday night.

Me: Unfortunately, no, but I think you'll like it and it does mean a fun Saturday night and a nappy Sunday afternoon.

Finn: I'm in.

I laugh at that and put my phone down. Every few seconds I check the clock, and as three approaches, I call it quits for the day and head outside. I drive the short distance to the bakery, and Finn is already standing at the door waiting for me. He's professionally dressed, which is a good reminder that today is all about business.

His grin is big and adorable as I approach, my steps fast, and I wish I could go up on my toes and give him a kiss. He leans into me when I reach him, his breath warm on my neck as he whispers, "You look good enough to eat, Luce."

A fine quiver goes through me and I inch back and look him over. "You look amazing as always."

He tugs on the band of his kilt, showcasing a big gap. "I brought my eating kilt."

A laugh bubbles out of me. "You have an eating kilt?"

He stares at me aghast. "You don't?"

I shake my head, and wonder exactly when it was that I fell in love with my sister's gay event planner.

FML.

There's a strange sense of loss in my gut as I glance at the bleachers and catch sight of the group of football wives chatting. Luce should be there with them, here with me. She's not my girl, so really, why would she want to be here? But I liked having her here, and when I first arrived on the pitch, everyone was looking for her. I hate that her work keeps her chained to her office for so long. Maybe I'll pop by later and surprise her, and help her unwind.

With that thought giving me a burst of excitement, I run the length of the field to warm up, and get into position. I can't even explain how happy I am to be back on the pitch with the guys. But as soon as I think about that guilt invades. Da is back in Scotland and I shouldn't be out here having the time of my life.

The ref blows his whistle and we all take our spots. The game flies by in a blur and I'm happy to report I scored the only two goals, which gives us the win by two. As soon as the game is over, Spencer comes over and I rib him.

"What did you guys ever do without me?"

"Lost," he says with a laugh. "You're staying in Boston, right? Not bailing back to Scotland?"

I open my mouth, but what do I say? When I agreed to help Finn out, it was with the understanding that I'd be going back. If I was fully committed to going back, why then, did I look at leasing a place downtown, or even put it out to Luce that we could be partners? It just popped out of my mouth, but really, I'm not sure it's a bad business idea.

Beck comes barreling across the field and jumps on my back. He rubs his knuckles into my hair. "Good game, Gavan."

"Finn," I say quickly, and he laughs as I shake him off.

"Right." He glances at the bleachers. "Your girl's not here. Don't need to pretend."

My stomach clenches. Jesus, I hate that I have to lie to her. But I know what telling her the truth will do and it's best we part with her none the wiser. No one gets hurt that way and yeah, running a pub and the two of us business partners is not going to happen because Finn will be back soon and I can't go on pretending forever.

I grab my towel from my bag and wipe my face off. "Hey *Finn*," Spencer says. "We're hitting up the Crow. You coming?"

"I'm going to try. There's something I have to do first."

He gives a nod and kicks off his shoes as I tug on my boots and pack my cleats. I hop into my car and drive straight to Luce's office tower. I park and head inside and I'm greeted by a new security guard. I guess Lester is off tonight.

"I'm here to see Lucille Johnson," I tell the guy sporting a gray jacket, the word security emblazoned over his right pectoral in big black letters. I don't think Cherise will be guarding Luce's door when I make it to her floor, though. It's past office hours.

He frowns, as he checks something on a monitor. "She's not in, sir."

"Can you check again? She told me she had to work late tonight."

He checks again, but honestly was there any need for him to screw his face up first, like I was dense and knew nothing, and he was the king of the world and always knew everyone's whereabouts.

"Like I said, she's not in. She left at three, and hasn't been back."

At three, we went dessert tasting, because Sarah didn't like the desserts at the steak house, and she told me then she was headed back to work. Maybe something came up. "Thanks." I walk away, tug my phone from my pocket and shoot her off a text. I wait, and nothing comes in return, and I can't help the worry in my gut. Why would she tell me she was working if she wasn't? Something must have come up, or...

Fuck, she's not with Ryland, is she? She seemed a bit off when I asked about him, but Luce is a smart girl who knows her self-worth. She's not going to let her parents push her back into his arms. I'm being ridiculous, and when it comes right down to it, what she does isn't any of my business. We're having sex, but we're not in a committed relationship—hell, she thinks I'm gay, or at least bi. But she is my friend and I care about her well-being.

I walk back to my car, and check my phone a few more times, but no messages come in. Not wanting to go back to an empty house, I head toward the Crow and find a parking spot. I'm still sweaty from the game as I walk down the street and freeze when I see three figures sitting on the sidewalk, and one of them has fangs.

I quickly remember that I'm not wearing a kilt with delicious, homemade liver treats for dogs. Killer doesn't growl as I approach, and Kev lifts his head.

"I know you."

"It's me, Finn." I step a bit closer as night closes in on us, to give him a look at my face. "I'm a friend of Jane's."

"Where's your kilt?" he asks and smirks.

"Home, I was just playing football."

"Did you win?"

"Yes."

He eyes me like he's not sure what I might want from him. "Jane isn't here."

"What?" Okay, I wasn't even thinking she was here, but since he brought her up. "Do you know where she is?"

He gestures with a nod to the restaurant Prime. "She's inside. You missed her."

"She's popular tonight," Larry says.

I turn my focus to Larry and even though I don't have treats in my pocket, I keep my distance from Killer. "What do you mean?"

"Her ex. Ryland. I don't like that guy. He came out of there." He tips his chin and I turn to see an upscale jewelry store. Maybe he's going to put a ring on Chloe's finger. If so I hope she doesn't show it off at the bachelorette party or any other event that Luce is organizing. I still can't wrap my brain around the fact that Chloe is Sarah's maid of honor and Luce isn't. It has to feel like a slap in the face, and Luce is far too good and kind for any of them.

"Are you saying Jane is with Ryland?"

"No they broke up. If you're her friend like you say, I thought you'd know that."

I shake my head. "No, I mean, tonight. I know they're broken up."

"Yeah. Killer didn't like him. He seems to like you better tonight." Kev pats the dog and it lays his head on his lap. "Good boy."

"What was she doing with Ryland?"

"Don't know," Kev says. "They were standing close."

I glance up and down the street, even though I have no idea what I'm looking for. Ryland maybe. My gaze settles on the burger joint across the street. "Are you guys hungry?"

Larry nods a big smile on his face as he rubs his stomach. "Yeah, but Jane is going to bring us some food later."

I glance at the restaurant, and try to piece things together. Is she in there with Ryland? "From Prime?"

"I hope they have them little shrimp things left over," Larry says, as Kev turns to him, leaving me standing there forgotten as they begin talking about the menu from Prime, I don't bother asking any more questions.

"You guys have a good night." I step away, and pause outside Prime. Even if she is in there with Ryland, it's not my business, right? Right, it's not, but I'm going in anyway and if I see them, I'm going to say hello to Ryland. With my fist. I pull on the door and I'm immediately greeted by a young hostess.

"I'm sorry, sir, we're all booked up tonight." I look past her shoulder and scan the dining room, but Luce is nowhere to be found. Neither is Ryland. "Can I help you with something?"

"No, it's good. I thought I saw a friend come in here."

I step back outside and my mood is darkening, much like the night sky. I walk down the street, and glance at the space still for lease as I pass it. I pull my phone from my pocket and call Da. It rings numerous times, but no answer. I guess he must be busy. I leave a voice message and tuck my phone away, but there's an uneasy feeling inside me that I just can't shake, and I'm not sure whether it has more to do with my father, or the girl I've been shagging and having a great time with. Da would like her. Whoa, where did that thought come from? It's not like I'm ever going to introduce the two, unless he decides to move to Boston with me, and even then, it's still unlikely that I'll see her after the wedding. It's not like we run in the same circles, although she loved hanging out after foot-ball last time.

I head toward the Crow and tug open the door. I spot the guys and their wives playing pool and make my way over. "Hey Finn," Liam says and puts his arm around me. His wife, I think her name is Holly, takes a shot and hands me the cue after she sinks the eight ball.

"Take my place," she says.

"Sure." Both a beer and cue are thrust into my hands and I don't miss the way Holly is glancing around.

"Where's Luce?"

"Oh, she had to work tonight."

"That's too bad. I was looking forward to seeing her tonight."

That makes two of us, but she's off God knows where doing God knows what, and none of it is my business because I'm not her boyfriend or partner or any other label you want to give whatever it is—or isn't—that we're doing. "She's really sweet."

"She really liked you too, Holly."

"We talked about a girls' night. I know she's busy with her sister's wedding, but afterward. We're all actually talking about going to Atlantic City."

"Really, she never mentioned it."

"Oh, I hope she can come. A girls' night is what we all need."

"She would love it," I say with all honesty.

"Hey Gavan, are you going to flap your lips all night or are you going to play?" Beck says.

Holly frowns. "Wait, I thought your name was Finn."

I tug my T-shirt away from my collar. Did it suddenly get hot in here? Christ, lying is exhausting. "It's Finn," I mumble under my breath and excuse myself to head to the other side of the table to take a shot. Holly watches me, then glances at Liam, who leans in to tell her something. A frown tugs at her mouth and fuck me, I'm pretty sure I just ruined everything for Luce. If I could, I'd take myself outside and beat my own ass.

We shoot pool for a couple more hours, and then we all call it a night since tomorrow is a workday. Outside we all head toward our cars, and I walk past Prime again. Should I take another peek inside? Nah, if Luce wanted me to know where she was and who she was with, surely to God she'd tell me, right? I check my phone, but no messages from my Da, so I head on back to Finn's empty house.

Hours later, restless and antsy, I grab a beer from the fridge, head out back and plunk myself down into one of the lounge chairs and stare at the dark sky. My phone pings and I snatch it from my pocket.

Luce: How was the game?

Me: We won. I scored.

Luce: Sorry I missed it. I really wish I could have been there.

Me: Work?

Luce: Yeah.

I stare at the phone. I shouldn't be upset that she's lying. Hell, I'm lying too.

Luce: Are you home?

Me: Just having a beer out at the pool.

. . .

Luce: Feel like company?

Me: Yes.

Luce: Glance up.

I lift my head and spot Luce standing at the back gate and my heart jumps into my throat, not at all surprised by how happy I am to see her. I set my beer down and head straight for her as she opens the gate and walks into the yard. The second I reach her, I pull her into my arms, and kiss her deeply. Her hands slide around my back and she moans into my mouth.

"Wow, I should stay away more often if it means getting kissed like that."

I chuckle. "How was your night?"

She exhales. "Long." I put my arm around her and lead her to one of the chairs.

"Glass of wine?"

"Love one."

I hurry inside, pour her a glass of wine and she has her shoes off and feet up when I get back and I love how comfortable she is around me. I hand her drink over and say, "I ran into Kev and Larry when I went to meet the guys for a drink tonight."

She goes completely still, her drink halfway to her mouth, and I can practically hear her brain racing. Jesus, I don't like anything about her body language. Unease courses roughly through my veins and it's a little bit harder to fill my lungs as I watch her, knowing enough about her to realize she's searching for a response—one I might not like.

"How did that go?" she finally says, her voice low, and a bit shaky.

"I offered to buy them something to eat."

She takes a sip of wine, and sets it down. "That was nice of you."

"They said they were waiting for you, something about shrimp."

She turns a little toward me, her gaze searching my face. "What else did they say?"

"You know what, Luce? You don't owe me an explanation for anything you do, but Jesus please tell me you're not hooking back up with Ryland."

She blinks once, then twice, something so lost and vulnerable in her eyes it hurts my heart.

"They told you they saw us together?"

"It's not my business, I just care—"

"Finn."

"Yeah?"

"I should probably tell you something."

I pull up in front of Finn's place much later than we'd planned, and while my mood is dark after spending the morning with my sister and mother—apparently, nothing I've done for the wedding is quite perfect enough—I can't help but smile as the front door flings open. Was Finn inside waiting for me, pacing restlessly until I arrived? Is that just wishful thinking and the only reason he's anxious is because he's more excited about the game at Fenway than he let on.

I smile and work to push back my bad mood as I wave and gather up the bags beside me. My mind goes back to when I showed up here, unannounced last Wednesday night after work. I have no idea why I was worried about telling Finn the truth about me moonlighting at the restaurant. He's good at keeping secrets and who is he going to tell, anyway? It's not like he's going to run to my mother and father, or my sister. Unlike them, he supports me in what I want to do and he was excited for me, happy that I am doing something I'm passionate about.

After my confession, I went on to explain that I ran into Ryland, and douche bag that he is, he asked my advice on a ring for Chloe. I loved Finn's incredulous reaction and that he wanted to hunt Ryland down and tell him—more like show him—exactly what he could do with said ring.

I didn't bother going into detail about Ryland's recent texts or how he quizzed me again regarding my relationship with Finn. Not Ryland's business by any stretch of the imagination, and I really wish my sister wouldn't spread rumors. Truthfully, I'm glad he's going to give Chloe a ring. At least then Mom and Dad will get off my back.

As I step closer, Finn rubs his chin, like he has something unpleasant on his mind, and his smile falters. Okay, what is going on here? Does he not want to go to the game? Is he ending this fling, or whatever it is, between us? I try to quiet my racing brain that always thinks the worst. Is it any wonder why? I go up on my toes, give him a kiss and note the way his gaze is moving over my face.

"What's wrong?" he asks, sliding his hand around my neck his fingers lightly grazing my skin.

"I was going to ask you the same thing."

"You first."

He shuts the door, takes the bags from me, and leads me into the living room. I drop down onto the sofa.

"Spill."

"Mom...Sarah..."

He sits on the coffee table and our legs bump. He takes my hand in his. "Are you okay?"

"I am, or rather I will be." I take a rejuvenating breath. My worries always seem to fade a little when I'm with Finn. "Apparently, Sarah didn't love the decorations, and while she liked the cake flavors, she didn't like the design."

"Then maybe she should have picked those things herself. She can't have you running around trying to guess what she wants."

"I told her to go online and figure out what she wants. You know, she wasn't even happy with the invitations we picked out. Actually, she was until Mom said she wasn't and then she sided with her." I exhale a hard breath.

"Sounds like she's heavily influenced by your mother."

"She is."

"Does she even want this marriage?" he asks, and my stomach tightens.

"I think so...I mean, I don't really know." I've been so busy with work and climbing the corporate ladder, I haven't paid much attention to her and Glen. Guilt once again swamps me that I haven't been there for my sister when she needed me. "She tried Mom's dress on."

"She's not getting her own dress?"

I cover my face with my hands. "It looked terrible on her, Finn. I gently suggested, much to Mom's disappointment, that she get her own dress, for today's fashion. She agreed and wants me to help her pick it out, and when I say help, that means pick it out for her, because she's off on another shoot, but how can I pick a dress out for her? I can't even try it on. I'm inches shorter and inches wider. She'll no doubt need alterations and she'll need to be there for that. I swear if I ever get married, and I don't see that happening, I'm eloping."

Finn laughs. "That sounds just about right."

"You too, huh?"

He nods. "We've got this, Luce. We can do this. I can help you." He cups my face, and kisses me. "It's been a pretty stressful morning for you."

"Totally and I just want to have fun today. No drama and no trouble. Can we just forget about life for a while and go to the game?" I reach for the bag and pull out Red Sox ballcaps and jerseys. "Look what I got for us."

He laughs. "If it's not Celtics football, I'm not wearing it."

"You can't wear Celtics to an American baseball game, and yes, you're wearing this and you're going to like it and cheer like a maniac. I shopped all over town to find these things, so put it on and I better see a smile." I toss the shirt to him. "Just be thankful I'm not making you paint your face or body."

"Now I get what my cousin was talking about," he says under his breath. "Ball buster."

"What?"

"Nothing." He tugs off his T-shirt and pulls on the jersey, which fits him perfectly. "Just so you know, I wouldn't be opposed to you painting my body, if I got to do the same to you." He wags his brow playfully, and it's a painful reminder that we're not serious and are never going to be.

"Do you have a one-track mind?" I ask.

"Two, sex and football."

I laugh. "Well, you look great." I sigh as tension leaves my shoulders. "I'm sorry I'm so late. We're not going to be able to grab a bite before the game now." After the morning I had, food is the last thing on my mind.

"I made us something and you're going to like it, and praise me like a maniac."

Grinning at his antics, I sit up a little straighter, my appetite coming back. "Really?"

"Yes, put your jersey on and I'll show you."

I eye him. "Are you just trying to get me out of my clothes, and distract me so we don't have to go to the game?"

"Yes, and no. Naturally, I want you naked, but I want to go to this game and see what your fascination is all about."

My heart wobbles. I like that he's interested in my pastimes, not that I've been to a game in forever. I unbutton my blouse and seductively let it fall from my shoulders. His groan wraps around me and elicits a giggle. I pull on the jersey and go still.

"Wait, what was it you wanted to talk about?"

He frowns, and scrubs his chin. "Nothing important."

"Finn."

"I just want us to have a fun day, now come on. Your gourmet lunch awaits." He pulls me to my feet and I eagerly follow him.

"What did you make?"

We enter the kitchen and I glance at the stove. There's a casserole dish with cheese oozing over the sides and getting all over the stove top. I'm aghast but I'm suddenly too hungry to worry about the mess.

"Mac and cheese," he announces with a big smile. I search the cupboards for the empty box and he's quick to notice what I'm doing. "I'll have you know when you messaged that you were going to be late, I went online and found a gourmet mac and cheese recipe." His grin is so adorable, and he looks so damn proud of himself I can't help but go up on my toes and kiss him.

"It looks amazing."

He winces a bit. "I just hope it tastes as good as it looks." He grabs two bowls from the cupboard and scoops a generous amount into each bowl. I grab forks and we sit at the table and dig in.

"Finn, this is delicious," I say and dive in for more. "You should put this on your menu when you open your pub downtown." He frowns and I set my fork down. "What?"

"The space was leased. I waited too long."

"Oh, I'm so sorry. I'm sure something else will come along."

"Yeah, maybe," he says, like he doubts it and I get it, it was the perfect downtown location, and while he's not showing it, disappointment radiates off him in waves. It's no wonder it didn't take long to lease it.

"So you want to elope, where would you go and what would you do?"

Okay, so he doesn't want to talk about it. "Let's see," I begin and think as I take another big bite. "Somewhere tropical, on a beach, or maybe a vineyard. Really simple, you know. I'd want everyone there to be someone special to me. Half the people going to Sarah's wedding are Mom and Dad's friends. I want to look around and have a special bond with everyone who is there."

"That makes sense."

"What about you?"

"I've never given it much thought, but I'd have to invite everyone at Da's pub or they'd kill me."

I laugh. "The pub sounds like one big happy family."

"They're not perfect, not by a long shot, but they're the only family I know. I've spent many a night hanging out at that pub, serving drinks to many lonely people."

I reach out and touch his hand. "You really miss them."

"I think Da has a new girlfriend."

"Really? Wait, is that a good thing or a bad thing?"

"It's a good thing. I want him happy. I might not ever be able to convince him to come here now, though."

I take in the worry and pain in his eyes. "Do you have to, though? If he has someone, maybe they can take care of each other."

He frowns and stares into his bowl of mac and cheese. "I guess I never thought of that. It was always just the two of us."

"You'll always be his son, Finn. Always, nothing will change that, and I bet he'd love to see you follow your passion and build that pub in honor of him."

His head lifts and his shoulders seem a bit lighter. "He wanted me to look for space while I was in Boston."

I frown. "While you were in Boston?"

He opens his mouth, his eyes a little dazed, and I get the sense he wants to say something, but when I drop a noodle onto my Red Sox jersey, his eyes snap shut for a second and his vision is clear when he opens them again.

"You can't go to a game with cheese all over you." He jumps up, grabs a cloth and comes over to me. He wipes me clean and I breathe in his fresh soapy scent as he leans close. He glances at the clock, and his voice is low. "We better get going."

"Okay," I say, missing his warmth as he inches back. "I'm going to have the company car drive us so we don't have to worry about parking."

He nods and takes our dishes to the sink, and I call for our car. Twenty minutes later, we're on our way to the game, and Finn is unusually quiet. I'm not sure what's going on with him, but he definitely seems to have something on his mind. We get dropped off into the crowd and Finn keeps hold of my hand as we make our way to our seats. The crowd is alive and full of energy today, and Finn's mood is a bit lighter.

"These are great seats," he says and takes a look around the field.

"I'll make a fan out of you yet," I teased.

"Okay, tell me the rules," he says, and I laugh.

I tell him everything, or as much as I can before the game starts and he sits there like an apt pupil wanting to learn. Once the game starts, he begins cheering and screaming like the rest of us. Just when I think I've had the best day with Finn, the next day gets better. Honestly, every day is a new adventure with more fun than the last, and I have no idea how I'm going to function when this is over.

"You're a fast learner," I tell him when he criticizes the ump for a bad call.

"Maybe you're a good teacher."

As the game continues, Finn gets us hotdogs and beer, and when the seventh inning stretch comes around, we all stand up and sing, Take Me Out to the Ball Game. He has a big smile on his face, so clearly, he's enjoying himself. Soon enough the jumbotron focuses in on a couple and the guy gets down on his knees and proposes.

The crowd goes crazy and I just groan. Finn turns to me. "You wouldn't want that?"

"Did you just meet me?"

He laughs, and brushes my hair from my shoulders. "You should be in the limelight, Luce."

"I have been, and it's never been pleasant. The shadows are just fine for me, thank you very much."

He grins and leans into kiss me, but the second he does, the camera turns to us and the next thing I know our intimate moment is broadcast on the jumbotron for all to see. Great, now our secret might not be so secret anymore, and I can't even imagine what this will mean for his image and business, or the shock and disapproval my family will throw my way if they discover I've been shagging the wedding planner.

23

GAVAN

I take a glance at my phone to check the time, and to also see if Luce messaged and disappointment curls through me, partly because it's only nine o'clock in the evening, and I hate everything about this bachelor party I've been forced to attend, and partly because I miss Luce.

Christ, I'd had all intentions of telling her the truth about who I was when she showed up at my place last Saturday before the game—even though I knew it would hurt her and would undoubtedly be the end of us. But lying and pretending is exhausting—not to mention the guilt that is eating me up —and I've become everything I hate.

But Luce was upset, wanting nothing more than a simple and fun afternoon, and I wanted to give her that, and yes, I am a goddamn chicken shit. Fuck me. We both had a blast at the game, and that led to a busy Sunday with both of us redesigning the country club's decorations, working on a new cake decoration and looking at dress designs—the more we did, the more convinced Luce was that she wanted to elope, not that she thought she'd ever get married.

But that Sunday should have been spent reading, napping and sex, but no, her mother and sister had her running all over town because they didn't like what she'd come up with for Sarah's wedding, although I think it was more her mother than her sister. Don't even get me started on where I'd like to tell them to shove their decorations. Luce is too good of a person for that family, and they don't deserve her.

Do you deserve her, Gavan?

Shite, when this lie began, I never thought I was going to fall for the sweet girl who put everyone else's needs above her own. That might be the case, but it still doesn't make it right. She's been fucked over enough, and I don't want to be adding to the list of men who did wrong by her. But I'd better figure out where we stand, and what the future holds now before Finn returns home at the end of next week and I make plans to return to Scotland.

A noise at the front of the room pulls my attention, and my gaze drifts to Ryland as he jumps on stage and I'm not sure the posh hotel has enough alcohol behind the bar for me to get through his speech. I push to my feet and order another scotch. We all have rooms here tonight, but I'm pretty sure I'm going to bail before long.

"Who's ready to party?" he shouts into a microphone. It's clear that douche bag likes to be the center of attention, and as I stare at him, I have a hard time trying to figure out what it was Luce saw in him. He did a shitty thing cheating on her, and while it hurt her, in the end she dodged a damn bullet.

Shouts come from the guys and I lean against the bar and nurse my drink. The last thing I want is to get drunk and tell the Baxter brothers what I really think of them. It's not my place, unless, of course they provoke me. As much as I'd like that, I don't want to do anything to upset or embarrass Luce. She deserves better than that from me. I also have Finn's business to think about.

"Are you ready for tonight's entertainment?"

The guys all start fist bumping and I stand up a bit straighter. Shite, Sarah didn't want strippers and I have a bad feeling about this. The lights dim, and a dozen women walk onto the stage and all strike a pose as the music begins. They begin a dance routine, and I relax. Okay, this is nice clean fun—providing they keep their clothes on.

I catch Ryland walking across the wide expanse of floor, coming directly at me, and I lift my glass and pretend I don't see him as I focus on the dancers.

"Having a good time?" he asks.

Shite.

"Great time," I lie.

"Flew the dance troupe in from Vegas." He nudges me, and my drink spills over my shirt. "What happens in Vegas stays in Vegas, am I right or am I right?"

"We're not in Vegas," I tell him.

"Yeah, but come on. Vegas showgirls. We might as well be, right?"

I get the sense he's feeling me out. "Do you plan on doing something you want to remain a secret?"

He laughs. "Aren't we all?"

I turn my attention back to the dancers as he orders a drink and downs half of it in one gulp. I almost tell him he might want to slow it down, but what do I care if he gets whiskey dick and can't cheat on his fiancée. I'm actually doing the women on stage a favor.

"So you and Luce, huh?" he sets his drink down. "You're..." He bumps his fist together.

"Bumping fists?"

He laughs. "I never knew you were funny." I just stare at him. "You tapping that?"

My entire body stiffens and I squeeze my drink glass so hard I'm sure it's going to shatter in my hand. I want to punch him in the face for talking about Luce like that.

Keep it together, Gavan.

"I think your brother might need you," I say as a very drunk Glen tries to climb on stage. If he knocks into one of the dancers, they're going to go down like dominos.

"I knew it," he says and tugs his phone from his pocket. His fingers fumble over the screen as he tries to find something. "You see, Sarah told Glen you weren't gay and Glen told me and when I asked Luce—"

My gaze jerks to his, and my heart jumps into my throat "You asked Luce?"

"We were texting..." He holds his phone out, and I take a fast glance at the screen. "She wouldn't come right out and say you two were shagging, which means—

"It means nothing. You don't know her, Ryland. You have no idea who she is, and if she was being vague, it only meant her business is hers and not yours."

Do not punch him in the face, Gavan.

"What the fuck is your problem?"

"As of right now you are, and if you don't walk away, *I'll* be your biggest fucking problem."

With his glass halfway to his mouth, he stares at me, like he's trying to figure out if I'm joking or not. I'm not. "Go get your brother."

He stumbles off toward the stage, and I turn my back and lean against the bar. I catch the bartender's eye and we exchange a knowing look. Yeah, he hates these rich arrogant motherfuckers as much as I do.

My phone pings and I pull it from my pocket. Despite the situation I'm in, a big smile crosses my face as I read Luce's text.

Luce: Kilt me now.

Me: Don't you mean kill me now? LOL I take it things aren't going great.

Luce: Cops are here. Sarah just got arrested.

My heart jumps into my throat. What the hell kind of bachelorette party are they having? Hell, I booked the spa and unlimited champagne.

Me: What happened?

Luce: Chloe hired stripper cops, and one has Sarah in handcuffs and now they're making out and I've lost all control.

Me: Ryland hired Vegas dancers. I told you those two deserved each other. Want to meet somewhere?

Luce: I probably shouldn't leave.

Me: I can come to you.

Luce: While I'd like that...

Me: You don't want anyone to see me.

Luce: We don't want to start rumors.

What if I do, though? What if I want to start rumors that the gay wedding planner, who isn't a gay wedding planner at all is falling for Lucille Johnson? Would it be so bad? I'm getting past the point of caring, but what if I'm the only one with feelings here, and I'm really nothing more than her dirty secret? There's a part of me that hates that, but there's also part of me that knows we can't have anything more because once she knows I've been lying, she's going to hate me. Fuck. I guess she's glad no one noticed it was us on the damn jumbotron. Sure, her sister has her suspicions, but no one can prove anything.

Me: I can be there in thirty minutes, and I can be stealthy.

Luce: Meet me by the elevators in the front lobby.

I tuck my phone away, push what's left in my glass away, and head for the doors. The guys are all busy drooling over the dancers, and I doubt any of them will even notice I'm gone. I shake my head as I steal one last glance over my shoulder to catch Ryland groping one of the women. I wouldn't be surprised if one or more of them get arrested.

I get my car from valet, and head straight for the Four Seasons. After handing my vehicle off to a young man standing outside the doors, I take my overnight bag from the trunk, not that I'd really planned on staying overnight with the guys, and head inside.

I spot Luce near the elevators, glancing around nervously. Her eyes light, and she waves when she sees me, but then she glances around again to make sure no one from the bridal party has eyes on her. Okay, that's fine. This is what we both wanted going into this, and I don't have any right to adjust the rules now, just because I'm falling for her.

Oh Gavan, you are such an eegit.

"Hi," I say and stand beside her, and can feel the needy, sexual energy radiating off her body as we wait for the elevator to arrive. "Do I know you?" I tease as I angle my head and look her over.

"I don't think so, I have one of those faces."

My gaze rakes over her perfect, curvy body. "It's not the face that seems familiar," I say, and her chest rises and falls in her tight little black dress that won't last two seconds on her body once we're behind closed doors.

"What's your name?" I ask.

"I don't give my name away to strangers."

I grin at the little game we're playing. "I have ways of making you talk, you know."

"Are you threatening an interrogation?"

"Yeah, I'm pretty sure if I put my hands and mouth on you, I can make you say or do anything I want." I hear her throat make a sound as she swallows and now I'm not even sure we'll make it to the room before I ravish her. The elevator doors open, and we step on, unfortunately an elderly man yells, asking us to hold the elevator. Luce and I exchange a glance, but in the end, I stick my arm out, because come on, when a little old man asks you to hold the elevator, you hold the elevator, no matter the stiffy between your legs.

"Nice night," he says as he climbs on. He narrows his eyes at Luce. "Do I know you?"

"I don't think so. I have one of those faces," she says, and I swear to god if he says it's not her face that's familiar, I'm going to lose it. I bite the inside of my cheek to keep myself from laughing and avoid eye contact with Luce, because I know she's having a hard time keeping it together too. The elevator stops on our floor and we both hurry out, and we burst out laughing as the doors close. She grabs my hand, and tugs.

"Let's get out of here before someone else recognizes us."

We reach the door and she slides the key card in and opens it. I step into the spacious room, and note the clothes and bags on the bed. I turn back to her as she locks the door and sets the deadbolt. The sound of it sliding home teases my cock.

"Are you sharing this room?"

"Yes."

If she still wants to keep this a secret, I can't be here. Someone else has a key and could come barging in. "Luce..."

She steps up to me, and loosens my tie. "I'm sharing it with you and you have all night to put your hands and mouth on me, providing I can do the same to you."

My cock stands up to take notice. "I can get behind that."

"One thing," she says and frowns.

"What?" Unease settles in the pit of my stomach. What is going through that pretty head of hers?

She produces a pair of handcuffs and as she dangles them, a coy grin tugs at her lips. "I believe all good interrogations begin with these."

My cock twitches as I eye the handcuffs. Who knew sweet little Luce had such a naughty side, and damned if I don't want to explore that. I snatch the handcuffs, spin her around and put my mouth close to her ear.

"Up against the wall, legs spread."

24

LUCE

y entire body quivers as Finn whispers in my ear, and rattles the handcuffs behind my back. Did I really steal those shackles from one of the cop strippers and suggest Finn use them on me?

Why yes, yes I did.

And I regret nothing.

He nudges me with his body and I step toward the door I just shut and locked, every nerve in my body alive and on fire. OMG, we're doing this. We're really doing this. I press myself against the door, my nipples so hard I'm sure I'm going to score it, and widen my shaky legs.

"Hands behind your back," he orders in a commanding voice that thrills me to my core. Until Finn, I never knew sex could be so much fun. Never knew I wanted to be restrained. I do as he says and the click of the handcuffs securing my hands behind my back pulls a groan of pleasure from the depths of my throat. He pushes my hair to the side to expose my neck and he breathes in the scent of my skin before he presses hot, open-mouthed kisses to my sensitive flesh.

"Are you going to tell me your name?" he asks, continuing on with our game from the elevator.

"No," I say, wanting more, everything. "I'll tell you nothing."

"Then you leave me no choice but to torture you."

I try to fill my lungs, try to sound normal and not so completely breathless, when I say, "No amount of torture will make me talk." It's a lie. I'd do or say anything to get him to touch me. I am just that easy.

"I bet there's something I can do to make you scream my name."

Oh, God, yes please.

My zipper hisses as he slowly drags it down my back. He slides his hands inside my dress, and reaches around to cup my breasts. I arch into him as he brushes his thumbs over my engorged nipples. He teases my nubs, pinches them between his fingers until the ache settles deep between my needy legs. I rub my ass against his body, everything inside me pleading for more as his hard cock presses against my back.

He pulls his hands out from my dress and I groan with displeasure, but it turns into a moan when he grips the hem and lifts it. He sinks to his knees, his mouth trailing kisses down my back as he settles on the floor. Big warm hands touch my inner thighs and climb higher, stopping at my soaking wet panties.

God, I can't believe how much I love everything about this.

Between my legs, he tugs my panties to the side and dips into my dampness. "So, so wet. Did that stripper cop get you all worked up?" he asks.

"Yes," I say, even though it's not really true. Thinking about Finn joining me tonight, and all the fun we could have with the handcuffs is the reason I'm soaked between my legs.

"You want me to put my fingers in you?"

"Yes," I practically scream and move my hips.

"Yeah, just like that," he says, and slides a thick finger all the way inside me. Small quakes begin in my core. I am so damn close it's almost embarrassing. He moves his finger in and out of me, and I rock with him, bending to grind, and rub up against the door like a damn cat on a scratching post. Knowing exactly what I need, and unable to touch my clit with my hands secured behind my back, he rubs my nub, and a keening cry erupts from my throat.

"Please..."

"You need something?"

"Yes."

"Are you going to tell me your name?"

"No."

He slides another finger into me, and lightly brushes the bundle of nerves inside that sets off a chain reaction in my body. The quivers grow stronger, and I clench down as I hover on the brink of an orgasm. He pulls his fingers from my body, and I cry at the loss. A snapping sound fills the air as he presses a button to unhook the handcuffs. He spins me to face him and I swear to God the intensity in his eyes is enough to make me come.

"Undress, now."

His eyes remain latched on my body as I shimmy out of my dress, and he unzips his pants to free his hard cock. He takes it into his hands and rubs it viciously as I drop my dress and reach behind my back to unhook my bra. I free my breasts and I love his groan of approval. He glances around the room and I follow his gaze having no idea what he's searching for.

I bend to remove my panties, and he whispers, "Slowly."

I can't help but grin, enjoying what my body does to him. I move my hips, swaying them ever so slowly, wanting to tease him, and hoping I'm pulling it off as I slide my panties down my legs, keeping them straight, and turning to the side slightly so I can really put on a show. I think I love this as much as he does and I can say with all confidence no man has ever looked at me with such need and hunger. It inflates my ego, and fills me with a confidence I never knew I had.

"You're such a tease," he murmurs, and I smile. Mission accomplished.

"What, this?" I ask, as I lift one leg at a time to remove my panties and toss them to him. He crushes them in his palm before shoving them into his back pocket like they're a souvenir...like this might be our last time together. It very well could be, considering we've made a significant dent in my sister's wedding plans. But I don't want to think about that right now. Nope, I only want to think about the pre-cum pearling on the crown of his rock-hard cock. I step up to him, drop to my knees and lick him clean. He curses under his breath and my pulse jumps with excitement.

"On your feet. Now."

I complain with a murmur as I stand and he spins me again, rubbing his cock against my body as he cups my breasts and begins walking me toward the bed, but instead of tossing me on it, he throws the handcuffs over a sconce light, puts my hands above my head and restrains me. He steps back as my heart races with excitement, and lightly runs his palms over the curve of my backside.

"So perfect."

I wiggle and he growls in response. "Please."

"Are you ready to tell me your name?"

"No," I say, like a petulant child. But I want to experience his brand of sexual torture.

"Then you leave me no choice. One way or the other, I'm going to win." He steps up to me and kicks my legs apart, and I'm sure if he touches me, I'm going to explode. His hand slides between my legs, and I arch, giving him all the access he needs. I quiver as he slides into me, two thick fingers that fill me. He pumps in and out until my breaths are coming fast and ragged.

I'm seconds from release and he pulls out. "What's your name?"

I whimper and hold my ground, dying for more...everything. He taps the crown of his cock against my ass, and he grabs my ass cheeks and spreads me wide. My pussy opens, and I glance over my shoulder, meeting his gaze as he jerks his hips forward, plunging into me, hitting so hard and deep, a hard quake begins at the top of my head and travels all the way to my toes, nearly shattering me in the most delicious way.

"Ohmigod," I cry out.

"That's right. I'm going to keep doing this to you until you talk."

I shut my mouth, never wanting to talk because I never want this to end. He grips my hips for leverage and pounds into me, and my moan is broken from the impact as I cry out.

"More," is all I managed to say as his fingers bite into my skin. Come morning, the bruises will be a beautiful reminder of Finn unleashed. Honestly, I love seeing him like this, dazed, focused on pleasure, one mission on his brain.

He pulls almost all the way out and as he jerks forward, I push back, meeting his every thrust until he's a panting mess, just like me. I sense it's taking every ounce of his control to hold off so I can come first, and while he's going at me like a wild beast, beneath it all lives a man who worships my body, and wants nothing more than to give me pleasure.

He pumps, beautifully brutal, and my eyes fill with tears. I'm not sure what's wrong with me. But I'm guessing the intimacy in what we're doing, the way we're both giving and taking is affecting my heart as much as my body. I blink to wash the tears away, not wanting anything to ruin this perfect moment between us.

He slides a finger around my body and I gasp, small quakes beginning in my core as he caresses my clit. "Are you ready to scream my name?"

"Finn," I yell. "Please, Finn. Yes, just like that." He pumps into me, hard blunt thrusts that turn my brain to mush and send pleasure shooting straight to my sex. My entire body breaks around his pistoning cock and I practically sob as the handcuffs clink on the sconce light.

"Fuck," he growls into my ear, his hot breath burning me from the inside out. "You are so hot." My cum slides down my legs as he slides in and out of me. I whimper, and he puts his arms around me, holding me tightly to his body, his heartbeat strong against my back, as he curls into me and releases high inside my body.

"It's Luce," I whisper, finally giving him my name, and his light, carefree chuckle curls around me. "And this was the best bachelorette party I've ever been to."

He laughs harder. "Best bachelorette party I've ever been to as well." He kisses my back, his palms gently cupping my full breasts and we stay like that for a long time, neither wanting to move and break the connection.

He lets go of me, and runs his fingers up my arms. "Are your arms getting tired?"

"Maybe a bit." He unhooks the handcuffs, brings my arms to my sides and lightly rubs them. "Sorry about that."

"Sorry? No way, Finn. Don't be sorry and don't lose them. I might want to use them on you next time."

He chuckles against my ear, pulls me to him and walks me to the bed. "Or I can use them on you again."

"Okay," I say quickly, unapologetically and he chuckles.

"I do love a girl who knows what she wants." He pulls the sheets down and gestures for me to get in. I slide between the soft sheets, my body so sated and weak that I sink into the mattress. He smiles at me for a second, before covering me up and walking to the fridge to grab a bottle of water. He cracks the lid, takes a pull and drops down onto the mattress beside me.

He puts the bottle up to my mouth. "Drink."

I take a long pull and sigh. "I needed that."

"You were thirsty."

I grin, and gesture toward the wall sconce, which might be hanging a little funny. "I meant, I needed that."

He laughs. "So did I." He angles his head, looking completely adorable as his gaze moves over my face, and my insides are so high, I swear I could take flight. But then his smile falters, and I notice he's still perched on the edge of the bed, and not lying down beside me.

"Finn?"

He scrubs his face, his brow knitted together. "Luce," he begins, but his entire body stiffens when someone pounds on my door. He turns at the sound. "What the fuck?"

I jackknife up as the pounding continues. I stare at Finn, trying not to panic. What if it's my sister or someone else from the party. What will they say if they see Finn in here? Lord knows he wants to keep this a secret.

I point to the bathroom. "Can you..."

He pushes from my bed, and I stare at his gorgeous body as he steps into the bathroom and closes the door. I open my overnight bag, pull on my pajamas, and run to the door. I fling it open to find a very tipsy Chloe standing there.

"What's going on?" I ask.

"Sarah is sick."

"Oh no. Where is she?" Chloe stands back a bit and points to the door across the hall from mine. "She's in the bathroom, vomiting."

"I'm not surprised, considering how much she'd been drinking."

"Shouldn't you be taking care of her? She is your sister." I resist the urge to tell her she's the maid of honor and maybe she could step up occasionally. She stumbles and I'm about to reach for her to steady her on her feet, when she pushes me, and I practically hit the door with a thud. "You're in here with someone?" She looks completely aghast, but who I'm in here with is none of her business. "So you're fucking around during your sister's bachelorette party. Everything is always about you, isn't it, Luce?"

I stand there, dumfounded, my mind racing, trying to figure out how I'm supposed to respond to that. "I'm...you're...how the hell..."

"Let me guess, it's the wedding planner." She snorts a laugh, and it totally pisses me off.

"You should go."

"I had no idea fucking was included in the bridal packages he sells. Or maybe you bought the slumming package. Are you really so desperate, Luce?"

I'm two seconds from making a fist and punching her square between the eyes when she hiccups and groans. I back up, sure she's going to be sick and slam the door closed in her face. I hurry to the bathroom, and find Finn standing there, leaning against the sink. I have no idea if he heard Chloe, but I sure hope he doesn't think I'm slumming.

"Sarah is sick. I'm so sorry, Finn. I have to go take care of her."

"Okay," he says quietly, and reaches out to push my hair from my face. "I'll get out of here."

"Or you could stay. I shouldn't be long."

"No, you go take care of Sarah."

I nod, and he walks past me. He gives me one quick glance over his shoulder before he leaves the room and my heart squeezes tight in my chest because it doesn't just feel like he's leaving the hotel, it feels like he's exiting my life—for good. I hope that's not the case, because I did something insane, something so incredibly crazy I still can't quite believe it.

Is it possible I just made the biggest mistake of my life?

25

GAVAN

I tug on Finn's best looking party kilt, the one he insisted I wear to the engagement party even though I begged him to let me find an excuse to cancel. He sharply informed me that when the Duncan men commit to something, they follow through. For the most part, he's right. I always follow through, but this charade has gone too far. I'm sleeping with Luce, pretending to be Finn, who is home tomorrow and the only thing that can happen is this fiasco blows up in our faces. I honestly can't see a way out of it that doesn't fuck at least one of us over.

I stand in Finn's bedroom and button up my dress shirt and tug on my boots. I probably should have touched up my hair, but this is the last official event where I have to play my soon to be dead cousin. Guilt swamps me as I stare at my reflection. Guilt for leaving Da, guilt for lying to Luce, guilt for enjoying my time here in Boston.

My hands fist at my sides, and I exhale a hard breath. I hate everything about what I'm about to do, but have no choice but to do it. I wish I never answered his call and jumped on a plane. Maybe that's not entirely true. If I hadn't, I wouldn't have met Luce. What is it they say, it's better to have loved and lost. What a bunch of bullshit that is.

Channeling my cousin and calling up my best Scottish accent, I head outside into the bright sunshine and in the car, I punch in the directions to the Johnson estate. My nerves jump in my gut as I approach the gate and note the media vans parked just inside. Of course, this is going to be broadcasted. Why wouldn't it be? Finn did say it's the wedding of the century, and he damn well should have been here to oversee it himself.

I park and smooth my sweaty hands over my hot fucking kilt as I step from the vehicle and hand my keys to a valet. They have a valet at their house? Guests of all ages, and all dressed in designer clothes make their way to the backyard and I keep to myself and follow along. My gaze instantly searches out Luce, and disappointment shoots through me when she's nowhere to be found.

I take in the decorated gazebo, the banners and balloons and over the top decorations. It's a little too overdone if you ask me, but I'm not the event planner. Finn might eat this right up. Wait, how do I know the girl laying out food on the table? I stare at her for a second longer, and that's when it hits me. She's from Prime. They must have hired the restaurant to cater this event. I just hope no one recognizes Luce.

Needing a drink, I walk toward the bar and order a scotch. The bartender catches my eye and that's when I realize it's the guy who was working the bar at Glen's bachelor party. He gives me a grin, and I lift my glass in salute before taking a long pull.

I scan the yard again and spot Luce. She's looking at me. There's a nervous energy about her that raises the hairs on the back of my neck. Is she nervous about this party, or is there something else going on? I've barely spoken to her since the bachelorette party, when she was dragged away by Chloe to take care of her sister. I'm not one-hundred percent sure what kind of exchange the two had, but judging from how rattled Luce was when she came to the bathroom and told me she had to go, I'm guessing it wasn't a very pleasant one.

She stands there, and doesn't come my way. I angle my head, and look her over, my eyes questioning her. But I have a very terrible feeling in my gut. A loud laugh fills the air and I turn and spot Sarah playing it up to the media as they snatch pictures. She looks gorgeous in her designer dress, but I only have eyes for Luce. Except when I turn back to her, she's gone, and my stomach coils, warning that something is definitely wrong.

I push off the bar and go in search of her, but stop when I find her in a corner talking to Ryland, their words whispered, clearly not meant for anyone's ears. I go still but she catches me from the corner of her eye and offers me a wobbly smile. The next thing I know, Chloe is standing in front of me with a big glass of wine in her hand, blocking my view.

"Did you have fun at the bachelorette party?" she asks, a smirk on her face like she knows something I don't.

I stare at her, and get the sense she's feeling me out. "Not sure what you're talking about," I say, hedging and trying to feel her out. I guess if Sarah told Glen I wasn't gay and Glen told Ryland, then Ryland must have told Chloe.

She gives a fake laugh. "Oh, come on. You can't tell me you and Luce haven't been messing around." She steps a bit closer, going up on her toes like she wants to go nose to nose. "What is your angle anyway?"

"I don't have an angle, Chloe," I tell her doing my best to remain calm as a few guests walk by and stare at the two of us. I think Chloe might have started drinking too early, and she's got something on her mind that needs out. I back up an inch to put distance between us.

"This family will never accept you." She glances up and down the length of me, disgust on her face. "Look at you. You're in a kilt. Do you know how ridiculous you look, and don't even get me started on your hair."

"Then why do you keep looking?" She looks aghast. Way to poke the bear, Gavan.

She quickly pulls herself together and shoots back with, "Because I haven't had a good laugh in a long time."

"Then maybe you should rethink the family you're marrying into. If I were you, I'd want a partner who made me laugh, at least once a day."

"Oh, is that what Luce does for you? She makes you laugh? Does she make you laugh when she's down on her knees? Or maybe your contracts only require you to go down on yours."

I stare at her, and her face goes tight when she doesn't get the reaction from me she was clearly hoping for. "What did Luce ever do to you?" I ask.

She falters a bit. "What..."

"You hate her so much," I state. "What did she ever do to hurt you? You're the one who stole her fiancé, not the other way around, and she doesn't hate you, Chloe. She actually misses you. That says an awful lot about who you are and who she is."

"You...you shut up."

"Seriously, Chloe. What did she ever do to you? I really want to know."

"Do you...do you...really?" She stumbles over her words a bit. "Little miss perfect." She searches the crowd and zeroes in on Luce. As if sensing the attention, Luce turns our way, and Chloe shakes her head and glances back at me. "Always the best at everything, so goddamn privileged. Throwing her money and name around to get what she wanted. That's what it's like in the Johnson family, but I'm guessing you know that and that's why you latched on to Luce."

"You have no idea what you're talking about." I'm about to tell her she probably had too much to drink, but I'd like to keep my nuts between my legs, so I don't.

She takes another drink of her wine, and it sloshes over the edge. "I was the one who liked Ryland first, but that didn't matter to her, and now...now I think he wants her back." A pained noise crawls out of her throat. "Just like a typical guy, he only wants what he can't have, and if it weren't for you, we'd still be happy. This is all your fault." I glance at her ring finger and find it empty. What kind of game was Ryland pulling when he asked Luce about engagement rings? Was he trying to make her jealous? Trying to win her back because he suddenly wanted what he couldn't have? "Everyone..." She sniffs and I almost feel sorry for her, but I can't. No one gets my sympathy when they talk trash about the woman I love. "Everyone wants them back together. Her parents...her sister."

"I don't want them back together."

She blinks up at me, like her thoughts are a million miles away. "What?"

"I think you and Ryland are perfect for each other."

"You do?" she asks with such hope in her eyes, I feel a tinge more pity for her. I honestly don't know her story, but her jealousy of Luce is destroying her. Does she even love Ryland or was he a conquest, a means of revenge?

"I don't think Luce is the kind of girl who'd go after a guy you liked first."

"You don't know her."

I'm about to tell her she's wrong, but as I glance over at Luce and Ryland, he has his hand on her arm, and worry zings through me. Do I know her? Sure, we've been having fun and shagging, but do I really know Luce?

"Don't think for a minute you do," Chloe says, "and if you're trying to work your way into this family, you should forget about that right now. She was slumming. She pretty much told me so the night of the bachelorette party when she hid you in the bathroom." She gives a very unladylike snort that draws attention. "Would she be hiding you away if she was proud of what she was doing?" She waves her hand as my stomach knots, old fears and insecurities poking at something deep. "Wouldn't she be introducing you as her guy if you two were a real couple, *Finn*." Jesus, something in the way she just said my name sends alarm bells racing through my blood. "But you're not her man, and I'm onto you. Everyone else will soon be onto your game, too, and Ryland will see that she's nothing but a loser." Her smirk is devious and so full of hatred and jealousy, my heart jumps into my throat, and I look over her head to find a very shaky Luce staring at me as Ryland walks over to the bar to get a drink.

I step around Chloe and head toward Luce. I don't care who is watching, this charade has gone on long enough and we have to talk. I put my hand on her shoulder and her eyes are damp as she lifts her head to mine.

"Are you okay? What did Ryland say to you?"

"He said...he said...he wants me back, and..." She swallows and stumbles over her words and my ears start ringing, but it's not coming from inside my head. No, it's her sister tapping her spoon against her champagne glass, and a hush falls over the crowd.

"I want to welcome everyone here today. I'm so glad you could all make it to my party, and on such short notice," she says with a laugh. "Speaking of short." She scans the crowd until her gaze lands on Luce. She laughs... "Ah, there's my sister. Hard to see her over the crowd." What the fuck? Everyone laughs, but I'm fucking appalled.

"I would like to give a big thanks to Luce and our wedding planner, Finn, for jumping in, with two feet and a kilt..." She pauses as everyone laughs again, and once again that bad feeling is mushrooming inside my stomach. "I think a few of you know Finn and have used his services before, and oh, Finn, there's an old friend of yours here who knows you rather...intimately. I'm not sure if you ran into him yet."

The backyard closes in around me, as a man about my height spreads his arms and the crowd parts to give him room as he makes his way toward me. Oh, Jesus I have no idea who he is. Did I do his wedding, or worse, was he one of Finn's lovers?

"Finn, darling," he says, but gasps and stops abruptly as he reaches me. "Finn?"

I scrub my face, trying to hide it. "Aye."

"Do you not remember your own ex?" Sarah says. Luce stiffens beside me and I catch the 'gotcha' way Sarah is looking at me, and making a mockery of her sister—after everything Luce has done for her. Why is everyone so fucking hateful? And if she knows I'm not Finn, why the hell would she do this here and now, at her own party in front of her family, friends?

Luce gulps and takes a small step back, and my heart leaps into my throat at her physical and emotional distancing.

"Luce," I reach for her but she shakes her head in sheer confusion.

"Finn, really?" my supposed ex says. "It's me, Danny." He puts his hand on his chest and feigns exasperation. "We dated for months."

"Right, aye," I say, half my attention on him and the other half on Luce as she gets further and further away from me.

Danny leans into me and touches my hair. "Oh, this is precious." He gives a huge laugh and turns to the crowd. "He doesn't remember me, because he doesn't know me," Danny says, making eye contact with Sarah, because obviously they were both in on this. Sarah's done her research and now it's all coming back to bite me in the arse. I'm going to kill my cousin, but really, is any of this his fault? I never should have gotten involved with Luce, never should have lied...never should have fallen in love.

Panic grips me by the balls, and I reach for Luce. "Luce, let me explain..."

"Explain what?" she says weakly, pulling away from me, as the media crew surround us and begin snapping pictures, which will be splashed all over the papers tomorrow, once again showing Lucille Johnson's bad choices in men.

"I'm sorry. I'm so fucking sorry." I hold my hand out, trying to stop the flashes, but there's nothing I can do. This couldn't have gone down any worse for Luce. She hates being the center of attention. Christ, she once told me she prefers to stay in the shadows because being in the limelight was never good for her, and this is all my fucking fault.

"This man is an imposter," Danny says.

The crowd gasps, and Luce tries desperately to hide her tears as she backs up, her world crashing around her.

"What...why? I don't understand," she murmurs, and she looks down, like she's reliving every moment with me, putting all the pieces of the puzzle together. "You're....you're Gavan?" I nod and she gives a humorless laugh full of pain. "I am so stupid."

"You're not stupid. This is my fault."

She laughs again, and I'm not sure she can even hear me. Her mother and father walk up to her, disapproving scowls on their face—directed at Luce.

"This is scandalous, Luce," her mother hisses, and tries to flash smiles to the cameras. "How could you have done this?"

Her father adds, "Again."

"It's not her fault," I say quickly.

"I don't know what you're trying to pull, but you need to leave," her father says, and I glance around at the crowd, hating everyone involved in this fiasco, myself included.

"Luce, will you please hear me out. Give me two minutes."

"Is your father even sick?" she asks, disbelief and horror all over her face.

"Yes, please if we can talk, I can explain?"

"Explain? How can I believe anything you say? I have no idea who you are."

"Yes, you do," I begin quickly, desperately. "What we did, the things we talked about, that's who I am." I make a fist and hit my chest. "That was the real Gavan."

"What you showed me, that was the real Gavan?"

"Yes, yes, Luce," I say a measure of hope in my gut. "That was the real me."

"I could never be with a guy like that."

Once again, old insecurities come racing to the surface as one word Chloe said bounces around inside my head. Slumming. "Are you saying you couldn't be with a guy who doesn't own a huge event planning business and simply wants to open a pub? Is that guy not good enough for you?" I shoot back, as her words gut me.

She snorts, and shakes her head. "To think I bought the space..." She stops talking as a sob catches in her throat.

Air evacuates my lungs in a rush and my throat is painful as I try to swallow. "You...you bought the space, Luce?" I ask incredulous. Why? How? Why would she do that? I must be wrong. The space had already been leased. "Luce?"

"I found the guy who owned it, and I made an offer he couldn't..."

From the corner of my eye, I spot her mother calling Ryland over. He pushes through the crowd and steps up to Luce, his eyes shooting daggers as he looks at me.

I work to get my focus on Luce's words and make sense of them. "You bought it? You bought the downtown space?"

"Yes," she says weakly, her face turning red with shame and embarrassment—like she'd made the stupidest mistake of her life.

"Luce, you can't just do that," I say, my voice low, both shocked and touched by her thoughtfulness. "What about the guy that leased it? You can't just push him out." I glance at the crowd, once again Chloe's words pinging in my brain. "You can't just throw your name and money around and take what you want, because you want it."

She shakes her head. "That's what you think of me?" Before I can answer, and I'm not even sure what to say, because I hate everything about myself and the stupid way I'm lashing out, she shakes her head. "None of that matters now. You're not at all who I thought you were either, and I could never be with a guy like you because—"

"Because I'm not good enough for you."

"I don't ever want to see you again, Finn." She briefly closes her eyes. "Or rather, Gavan."

26

LUCE

I am so numb, so completely shocked, I don't even realize Mom called Ryland over, and he currently has his arm around me and is guiding me away as Gavan turns his back to me and walks out, everyone jeering and whispering and cameras flashing. I can barely see a thing through the tears flooding my eyes. I try to blink them back, try to appear strong, as those cameras turn to me. How can this be happening again? Will I never learn, and constantly go for the wrong guy?

Gavan was pretending to be Finn.

I shake my head and try to wrap my brain around that, but honestly the signs were all there, I was just too damn stupid, too infatuated to actually see it. God, I don't even want to use the word love.

"Take her inside, Ryland," Mom says and my stomach cramps. What the hell. Is she kidding? I don't want or need Ryland to take me anywhere and if Mom is using this opportunity to try to get us back together, she's out of her mind. Why again is it

I go out of my way, and play by all the rules to win their adoration, when they clearly never put what's right for *me*—and not the family image—first? I'm not sure, but one thing I do know is I'm sick of it.

"Come on, Luce, let's get you inside and you can lay down."

As Ryland's voice grates on my very last nerve—who the hell does he think he is, anyway?—I shrug him off. But the second I do, and tell him to back off, the cameras flash like crazy. I stand there, completely lost and alone in a crowd, my eyes searching for a friend, when they land on Ivy, one of the staff from Prime, whose jaw is practically on the dessert table, to Chloe who is grinning at me. Was she behind all this? My gaze goes to my sister, and her eyes are big, horrified. Does she realize how much she just hurt me? Maybe I deserve it, leaving her alone with my parents influence while I was off at university.

I square my shoulders and present a calm that I don't feel. "If you'll all excuse me." I keep my head high and my steps even as I walk through the back garden and open the gate. The second I'm out of sight, tears fall down my cheeks and I practically run to the driveway. I find Nathan, the young valet Mom and Dad always hire for their parties, standing there. He takes one look at me and he tugs at his collar.

"I need my car." He stands there for a second. "Please, I just need to get out of here."

"Okay, sure but I'm not sure you should be driving."

Just then, Parker, the other valet, comes up to him. "Ms. Johnson, are you okay?"

"No, not really," I admit, and he pulls a couple of tissues from his pocket and hands them to me.

"How about I drive you home?"

I glance at the young man, and nod. "Okay." Parker, who is only about twenty years old, nods to Nathan, who goes and gets my car. He doesn't speak and for that I'm grateful. Nathan comes back with my car, and Parker opens the door for me. I slide in. I've had more kindness from strangers today than anyone. That thought brings on another burst of tears and as Parker circles the car, Ryland comes racing around the corner.

"Luce, wait."

Parker stops at the door. "I'm taking her home."

"I need to speak to her."

Parker glances into the car. "Ms. Johnson?"

"I want to go."

Parker nods and slides in. "If you leave with her, you're fired," Ryland says.

"I guess I'm fired."

I glance at Parker.

"I can't—"

He holds his hand up to stop me. "If you don't mind me saying, I never much liked that asshole." My tears turn into a big hiccupping laugh. "Between you and me," he begins, "I took his Ferrari for a little spin around the block before parking it." I grin a little more, and he moves his hand like he's shifting a race car. "Really gave it a workout."

"Thank you, Parker. Wait, how are you going to get back to the party?"

"Uber."

I reach into my purse and he holds his hand out. "It's okay, Ms. Johnson. You've always been really nice to me, so I don't mind helping out."

I pull out a fifty and put it into his hand. "This isn't for the Uber. It's for putting up with assholes all day."

He grins. "Well then...when you put it that way." He crumbles the bill and shoves it into his pocket.

I sniff, and wanting my mind off the disaster that has become my life, I say, "What is it you do, Parker, beside park cars?"

He lights up. "I'm in culinary school. I want to be a chef."

I smile at that, but then frown because it reminds me of Finn —Gavan—and his stupid idea that we go into business together. I turn and look out the side window as he drives me home, and once we're there, I thank him and head inside my big empty house, but everywhere I look, I see Gavan. Great, now I'm going to have to move. But before I do, I need to call the agent that oversaw the deal of the downtown space and have him put it back up for sale. I don't want anything to do with it. After I make the call, I stare at the wall for a good forty-five minutes. I'm not one to feel sorry for myself, but I'm pretty sure today was the worst day of my life, and yes, it's worse than when I found out Chloe and Ryland were having an affair.

I turn my head and look outside as clouds begin to knit together overhead. Looks like Sarah's party is about to get rained on. What a shame. I snort, push to my feet and even though I'm not hungry, I walk to the kitchen and grab the ice cream. I dig into the tub with a spoon as my cell phone continues to ring, but I'm not interested in talking to anyone.

I pull it from my purse and I'm about to power it down when I see it's Chef calling from work. "Hello," I say, trying to inject a bit of happiness into my voice.

"Jane."

"Yes, that's me."

"It's come to my attention that you've been trading your Saturday night shifts for the last month."

"Yes, I've had—"

"We hired you for weekend shifts, and since you can't seem to make them, I'm afraid we're going to let you go."

"Wait, I can explain. My sister's wedding—"

"We're well aware of your sister's wedding....Lucille," he says, and my heart falls into my stomach. "We're also well aware that you've been lying to us the entire time you've been working here."

Oh God.

"If you'll just let me explain."

As soon as the words leave my mouth, my thoughts go to Gavan. I didn't want to hear his explanation, and I'm guessing Chef doesn't want to hear mine.

"No need for explanations. Your last paycheck will be mailed to you." The line goes as dead as my damn heart. No, my heart isn't dead. I just wish it was. That way it wouldn't hurt so much. And here I thought my day couldn't get any worse. I toss my phone, and it clatters on my table and I don't much care if I shattered it. I dig back into my ice cream and walk around my big empty house. Not even the flower garden in the back can bring a smile to my face.

My doorbell rings and I practically jump ten feet in the air. I spin toward it, and go perfectly still. Maybe whoever it is will think I'm not home and leave.

"Luce, open up. I know you're in there," I hear Sarah say as she pounds on the door.

I nearly choke on my ice cream. What, my sister didn't humiliate me enough? She had to come to my house to rub my mistakes in a little more. Well, she can bang on my door all she wants. I'm not opening it.

"If you don't open up, I'll use my key."

I hurry to the door, to set the bolt she doesn't have a key for but I'm too late. The door is flung open and a very bedraggled Sarah stands there. I can't remember the last time I saw a hair on Sarah's head out of place.

"It's not a good time," I tell her, my heart pounding so hard, I'm sure I sound manic.

She looks at the ice cream. "Can I have some?"

"You don't eat ice cream."

"I do today."

I hand her the carton and she takes a big bite. "I forgot how good this was."

"What do you want, Sarah?"

Her shoulders sag. "Can we sit?"

Since I have a very hard time saying no to her, despite what she just put me through, I turn, and walk into the living room. I plunk myself down onto the sofa and she sits across from me, setting the ice cream on the coffee table. I scoop it up, and pay more attention to the chunks of salted caramel than I do her.

"I'm sorry," she begins, and my head lifts to find tears in her eyes.

"What are you sorry for, Sarah?"

"For being a horrible sister."

I frown and glance down, my stomach turning. I set the ice cream on the coffee table as I think about the years I wasn't there for her. "I'm the horrible sister."

"Are you kidding me? You're the best sister a girl could ask for. I'm the horrible one."

"Sarah—"

"I've always been so jealous of you, Luce." Okay, now that takes me by surprise. I sit up a little straighter, hardly able to believe what I'm hearing. "I could never be as smart as you, could never get an MBA, could never get a place in the firm, let alone a well-deserved corner office." She shakes her head. "Dad always praised you. Telling everyone how proud he was that you were following in his footsteps."

"Really?"

"I was jealous. I don't even know what else to say, but then today...I just...I really hurt you, and when I saw what I did to you, it was a much-needed slap in the face. My heart hurts, Luce."

"You did hurt me," I say quietly, as tears fill my eyes. "My heart hurts too."

She crosses the room and sits next to me. "I'm a sad and pathetic and jealous sister. I saw the way Gavan looked at you. I saw the way you looked at him. I wanted that, Luce. I wanted Glen to look at me that way. I thought you two were the perfect couple, and I hated you for that, but that's on me, not you. I let jealousy get to me, and...I don't know, I just always wanted what you had, but I could never be you. It's not an excuse for what I did today."

"Sarah," I begin. "I had no idea you felt like that. I just...never thought I was good enough in Mom or Dad's eyes."

She snorts. "Same here."

"Parents," I say quietly, and it brings a small smile to her face.

"When I found out who Gavan was, I was going to tell you, but Chloe convinced me to do it publicly, to really put him in his place. She wanted to destroy him."

"And me." I guess Chloe wanted to publicly destroy me and show Ryland that I was a loser. God, she was right about that.

"I'm so sorry. I hurt you publicly, and I'll never forgive myself for that. She convinced me I was doing you a big favor. But this is on me. It's all on me." She looks down, embarrassed, and I'm happy to see her taking responsibility for her actions. "I don't think Chloe was the friend she pretended to be."

I nod and squeeze her hand. "She has a lot to work through." I briefly close my eyes. "Oh, God, the pictures, the things they're going to say about me."

"I'm working on that. I'll do everything I can to stop it." She takes my hand. "But seriously. I'm so sorry. What can I ever do to make this up to you? You were always the best big sister, and I don't want to lose you and I understand if you can't forgive me."

"There's only one thing I won't be able to forgive you for."

"What's that?" she asks, her chin quivering, as worried tears fall down her cheek.

"Don't marry Glen unless you really love him. Don't let anyone pressure you into it."

She relaxes a bit. "Things aren't perfect and I don't think any man will ever look at me the way Gavan looked at you. I guess I have a lot of soul searching to do, and maybe I shouldn't have agreed when Mom suggested a fall wedding. Maybe Glen and I need to spend some more time together first."

"I think that's a great idea."

She takes a deep breath. "Luce?"

"Yeah?"

"Thanks for putting this wedding together, but there is something that isn't quite right."

I stare at her, hardly able to believe she's bringing up my shortcomings right now. "What?"

"If and when I do get married, will you be my maid of honor?"

27

GAVAN

I try not to snarl at the flight attendant as she tells me I need to put my tray up and seat belt on. It's not her fault I'm a total fuck up, and made a complete fool out of Luce. No, the fault is mine and mine alone. Well, maybe it's her sister's too. Sarah didn't have to out me at her party, where everyone was watching and taking pictures.

I do as she asks, and pull my phone from my pocket before take-off. I run my shaky fingers over the screen and shoot off a text to Spencer. I see a couple of texts from Finn, but don't respond. Instead, I power down my phone. After the party this afternoon, I went back to Finn's, packed my bag and came straight to the airport, wanting to catch the next plane back to Glasgow. Now here I am on the red eye, and Finn is on his way home from Fiji. I have no desire to talk to him, or even let him know I bailed.

I tuck my phone away, and try to dispel all the pent-up energy inside me. Christ, when I get back to Da's pub, maybe I'll pick a fight with McNally. He's always up for a good brawl and I really need a good shit-kicking. Tough son of a bitch that he is, he's just the guy to give it to me.

I push my seat back, and close my eyes, but spend the entire flight with the afternoon playing out in my brain. By the time we land, it's morning in Boston, but noon time in Glasgow, and I'm in need of a drink, and no, I don't care what time it is.

I power my phone back up to about a hundred messages from Finn. Out on the sidewalk, I grab a cab, and stare quietly at the landscape as he takes me home. While I'm happy to be back where I'm wanted—at least, I think I am—hell I haven't heard from Da in ages—I can't help the strange sense of loss inside of me. Loss of Luce, loss of my dreams...loss of my Da. No, that can't be true. Da has been busy without me, and I shouldn't have been off having such a great time, and leaving him behind. No sense in trying to get him to move to Boston with me. I'm never setting foot in that city again.

The cab drops me off in front of the pub, and music and voices spill from the open windows as I enter. The second I do, a hush falls over the crowd, and I catch Da's eyes from behind the bar. My heart sinks. He's not happy to see me. What the ever-loving fuck.

"Look what the cat dragged in," McNally says, as he sets his beer onto the wooden table a little too hard.

"You got a problem?" I ask, simply to provoke him. We're actually good friends, and spent many Sundays chatting here at the bar and playing cards.

I catch the curious way my father is staring at me, and don't miss Freya by his side. I guess he was quick to replace my company. Fuck, maybe I'm not wanted here anymore either.

McNally stands, and puffs his chest out, and I sense he knows exactly what I need. "Big shot American boy now, are you?"

"Don't call me that?"

"Too good for Glasgow now, are you?"

"You want to take this outside?" I ask, even though I'm being ridiculous and juvenile, and want my ass kicked.

Everyone starts cheering—everyone except my father, but he follows us out. He's never one to stop a good fight at his bar. A crowd of familiar faces—family—surrounds us, and my heart races, adrenaline pumping through my body. I'm about to lift my fists, but McNally gets a good punch off, square between my eyes. I stumble backward.

"What the fuck?"

"America's made you soft, Duncan," he says, calling me by my last name. Which I much prefer over Finn. I take a punch, but miss. Shite.

"Soft and slow," he says, provoking me as he dances around me.

"You're aft your damn mind," Buchanan says, and he's not wrong. I've never seen McNally lose a fight yet.

I take another punch, and he dodges it and hits me so hard in the jaw, I tumble backward and go down. He stands over me. "Are ye done?"

I'm about to stand, but Da comes up to me. "Stay down, Gavan." I nod, and Da turns to the crowd. "Back inside, nothing to see out here."

Everyone turns and conversation goes back to whatever they were talking about before I arrived, like my return meant nothing.

Da drops down beside me, and I sit up and cross my legs as I look beyond the pub and into the pasture. Silence surrounds us for a long time, and when I finally turn to look at Da, he arches a brow.

"That bad, huh?"

I snort. "Yeah."

"I wasn't expecting you home."

"Sorry to disappoint you." I look away, my heart crashing a little too hard in my chest.

"Gavan."

The way he says my name, the same way he used to say it when I was young, and there was a lesson to be learned, forces me to look at him. "You're right. I am disappointed."

My throat tightens to the point of pain, as love, hate, anger and betrayal, all the emotions I've experienced over the last month, come back to hit me in the face harder than McNally's fist.

"I should go."

His hand lands on my shoulder and he holds me down. "This is your home, son. It's always been your home and will always be your home." I turn to him, and work not to sob. I'm a grown fucking man, for Christ's sake. "It's my home too, and always has been, which is why I don't want to leave it, and move to America with you. Do you understand that?"

"I guess."

"I love you, son. More than the world. You are the most important person in the world to me."

My throat pains. "I love you too."

"I know that. I also know you gave up your hopes and dreams to take care of me when I was sick. I'm not sick anymore, and now it's your turn to go live your life."

"I can't—"

"Yes, you can and you don't have to worry about me. I sort of have Freya to do that now."

I nod. "I had a feeling." I look at my da, take in the fine lines around his face, and for the first time in a long time, he looks content. "Are you happy?"

"I'm happy with Freya yes. She makes me feel alive again, Gavan."

"I'm glad." I study his face. "I sense a but in there."

"You're right. There is a but. I won't be truly happy until you go off and fulfil your dreams. It's your turn now, son. I've been selfish keeping you here with me. I realize that now, thanks to Finn..."

"Finn, don't even mention his name around me." Fire races through my veins. "Wait, what are you talking about?"

"When your Ma left us, it made us hold on to one another a whole lot tighter." He nudges me. "It was just you and me against the world, right?"

"It still is."

"No, son. It isn't. Now it's your turn to go face that world alone, in America. I'll always be here in Glasgow, it's where I belong but it's not where you belong."

"I don't know where I belong anymore," I mumble, as I take in the beauty of Da's pub, and the green pasture behind it. I love it here, I really do, but I think he's right. I don't belong.

"That's not hard to tell."

"What do you mean?"

"You picked a fight with McNally, didn't you?"

I laugh unable to help myself. "I really am a dumbass."

"Yeah," he agrees, and I take a big breath. As I let it out, I expel a bit of the tension that's been building inside me.

I turn to my father. "I fucked up." He nods, and we sit there for the next hour or so, and I tell him everything, from the kilt rash to Sarah's fiasco of an engagement party. I left out a few parts of course, but as soon as I finish, I take in the draw of his brow, waiting for his words of wisdom.

"Finn made you wear a kilt?"

I shake my head. "That was your takeaway."

He laughs and claps my shoulder. "I can't tell you what to do, Gavan. Only that can come from here." He puts his hand over my heart, and it pounds a bit harder.

"I love her."

"Then you need to go and make it right."

"I don't know how."

"Figure it out, and you need to talk to your cousin."

"I'm never talking to him again." He nods and goes quiet. "Do you and Finn talk a lot?" I ask.

He shifts a bit and averts my gaze, like he doesn't want me to know something. My insides tighten. "Da?"

"He's my nephew. We talk, and now you need to talk to him. You might need to take a day or two, but you two have to talk." I'm about to tell him no way, when he stares at me and says, "You remember all those years you stood up for him, fought his battles."

I nod and laugh, my mind going back to the shit kicking I took and gave. "I remember."

"Then know this. Right now, Finn is fighting your battle."

I stare at my da, having no idea what he's talking about. I'm in this mess because of Finn. I also met the woman I'm in love with because of him too.

My phone buzzes in my back pocket, and I ignore it. If I answer it now, I can't be responsible for what comes out of my mouth. "I'll talk to him. Eventually."

"You do that. Right now, I suggest ice on that eye and a good night's sleep." He stands, and pulls me to my feet. I brush off my pants, and head inside. My gaze seeks out McNally, and he lifts his beer in salute—no hard feelings. I nod back and head upstairs for a good long nap.

I pull the blinds, crawl into bed, and exhaustion puts me right out. When I wake, it's bright out and I check the clock, a bit confused. How is it only late afternoon? I'm sure I was asleep for days. I rub my eyes, snatch my phone off the nightstand and realize it's the next day. As soon as I shake the fog from my brain, my thoughts go back to Luce. I groan and roll back over, wanting to sleep for another month or so, until the pain slicing at my heart subsides, although I'm guessing it never will.

I'm here with Da, in the comfort of my home surrounded by friends, and I can't even imagine what Luce is going through. She can't turn to her family, and her friend supply is short. Christ, the look on Chloe's face, the happiness in her eyes when her sister outed me was disgusting. Worry for Luce wraps around my heart, and I check to see if Spencer has messaged. I'd asked him if the wives and girlfriends would check in on Luce, and I really hope they do. She needs a friend and as much as I want to call and check up on her, I'm the last person she wants or needs to hear from. I should have kept my hands to myself and my tadger in my kilt.

I've got no one to blame but myself, and Finn. I can always blame Finn. Speak of the devil my phone pings again and I count numerous messages from him. What was that my da said about Finn? *Finn is fighting your battle.* What the fuck did he mean by that? I slide my finger across my phone. I guess I'm about to find out. I dial my cousin, drop back onto my pillow and put my arm over my head. I stare up at the ceiling as he answers on the first ring.

"Gavan," he says, sounding breathless.

"Finn," I answer.

"Why did you leave?"

"I don't want to talk about it."

"You don't have to talk about it. I know everything," he says, and there's something odd in his voice. He's usually so calm and collected, but he's distraught today. I sit up and brace my back on the headboard. Did he and Alistair break up, or did I totally fuck up his business?

"I guess the papers are having a field day at Luce's expense."

"Papers?"

"The party, the pictures, Sarah outing me."

"Darling, I know all that, but no pictures have been posted."

I breathe a sigh of relief. "Thank God."

"Sarah made sure of that."

I shake my head, confused. "Sarah did?" I rake my hair back, push from my bed and pull up the blinds. "What is going on?"

"Sarah filled me in on everything."

"Okay," I say for lack of anything else.

"You need to get your arse back here right now. It's an emergency."

I snort. "I'm not falling for that again."

"Gavan, you and Luce, you need to be together."

"Come on, Finn. I'm not the guy for her, and you know it."

"What makes you say that?"

"I'd never fit into her family." I think back to the cruel things I said to her and cringe.

Do you really believe she was slumming, Gavan?

"She told me she never wanted to see me again. She said she could never be with a guy like me and—"

"Why do you think that is?"

"Because I'm not good enough." I shake my head. "Come on, Finn. You deal with people like her all the time, don't you? Throw their name around to get what they want. Hell, how do you think we got the venue? Someone lost that space because the Johnsons swooped in and stole it, because they wanted it. What about the downtown space I was looking at?

She went straight to the owner and made an offer. What about the poor bastard who leased it and had plans of his own? Poof. All shot to shit."

"I know...," he says, a hitch to his voice. "I know everything."

"Then I'm wasting my breath."

"But *you* don't know everything," he responds sounding a bit nervous.

"What are you talking about?"

"Did you know Luce is paying for the entire wedding for the people who lost Cypress Gardens?"

My body stiffens. "What?"

"That's right, and did you know that she bought that space you wanted because you wanted it? And the guy she displaced? Well, she found him a new space. She bought another building and for the next five years, she's giving him a discounted rate on his lease."

My heart squeezes so tight, it produces tears in my eyes. Luce did that? I call my anger back, because being mad is easier than being gutted. "Tossing her money and power around again," I say, but it sounds weak even to me.

"Do you think she did any of that for herself, Gavan?"

"Uh, well..."

"Uh, well nothing." He huffs, like he's so over me. "She did it for her sister...and she did it for you."

I back up and drop back onto my bed. Luce has never done anything selfishly. I know that, deep in my heart. I also know she's good, deep in her soul, and cares about others. When have I ever seen her put herself first? Never, which is why I always wanted to take care of her and give her what she needs.

"She didn't tell you any of that, did she?" he asks.

"No." That one word comes out pained and tortured, mimicking the storm going on inside my body.

"I think it was your old insecurities and fears getting to you when she said she could never be with a guy like you," he says, his voice a bit softer.

"Meaning?"

"Meaning you lied to her. She could never be with a guy who lied to her."

I snort. "And whose fault is that?"

"Mine, and I'm sorry. I thought…"

Alarm bells jangle in the back of my head as Da's words once again race through my brain. "What did you think?"

"That if you saw her and got to know her, that the two of you would fall for each other. I knew you were perfect for each other, and you needed to start moving on with your life, Gavan. You belong here, in Boston. With me and Luce."

I go still, my brain racing so fast, I can't keep track of my thoughts. I jump to my feet. "You did this on purpose? You were matchmaking?" The tumblers fall into place. Of course, he was. Why hadn't I seen it? Oh, probably because I was dealing with a rash, and falling in love. But now it all makes sense. Seriously, maybe Finn was right and I took one too many hits on the pitch. I should have seen this coming right from the start.

"Yes, and on the bright side, I'm pretty good at it."

"Finn!"

"Gavan, please, hear me out."

Hear him out? If I could, I'd go through the phone and choke him to death. But I can't do that, and my life is shit, so I might as well hear what he has to say.

"Your da and I. We did this for you."

"He was in on it, too?" I shake my head, incredulous. I had the worst feeling that Da was pushing me away, and I guess he was, but he was doing it for my own good. I realize that now.

"We needed to do something to get your arse in gear. You're not getting any younger, you know."

"Yeah well, I fucked everything up and it's too late. I said horrible things, and there is no way she'd ever forgive me."

"Is she not the forgiving kind?"

His question stops me cold and I think back to Chloe. Luce was hurt deeply by both her and Ryland, but she told me she missed her friend. There isn't a mean bone in Luce's body. She's a woman of substance, a woman who deserves all the happiness in the world and deserves to be with someone who will love her the way I love her, but right now, as I sit here in my old bed—in my current state of limbo and despair—I'm not sure I'm the man she needs in her life. "No..."

"She likes you for you, Gavan."

"She thinks I'm you."

"No one can be me, not even you." I close my eyes and picture him throwing his arms around in pure Finn fashion that not even I could pull off without looking like a raving lunatic.

"But you told me I could—"

"I lied. Sorry."

He doesn't sound sorry. "She said she didn't even know who I was, Finn."

"Then maybe you'd better grow a set and show her exactly who you are."

28

LUCE

I push myself from my sofa and walk aimlessly around my living room. It's been two weeks since I found out who Gavan was, lost my job at the restaurant and took a leave of absence from work. I've not talked to my parents since the party. They're thoroughly disappointed in me, and trust me, that feeling is mutual. Why can't they support me? Why can't they tell me everyone makes mistakes and it's time to dust myself off, lift my head high and get on with life? I'm their daughter, for God's sake.

Instead, since they cared more about their image than me, they threatened to disown me if I ever brought shame like that to the family again. Honestly, I'm a bit angry. After Gavan left, they proceeded to remind me of all my past mistakes and when the caterers of the engagement party recognized me from Prime and mentioned it to one of the guests, my folks were mortified. I don't care if they think cooking is beneath them, it's what I love to do, and I'm sick and tired of trying to please them. They either like me for me and support what I do, or they can spend the rest of their lives missing out on my life and future. If I'm out of the picture, I just don't want them to put more pressure on Sarah to be the perfect daughter.

Gavan supported you.

Yeah, because he wanted something from me. Did he really think he could go on pretending to be a gay event planner if we went into business together? Ugh. Maybe he wasn't serious about that and once he got the space he wanted, he'd ditch me. I am such a fool.

My phone pings and I pick it up. My heart wobbles a little to see that it's Candace checking in—again. I'm not really sure how the wives of the guys Gavan plays soccer with got my number, but they've messaged nearly every day just to say hello, or ask if I was interested in coming out for a drink. I've declined every time. They're Gavan's friends by association, not mine. It would be weird and awkward, even though Gavan is no longer in town. My sister found that out from Finn, apparently. The two have been talking, as she canceled all wedding plans for now.

One good thing came out of this mess, and it's that my sister is starting to make her own decisions on what's right for her, and she's even talking about going to college to take some courses, although she has no idea what she wants to do, but at least she's thinking for herself. I'm happy with that. I'm not happy that my parents aren't talking to me, but at least they're not pushing Ryland on me, or straight up informing me that I need a powerful man on my arm. I don't need a man to be happy.

But Gavan made you happy.

A loud grumbling sound crawls out of my throat and I shoot Candace a message back, letting her know I'm not up for company. I drop my phone, walk past the mirror in the hallway as I head to the kitchen for more ice cream and nearly scream at the horrific vision before me. I'm about to finger comb my hair, but why bother? I don't have anyone to impress, and I'll never know if Gavan liked what he saw or was just humoring me.

I'm about to walk away, but stare at myself a bit longer, and that's when it occurs to me that I like what I see. I might be short, studious, and missing the glamor gene in the family, but I like who I am. I'm a good person, wouldn't harm a fly and I truly and deeply care about others. If a guy can't see that, then he's not worth my tears.

"...I don't think any man will ever look at me the way Gavan looked at you."

I suck in a breath as my sister's words ping around inside my brain. Is it possible that I'm wrong, that Gavan wasn't just messing around with me for his own selfish pursuits? I can't deny that I felt something in my soul, something I've never felt with another man, not even Ryland. Yes, he lied to me, and I'm still not sure what that was all about, or if I'll ever find out, but did he care for me the way I cared for him?

Maybe you should find out.

A knock comes on my door, and I hesitate. My gaze goes from the door to the kitchen where ice cream awaits. The knock comes again. Whoever is on my stoop is pretty insistent. Maybe it's Sarah. She's been stopping by unexpectedly a lot lately, and while I usually hate drop-ins, I don't mind hers. We've grown a lot closer over the last couple weeks and everything about her fills my heart with joy. I've missed her terribly.

Sarah is no longer friends with Chloe, and honestly, that hurts my heart. Maybe someday, after we've all done a little work on ourselves, we can all be friends again. Ryland and I will never get back together, and I heard he and Chloe broke up and I think it's for the best for both of them. Honestly, I hope they find what they need to fulfil their hearts.

I pull open the door, despite my appearance—Sarah has seen me at my worst—and my eyes bulge out of my head to discover Candace, Shyanne, Emma and Holly standing there, all looking a bit worried and sheepish about this surprise visit.

"What...how...hi."

"We're sorry to just stop by like this, Luce," Candace says. "We really missed you and we want to take you out for dinner."

"It's dinner time already?" As soon as the words leave my mouth, Shyanne steps forward.

"You have been inside too long." She tucks a strand of hair behind my ear, and crinkles her nose. "Come out and play."

"I'm a mess."

"I'm a hair stylist. Take a shower and give me five minutes."

"You guys don't have to worry about me," I say, but the truth is that I'm so touched that they do. These are the kind of friends I need. I realize they're all still standing outside, and I'm being rude, so I back up and wave them in. "Please, come in. Let me put on some coffee."

"Forget coffee. Where's the wine?" Candace says and I laugh.

"Wine it is."

Candace glances around. "Point us to the kitchen and I'll pour the wine while you shower and get ready."

"I'm not sure—"

"Please," Holly says, looking so forlorn. How can I say no?

"Just one drink."

"That's all we're asking for," Shyanne says, and puts her arm through mine.

"Wait, how do you all know where I live?"

Candace and Shyanne look down while Emma and Holly look around at the paintings on the walls. Why are they being so cagey? I stare at them for a second when understanding dawns.

"Gavan gave you my address."

"Don't be mad," Candace says quickly. "He was worried about you."

I frown and glance down as my heart jumps. Gavan was worried about me? I shouldn't like that so much, considering all the lies and how much he hurt me.

"Never mind that. Let's just go have a fun girls' night."

I lift my head. "I could really use that."

"To the shower," Shyanne says.

I head upstairs as they all talk quietly, like they don't want me to hear as they head to the kitchen. It's so incredibly sweet that they want to include me. Holly once talked about us all going to Atlantic City, and maybe a weekend away would be good for my soul and help me get on with life.

Thirty minutes later, dressed in jeans and a nice shirt, much like the ladies having wine downstairs, I tug on a pair of comfy shoes and head to the kitchen. They hand me a glass of wine and hold their glasses up.

"What are we drinking to?" I ask.

"To not being mad at us."

I clink glasses with them. "I'm not mad that you showed up. It was really nice, actually."

They all exchange a look that I don't understand, but maybe, if I spend more time with them, I'll understand those secret looks and the meaning behind them. I take a sip of wine, and they finish what's in their glasses.

Ten minutes later, I'm sitting in the front seat of Candace's car, the other ladies vying for the back seat and we all head downtown. "Are we going to the Crow?" I ask, their usual hangout place after soccer, but it's not Wednesday night, it's Saturday, exactly two weeks since I last set eyes on Gavan.

"Close to that," Candace says and begins to tell us all about this marketing campaign for a new pub that's opening. I listen, even though my stomach is in knots. It's crazy how much Gavan's idea had grown on me. Heck, I went and purchased the damn property, hoping I could make a career out of my passion. But it wasn't meant to be, I guess. Honestly, was I going to give up a well paying job to cook? Yes, yes I was.

We park in a lot downtown, and the air is warm as we head down the sidewalk. I try to keep my spirits high as we walk past Prime, try not to glance into the window to see who replaced me. I guess I deserved what I got. I shouldn't have lied about who I was, but maybe they could have heard me out and given me a second chance.

Did you hear Gavan out and give him a second chance?

My stomach cramps because I don't like the answer to that question. Did I ruin things by not listening? Was he going to explain why he pretended to be his cousin, and would I have understood? I guess I'll never find out.

I hurry my steps, taking the lead even though I have no idea where we're going. We walk past the Crow, and I see a flurry of activity outside the space I bought—and sold—as a group of men on scaffolding hang a sign over the much-coveted retail space. The women slow their steps and I turn around to glance at them.

"What's going on?"

Candace reaches out and squeezes my hand. "Don't be mad at us."

"Mad...why would I be mad?" Candace nods and gestures for me to turn back around. The second I do, my eyes land on the sign.

Kilting Around.

My heart leaps into my throat and I falter backward. Candace rights me, and at that second, none other than Gavan Duncan walks outside, dressed in a kilt, tears flood my eyes.

"What's going on?" I whisper, almost to myself.

"Luce," he says and walks straight up to me.

"Gavan..." I choke. "You...bought this."

"Yes, I'm opening my pub."

"That's...great." I blink hard, trying to stop the tears. He takes my hand in his as his gaze moves over my face. Honestly, no man has ever looked at me quite the way Gavan does. My heart swells, and I don't pull back.

"I'm sorry, Luce. I never meant to hurt you. Finn called me and told me he needed me." He shakes his head. "You see, I can't say no to family. He asked me to take over for him and insisted I wear a kilt." He briefly closes his eyes. "He thinks women find it charming."

"It was charming," I say quietly.

"There were a couple of things I didn't know when I agreed to help him." He pauses for a second, glances over my head and smiles at the women who brought me here. "I didn't know he was matchmaking, and I didn't know I was going to fall in love with the sweetest, kindest most beautiful woman on this planet."

My legs weaken, and this time I can't stop the tears. "Gavan—"

"Please, let me keep going. I've been practicing."

I nod and tug my bottom lip between my teeth because he looks so lost and so adorable it's all I can do not to hush him with a kiss.

"I never meant to say hurtful things to you. I know you don't judge people based on who they are and what they do. You care about everyone equally. You're the nicest person in the world, and probably too nice for the likes of me." I stay quiet, and he adds, "Ah, this is where you tell me that's not true."

I can't help but laugh as my heart fills with love. "That's not true."

"Whew," he says, and I look around him as the door to his pub opens and closes. Out walks my sister and the real Finn.

"I love you, Luce. I never want to lie to you or hurt you again. I never even knew what love was, or thought fidelity was a thing until I met you. You're the only woman I want to be with. I think I knew that the second you walked into the backyard, found me in the pool and made fun of my dangly parts." Murmurs sound from behind me. No doubt they're wondering what he's talking about, but that's our secret, and I like having secrets with him. Just not about who we really are. "Will you forgive me? Will you give me a second chance at figuring out how to be the man you need?"

"No," I say and his face crumbles. He takes a deep breath, only a modicum of hope left in his eyes.

"Luce," he begins, no doubt trying to come up with another way to convince me, and I like that he's not giving up so easily.

I put my hands on his face. "No, Gavan, you don't need a second chance at figuring out how to be the man I need. You *are* the man I need."

Squeals sound from behind me and my heart is so full I fear it could burst. "You mean that, Luce?"

I smile, and joy races through me. Never in my life have I been happier than this minute. Honestly, every day with Gavan was better than the last, and I can't wait to see what our future holds. "Yes, I mean that. I love you too, Gavan. I love you for who you are."

"You know who I am?"

I laugh at that. "You are the kindest, most caring and giving man I know. You are worthy and deserving, and protective of those you love."

"I love you."

"I know and you didn't need to do this to become what I wanted, but I'm glad you're doing it to finally fulfill your dreams."

"Not just my dreams, Luce, yours too." Before I can say anything, he grabs my hand and tugs. My sister, who can't stop grinning, moves to the side to let me in and the second I see the sign over the bar, a big burst of laughter climbs out of my throat.

Luce, Duncan Disorderly!

"Ohmigod, Gavan. That's hilarious."

Childlike wonderment fills his eyes as he smiles widely. "You like it?"

"I love it. It's crazy, just like you."

"Will you take a chance on me, and more importantly on yourself and see your dream of running your own kitchen to fruition?"

"Gavan," I begin, hardly able to stop my spinning brain long enough to find my words.

"You can be the chef, and I'll bartend and we'll make this place everything we want it to be, but I want to do it together. It won't mean a thing to me if you're not by my side. Equal partners in everything."

"Running a pub is hard work, Gavan, but with you by my side, it's going to be a whole lot more fun."

He lifts me up and spins me around and my sister and the rest of the girls, along with Finn, all come inside. I can't believe they were all in cahoots, putting this together with Finn. Here they were worried I'd be mad, but I'm not. Not only do I have the man I love offering me his heart and wanting us both to fulfill our dreams together, I have my sister back and a handful of wonderful, caring girlfriends that care about me.

My sister pulls out a couple bottles of champagne from the fridge and hands one to Finn. They shake them, pull the corks and we all gasp as they spray us.

"Time to celebrate," Sarah says.

"No," Gavan corrects as he presses his lips to mine. "Time to get loose, drunk and disorderly."

"You're crazy," I say with a laugh.

"Crazy about you, Luce."

My heart soars as I glance around the new pub. "I can't wait to get cooking."

He winks at me. "How about we kick these guys all out, and start now?"

I laugh and accept the glass of champagne from my sister. "I'll drink to that!"

EPILOGUE

Gavan

One Year Later

I reach over and give Luce's leg a loving squeeze as Sarah and Glen walk to the dance floor for their first dance as a married couple. Luce turns to me, tears in her eyes and my heart fills with love. I am seriously the luckiest man in the world—thanks to Finn. He pushed me out of my comfort zone, and helped me become the man I was meant to be. He, of course, likes to remind me of this every day.

"Having fun?" I ask, and Luce leans over and presses her lips to mine. My gaze rakes over her face and once again takes in the maid of honor dress she's wearing. I love that she stood up for her sister, which is how it should have been all along, and I'm so happy the two have put the past behind them and have become the best of friends. We hang out with them a lot, and Glen has mellowed in my presence. I think both he and Sarah just had some growing up to do.

I take Luce's hand in mine. You'd think after working together at the pub we'd be tired of being around each other all day, but we're not. I still can't get enough of her. My gaze searches the beautifully decorated room, compliments of Finn's great eye, and I spot Luce's parents.

Her mom is watching us, and I give her a smile. She smiles back. It wasn't easy with them at first, but Luce stood her ground and followed her passion, and we now have one of the busiest pubs in Boston, offering authentic Scottish foods and fresh local market cuisine, all made by the talented beautiful woman beside me, and her sous chef Parker, who used to work as a valet for her parents. Kev, the guy Luce used to bring food to, also works for us. He clears tables and does the dishes and has found himself a little apartment that he shares with Larry and Killer. Her parents now come into our little place, and they can't deny that their daughter is a master chef. I know they're proud of her, but more importantly Luce is proud of herself, and she's the only one she needs to please.

I love how much Luce thinks about others and when she asked about hiring Parker and Kev, I readily agreed. So, while she's always taking care of others, I take care of her. Yes, she's a strong, independent woman, but she's my woman, and I'd do anything for her.

Soon enough, the song ends, and Finn jiggles restlessly in his seat beside me. "It's time," he whispers.

I turn and hush him. He's so bad at keeping secrets. It's a wonder he was able to keep the fact that he was matching under wraps. I guess that's why he had to go all the way to Fiji. Otherwise I'm sure he would have spilled and I might have just up and left Boston.

The music dies down and Sarah grabs her bouquet. "Okay, single ladies, let's all line up. It's time to catch the bouquet."

The women jump to their feet, but Luce doesn't budge. "Get up there," I say.

"No. You know I prefer to be in the shadows."

Dammit, I really need her up there. I'm about to push, but stop when Sarah marches over, grabs Luce's hand and hauls her up. Luce protests, but when Sarah pouts, she gives in. She can't say no to her sister and in this case, I'm glad.

All the women line up, and Luce sort of stands off to the side, like she has no intention of catching the bouquet and putting herself in the spotlight. Sarah glances behind her, turns and throws the bouquet right into Luce's arms.

Perfect.

Everyone claps and Luce's eyes go wide as everyone stares at her. She dips her head, like she's trying to hide, but there will be no hiding today. In fact, she's about to be the highlight in a moment.

As the women all go back to their seats, I stand, and make my way toward Luce. She angles her head, her eyes questioning as the dance floor clears, save for the two of us.

"Nice catch," I tell her.

"I think Sarah threw them to me on purpose."

"She did."

"She did?"

I chuckle and the spotlight centers on us as I go down on one knee. Luce gasps, and puts one hand over her mouth.

"Gavan, what are you doing?" She looks around, her cheeks heating.

"Will you marry me, Luce? Make me the happiest man in the world."

She stands there and for a second, I think she's going to falter. Her gaze goes to her sister, and when she looks back at me, she says, "No."

A loud hush goes over the crowd and my heart sinks into my stomach. We've spent the last year living and working together, and falling into each other's arms every night, and waking up together every morning. Our lives have been perfect and the only thing that could make it better is if we were married.

"Luce," I choke out.

She sinks to the floor, drops the bouquet and puts her hands on my face. Her voice is low when she says, "We can't take the thunder away from my sister, Gavan. Today is her day. This is all about her."

I laugh, and fall deeper in love with her. Impossible, I know, but I love how she's always worried about everyone else. "We have her blessing. She helped me pick out the ring and this was her idea. She wanted to share her day with her big sister and best friend."

"Really." She catches her sister's eye, and Sarah is grinning and nodding.

"Yes, really."

"That was so sweet of her."

Down on our knees, we both stare at each other, everything so right and good between us as I wait for her to answer. When one doesn't come, I say, "Luce?"

"Yeah?"

"Will you marry me?"

She has a cheeky grin on her face when she answers with, "Only if you promise to wear your kilt to the altar."

"You're just kidding around, right?"

"No, I'm not kilting around, Gavan. I want that."

"Then you get that." I lean in and kiss her. "Wait, is that a yes?"

She laughs and throws her arms around me. "That's a yes, a million times over."

***

Thank you so much for reading Luce and Gavan's story. I hope you enjoyed it as much as I loved writing it. Please check out the next two books in the series! Kilt Trip and Off Kilter.

ALSO BY CATHRYN FOX

Hot Scots in Kilts:

Kilting Around

Kilt Trip

Off Kilter

Crazy Canadians:

Crazy Apologetic Canadians.

Scotia Storms

Away Game (Rebels)

Warm Up (Rebels)

Crash Course (Rebels)

Home Advantage (Rebels)

Shut Out (Rebels)

End Zone

Fair Play

Enemy Down

Keeping Score

Trading Up

All In

Blue Bay Crew

Demolished

Leveled

Hammered

Single Dad
Single Dad Next Door
Single Dad on Tap
Single Dad Burning Up

Players on Ice
The Playmaker
The Stick Handler
The Body Checker
The Hard Hitter
The Risk Taker
The Wing Man
The Puck Charmer
The Troublemaker
The Rule Breaker
The Rookie
The Sweet Talker
The Heart Breaker

In the Line of Duty
His Obsession Next Door
His Strings to Pull
His Trouble in Talulah
His Taste of Temptation
His Moment to Steal
His Best Friend's Girl
His Reason to Stay

Confessions

Confessions of a Bad Boy Professor

Confessions of a Bad Boy Officer

Confessions of a Bad Boy Fighter

Confessions of a Bad Boy Doctor

Confessions of a Bad Boy Gamer

Confessions of a Bad Boy Millionaire

Confessions of a Bad Boy Santa

Confessions of a Bad Boy CEO

Hands On

Hands On

Body Contact

Full Exposure

Dossier

Private Reserve

House Rules

Under Pressure

Big Catch

Brazilian Fantasy

Improper Proposal

Boys of Beachville

Good at Being Bad

Igniting the Bad Boy

Bad Girl Therapy

Stone Cliff Series:

Crashing Down

Wasted Summer

Love Lessons

Wrapped Up

Eternal Pleasure Series

Instinctive

Impulsive

Indulgent

Sun Stroked Series

Seaside Seduction

Deep Desire

Private Pleasure

Captured and Claimed Series:

Yours to Take

Yours to Teach

Yours to Keep

Firefighter Heat Series

Fever

Siren

Flash Fire

Playing For Keeps Series

Slow Ride

Wild Ride

Sweet Ride

Breaking the Rules:

Hold Me Down Hard

Pin Me Up Proper

Tie Me Down Tight

Stand Alone Title:

Crazy Apologetic Canadians

Hands on with the CEO

Torn Between Two Brothers

Holiday Spirit

Unleashed

Knocking on Demon's Door

Web of Desire

ABOUT CATHRYN

New York Times and *USA today* Bestselling author, Cathryn is a wife, mom, sister, daughter, and friend. She loves dogs, sunny weather, anything chocolate (she never says no to a brownie) pizza and red wine. She has two teenagers who keep her busy with their never ending activities, and a husband who is convinced he can turn her into a mixed martial arts fan. Cathryn can never find balance in her life, is always trying to find time to go to the gym, can never keep up with emails, Facebook or Twitter and tries to write page-turning books that her readers will love.

Connect with Cathryn:

Tik Tok: @cathrynfoxwriter
Newsletter https://app.mailerlite.com/webforms/landing/c1f8n1
Twitter: https://twitter.com/writercatfox
Facebook: https://www.facebook.com/AuthorCathrynFox?ref=hl

Blog: http://cathrynfox.com/blog/
Goodreads: https://www.goodreads.com/author/show/91799.Cathryn_Fox
Pinterest http://www.pinterest.com/catkalen/